American Season

ISBN 978-1-60145-864-3

Printed in the United States of America.

Booklocker.com, Inc.
2010

American Season

Doug Pinkston

Table of Contents

Prologue

Every life is a collection of memories and dreams. And while I have heard it said that the mind keeps a record of every moment, I don't really know about that. I do know that memories, and the emotions they bring with them, will sneak up on you sometimes unexpectedly, perhaps when you're cleaning out the garage, say, and you come across an old sweatshirt, or when on a late summer afternoon you find yourself watching your children race across the yard and you think back to your own golden childhood, or those times when an old familiar tune pops up on the radio, blanketing your mood with violet reminiscence. I know I shall never forget the autumn season of my senior year at Lassiter College, for it was a season filled with the deepest of memories. That season is now a part of me, and I will always be haunted by those memories and dreams.

There were two seasons for me in the fall of that year at Lassiter, Connecticut: one rich bronze autumn of ripening for my own heart and mind and one season in which I played, for the last time, a crazy and simple game that we call, here in the States, football. I remember, as if it were yesterday, one shimmering image from that year. It was the last few days of August and the summer was as hot in Connecticut as it would ever be. We were working out in full pads and I had a coach who would push us in these practices until the fibers of our jerseys were soaked with sweat and coated with dust from the trampled grass at our feet, and only then would he justify a halt to the scrimmage. In that brief break it was a tradition at that school to allow every player a single cup of ice cold water. The act was more ritual -- a sacrificial offering -- than real relief. Hell, I could've drunk a bucketful and still been thirsty! Yet in all my life it's doubtful I've consumed a sweeter taste than that spare swallow. The ice water ran across our tongues and swirled down our throats in a fleeting moment of absolute fraternity, virgin pureness and crystalline clarity. We became linked in that drama, not only with each other, but with the essence of our existence, the unclouded sustenance of our lives. The memory ties up for me much of the pain and unreachable desires of my last year at Lassiter. I came to terms with the magnitude of my thirsts that year: in me the presence of an unquenchable thirst for passion and triumph, a deep flowing thirst for love and respect and, finally, a thirst for justice. It was the season I came of age, and this is the story of that season.

Chapter 1
Shifting the Balance

This story is about - mostly - the events that transpired during my last year at Lassiter College. From time to time, as this story unfolds, you may think, distracted by a sudden familiar footstep, or an autumn breeze, that you've heard parts of this story before. You may even recall a scene or two from your own life and marvel at the detail of my re-telling. But it is all coincidence, believe me. Dreams, fiction and history are close companions. I am an American child, raised in the dust-hooves of the continent, dirt-faced and mean, and it is likely that we share a history.

It is true that much of my story is typical of many young Americans growing up in the last stages of the twentieth century. We were starry-eyed kids, feeling our way blindly through the ambiguities, challenges and delights of college towards the impending uncertainties, fears and freedoms of adulthood. This story takes place in a weird time, a time well after the disillusionment of Nixon and Vietnam, a time before the Roaring Nineties and the slurp of The Bubble. It has been described as a lost time, a time when inflation was the Big Enemy and Disco battled Punk and Metal for The Stage. We all have our histories, fictions and dreams. And we all have our secrets.

The year was 1981. It was the year in which I would reach my highest achievements as an athlete, the year in which I would encounter the most painful truths about the mortality of man and, indeed, my own mortality, and the year in which I would learn the hardest lessons of the powerful and the powerless. It was the year that I would explore the depths of Edgar Allan Poe through the greatest English teacher on earth, and a year in which I would begin to understand the demons caged within me and how they could defeat me in a single unguarded moment of fervor or ignite in me a fire whose tendrils could reach every slick and ivy-covered gutter of a quiet New England school. To this day I maintain that it was all my sister's fault.

What can I say about Lisa Rae? She was different. That's probably the best compliment I can give her right now, given my state of mind. Lisa Rae was two years older than me by the calendar, but leagues ahead when it came to intellect and intuition. I don't know how she came to such acute perceptions. She looked just like me -- God bless her soul -- and I can attest to the modesty of her upbringings and genetic pool. One or more of the Muses must've made her acquaintance at some point in her youth, because it was a fact: she had ways. She could teach a cat to fetch slippers. Tie sailor knots blindfolded. Climb Fealey's oak in a minute and a half, and do a one and a half into Winowee's Creek. She could make perfect sense of Shakespeare while still a sophomore in high school. I envied her and idolized her and resented her, in my best moments. She tolerated me, at best, most times, but we were all we had in our family.

Lisa Rae had her own perspectives on how the world worked. She spoke too well for her class, I believed. It probably had something to do with her voracious appetite for books. I hardly ever saw her without a book in her lap or at her side. It was as though she found escape from the slow, quiet reality of Lumberton in the pages of her novels. She believed in the power of dreams, but saw little value in the passions of sports. I couldn't side with her on that one. "Johnnie Boy," she'd call me. We'd be driving down some dirt road, on our way to Hendersonville to visit Aunt Rachel who lived near the lake, perhaps. "We're doomed, you know? Just look around. I can't pick out a single relative on either side that's ever amounted to anything. It's in the genes." Sometimes, in my bolder moments, I would counter her. "Well, Aunt Rachel's done alright by herself." Lisa Rae drove poorly, particularly on a back road with no oncoming obstacles. She had a mind for concepts, but not much of an eye for geometry or physics. When my big sister was driving I always kept one eye geared toward the road and one hand fastened to the car door.

Our Aunt Rachel lived in a large two-story home, sitting in the middle of about five acres. The front drive was framed by huge oak trees like something out of Gone with the Wind.

"Inherited it," Lisa Rae told me. "Got it all from Uncle Ned's folks, who inherited it from one of their grandparents, who struck oil in Louisiana. I hardly call that making it. Though she is just about the nicest Aunt in the bunch."

"Yeah, and she's got a ski boat."

"Yeah, that counts for a lot."

Lisa Rae and I saw eye to eye on many things within the family, but she never quite understood the dynamics of athletics, nor my own obsession with sports. Many books have been written about sport, but it is a subject still surrounded by the mysteries of human evolution. For most of my life competition on the field of play ruled my life. I think it was mostly because I was good at it. As a child I took quickly to the strategies of every sport I took up. Though never particularly big (even in college I was but 5' 10" and weighed a mere 175 pounds) I nevertheless had quick feet and a feeling for the angles, and I used every trick I could create if it would give me an advantage. Some folks called me just plain lucky. Usually, after some wacky touchdown, where I'd stop in mid-field, offering the defender one leg, then another, only to snatch them both away at the last moment, and slip by him to sideline. I insisted it was the natural warrior instinct of the Natchez Indian.

My father, or Sarge, as he was not so affectionately known around Lumberton, was my greatest fan and sternest critic. It was he who tossed me my first rubber football at age two. It was he who took me to Wal-Mart to pick out my first baseball mitt, he who nurtured my thirst for athletics when the challenges were greatest, he who cheered loudest when I faced adversity and emerged victorious, and he whose disappointment at my failures most often broke my spirit and endangered my love for The Game. Everywhere, Sarge saw a world of violence, where the meek inherit nothing but despair. Even at a young age he would line up against me and force me to try to tackle him, or bring out some old pugil sticks to stage mock battles in the back yard. I remember once catching him in the groin with an errant stab. His face turned red, then he whirled and batted me in the jaw. He stood over me and grinned as I looked for my teeth in the grass. No spanking went on in our house. It was called whippin'. I learned quickly to keep my smart mouth shut and if the thought of devilry crossed by mind I'd better be damn sure I could get away with it. My mother kept secret many of my larger transgressions, saving what little ass I have left. Even with her protection, however, I seemed to always be in trouble for something, as though I was at once at war with my father, while still his most trusted soldier.

I graduated from Jackson High School in 1975. Originally built in 1927, the gym burned down in 1940 and again twenty years later. A new stadium was built in 1962 and a new wing added in 1965, but these were the only major additions to the original ruby-red bricks. While the age of the institution provided some sort of pride to some members of the community, the students found the building awkward and outdated. Like much of southern Mississippi, large pines and oaks rose up in the courtyard, giving the grounds a scenic beauty. But inside it was different. Every day you could smell some strange, peculiar odor, not unlike the mixing of linseed oil and pine sol. Most of the classrooms had no air-conditioners and during the warmer months of the year we would literally drip perspiration onto the carved-up desk, struggling to follow the teacher's uninspired lessons. During spring the pollen from the yellow pines that surrounded the school would float in with the hot breezes and wreak havoc on everyone's nasal passages. The school was a dinosaur, lurching forward on the momentum of historic tradition. I did well there, both academically and athletically, but my case was not typical. Racial prejudice was pervasive in the town where I grew up. Though the high school had been desegregated in 1970, the cultures which created the segregation died less swiftly. I had been raised to be fair and honest and to judge people by the same measures, but it was a difficult stand to uphold. My mother was a devout Methodist. She viewed all humanity in terms of their capacity for goodness and the value of their eternal soul. In these regards she told us (and the preacher at least seemed to back her up) all of us are equal. Though my father had been raised in a segregated world, the Army had seasoned him to the realities of our time. There is something about war which awakens the humanity of all men, but one does not easily supersede ones time.

Coping is enough. Shifting the balance of a few hearts and minds, perhaps that is all one should aspire to. By the time I was old enough to give sociology much serious thought I could see only two conclusions: I liked women and I wanted the ball. I had tasted the recontre and it was sweet. In my senior year a transfer from Texas joined our team who could really throw, and our offense suddenly evolved into a lively force in southern Mississippi. We ran and threw with equal nonchalance and I began to recognize the true discrepancies between my own talents and those of my peers. We made it to the state finals, where we got beat narrowly by a much better team from Tupelo. I took the defeat graciously, for I'd contributed my share. I'd set a slew of records and had refined open-field maneuvering into an art form. Our bus trip back to Lumberton after the final game was quiet, but not sorrowful. We'd given it our best shot and been defeated by a superior team. We were outmanned.

I remember our fans awaiting our return in the school parking lot late that night. I recall their applause as the team stepped off the bus and the way they lit up as I began my descent. I'd entertained them for three years and led them to the best season the school had seen in seventeen years. I looked out across the crowd. I heard them raise their voices in praise, heard the cheerleaders call my name in unison, saw the faces, both white and black, giving me the finest curtain call I was capable of absorbing. My family and my girlfriend waited near the door and we all hugged in sympathy and celebration. My father shook my hand in firm military fashion. He pulled a twenty dollar bill from his wallet. "Take Susie out for a pizza," he said, handing me the keys to the Ford. "Fine season, son." I looked into his dark eyes, glossed over by the phosphorescent lighting and the lateness of the hours, and caught within them the approval and the recognition which he bestowed so rarely. He was at his finest in such moments. This is how I choose to remember Lumberton and Jackson High. The academic backwardness, the racism, the conflicts with my father, the lost loves: all are relics I prefer to keep hidden from my recollections, a dusty chest deep in the corner of my Freudian attic. It was the best of times, not only for me, but for my community, and we reveled in the excitement and brotherhood occasioned by our simple game. One can choose to forget or remember anything, but one must always pay the consequences.

Chapter 2
Who were these freaks?

How I ended up at Lassiter College is a tale of one girl's compelling energy and pure chance. My father thought Ole Miss was the top of the line when it came to colleges. He harbored regional prejudices and his only uncle -- Jimmy Sloan -- was an Ole Miss graduate. Located in Oxford, Ole Miss was Mississippi's largest university and close enough to Lumberton to make it a comfortable day trip. Though Sarge had never attended a day of college, he was a Mississippian and nothing would thrill him more than watching his son strap it on at the state's preeminent university. My mother was mostly noncommittal, but she knew better than to openly question my father's wisdom. Plus, I believed at the time, she wanted me close enough to keep an eye on, for her own reasons. She prayed the Lord would guide me to the right choice.

During my last semester at Jackson High I struggled with the implications and opportunities that the different scholarship offers presented. It had never occurred to me the importance of college athletic programs, nor how significant my selection might be for my own future. I knew nothing about the many schools that sent me scholarship offers, or the importance my selection might portend for my own future. With the exception of their geographical location and the record of their football team, they all looked alike. I was unprepared for the multitude of offers. Even before the season was over several members of the Ole Miss and Mississippi State alumni caught me in the parking lot to chat. They stopped just short of slipping me five-dollar bills, but their intentions were obvious. I let them banter, but their backslapping 'good-ole-boy' prodding didn't help their cause. They had mistaken my background and my motives. In the first week of eligibility the pace heightened. Nearly every division I and II school in the southeast and Texas sent letters of invitation, often followed up with phone calls and personal visits by recruiters. As I played out my last season of organized baseball I shuffled through these distractions clumsily.

It was my sister who noticed the odd letter from Dr. Francis Cannon, an alumnus of Lassiter College, an exclusive, private school just north of

Hartford, Connecticut. I certainly would have quickly disposed of the inquiry had it not been for Lisa Rae's persistence. Dr. Cannon had played tackle for Lassiter back in 65. He now was an ophthalmologist in Hattiesburg. The letter was quiet in its tone, but included an intriguing sentence intimating that he could twist some arms if I needed help negotiating the academic requirements at Lassiter. What the hell, I thought. I had a 3.5 G.P.A. Who were these freaks?

Lisa Rae did some research for me. Indeed, she often gave me a full review of the schools on my list before I knew where they were located. She was unforgiving of their academic mediocrity. To this day, I don't why I lent her viewpoint such credence. After all, she seemed satisfied enough with Biloxi State, a school of rather modest dimensions in all respects. She told me that love shaded her considerations. (Her boyfriend, and later, her husband, was a sophomore there). Besides, nothing in her prep record recommended her to a scholarship at such a prestigious school. A college education is an investment in the mind and spirit, she told me. When it was all said and done, not even professional tutoring would be sufficient to equal out the disparities between us; but it might give me an edge. She convinced me that I lacked the intelligence and ambition to overcome the environment that we both had inherited. If the Colton's were to make out of the swamps, therefore, the burden rested firmly on me. She would be the light, she told me. It was up to me to do the legwork. I knew she was right at least in this respect: I had to get out of Mississippi. Perhaps, like my father, I would one day return, set down roots in familiar soil. But the time was right for a gamble. The dusty air was full of chance. I could feel it my bones like a fresh cold. So it was that Lisa Rae called Dr. Cannon and set up the paperwork that eventually led to me being offered a full scholarship, including a travel stipend, to a prestigious northern university, in southern Connecticut, in the middle of New England, and as far away from my current world as the moon.

For a kid like me, used to playing it safe when off the field of play, it was a gritty call. Sarge was not one to be dismissed lightly; he had his prejudices and preconceptions about how the world worked. None of us knew anything about Lassiter, Connecticut - or New England for that matter - and my dad was not impressed with their academic resume. I think, in the back of his mind, he had given some thought to the possibility of me taking over his hardware business. We had grown up in different times, with different opportunities; it was too early to let him in on how different were our visions of the world.

The Boys were equally unimpressed. At one of the many parties thrown to celebrate the conclusion of our senior year, my closest friends tried their best to dissuade me of my crazy notions. We were at Reynolds farm. We'd dragged a couple of kegs out behind their barn, down where the lake had been cleared out, and things started to seem right with the world. On a moonlit night in Mississippi, when the hormones are raging and the cold beer is flowing, and a cheap stereo is honking out Lynyrd Skynyrd classics and over-played Led Zeppelin tunes, there's only one place on this earth to be - at Reynolds's farm. It was the prime spot for a party when Rabbit Reynolds and his wing man Little Dipper could work it out. Rabbit's folks were always making trips to New Orleans, or somewhere else exotic, so on those weekends Reynolds's farm became The Spot. We'd pool our cash for kegs or cases, devise stories for the folks, put on too much cologne, wait for dusk, and then head down the dusty dirt roads for Reynolds's Farm.

Most of The Boys had been there a while, when Susie had hiked her way to the house with some of the girls. The Boys and I made our way naturally toward the lake shore, where a huge oak supported a tire swing on one of its muscular limbs. Even at this hour someone would occasionally throw off their shirt and swing out over the lake and fall in with a howl. It was clear they'd had a head start.

At one point Red Simpson grabbed me from behind.

"You ready to go in, college boy?" he asked me.

Red was the shortstop and point guard at Jackson High, about the quickest little bugger in school, with hands like painter. Had he been a few inches taller the boy might've played a few years, but at 5' 5" he was always viewed as a novelty. So far, only Colleton Community College and Biloxi JuCo had showed any interest.

"Go ahead Red," I answered, "I'll join you in a few. The night is still young and the beer is still cold."

Jazz Kaufman, our quarterback and Romeo, chimed in. "Well, you better drink up boys, 'cause the keg by the barn is on its last leg."

"Not a problem," Scooter Leaks informed us. "I've got a bottle of Jack Black in the trunk." Scooter played center on the football team and was a state finalist wrestler. He was a good man to have on your side.

"Just one?" I asked him.

"As far as you know, Colton. Besides, aren't you supposed to be in training for big time college football? What's the name of that place: Connecticut School for Disadvantaged Women?"

"Lassiter College," I corrected him, "Though I hope to leave a few disadvantaged women in my wake."

Red continued the line of questioning. "Yeah Colton, what's the deal with that, anyway? I heard Ole Miss sent you a letter."

Heads seemed to suddenly turn our way from all around us in the shady moonlight.

"Who told you that?" I asked him.

"I've got my sources," was all he would say.

I suspected perhaps my sister had let it out, then, reconsidering, I realized it was probably my old man, running his mouth at the barber shop, or over the counter at the hardware store.

"Well I lost track of them," I fessed up, facetiously. "Who knows? I mean, after The Bear stopped by for supper, they all faded into mediocrity."

"The Bear?" Scooter queried. "Bear fuckin' Bryant? You're crazier'n a possum on moonshine."

"Sonafabitch could eat some pie, though. I'll tell ya that!"

Suddenly, Hallie Matson burst into our circle, with her 38 DD's tightly testing the fibers of her Ole Miss t-shirt.

"What's this about Ole Miss?" Her voice was as southern and seductive as a warm pecan pie.

"Colton thinks he's Shakespeare!" Red told her, stepping forward so his nose was mere inches from glory. "Or....at the least....Faulkner."

"Shakespeare?" Hallie wondered aloud.

Scooter spoke up. "Yeah, Colton is heading north. Mississippi's not good enough for him."

"Well, *I'm* going to Ole Miss, John," Hallie said, stepping too close for her own good. I tried to regain my composure, one eye on her t-shirt, one on the hill beyond, where Susie might soon be returning.

"I sure don't know what I'm going to do, Hallie. Ole Miss is a pretty big school, you know. I'm just a little peanut of a player. All that physical contact gives me the willies."

Hallie smiled and moved close enough to whisper in my ear. "That's not what I heard," she told me.

I looked straight ahead, nonplussed, across Sadie's lake, where the reflection of the full moon rode the light ripples of the evening breeze. I could feel the moisture from her breath on my earlobe and smell the sweet aroma of bourbon and I must admit it sent a charge throughout the weaker angels of my existence. I leaned toward Scooter Leaks and put a hand on his shoulder, as if to ground me from her electrical charges.

"Well, we'll see," I said. "Who knows? Perhaps I'll apply for admission in some first class Ole Miss fraternity. One of those houses with the big columns out front and keg parties every weekend, win or lose."

"Oh yeah!" Hallie encouraged me. And everyone else seemed to concur.

"Sounds good to me," Kerry said, slapping Scooter's hand.

"I can only imagine running into some coed like you, Hallie, on a wild Saturday night in Oxford after we just laid a butt whuppin' on The Tide."

Pete Kaufman brought me back to reality. "Well, the first part has some basis in reality. Seriously Colton: you don't think you can play in the SEC?"

I tried to answer the question in a way that was politically correct; and not make me seem too much of a coward. "That's a good question," I told him, distracted once more by Hallie Matson's perfume. A bullfrog jumped into the lake with a splash.

"I really don't know, guys. Truth is, I'm just not sure. You remember the semi-finals against Biloxi? You remember that linebacker that knocked Cooley out of the game and ran down Daughtery on the corner?"

Scooter certainly did. He answered. "Jason McKinney. I heard he's committed to Texas A&M."

"Yeah. McKinney. Kid was on the state champion 880 relay team. You guys think I got the moves to beat a whole field of McKinney's?"

The guys had to stop for a second and consider that one. They were the best judge and jury I could put together for such a verdict and they were unsure. After a moment, Red stepped in. "Couldn't catch me."

We laughed and imagined the scene. It was true. Red Simpson was quicker than a jackrabbit in the open field. Red and I had grown up together and in a backyard football game I don't think I'd ever seen anyone tackle him in the open field. Even in full pads, as a sophomore, he struck terror into the hearts of defensive backs. But it was no matter. He would always be too small. And he knew it.

Red's father was a true farmer. He grew peanuts on his arable land and catfish in the wetlands. Zeke Simpson was a mean sonafabitch, but you always knew where you stood. Red's mom, Lizzie, was as big as a bear and just as sturdy. It was no wonder Red had developed quick reflexes. I'd seen him snatch catfish out of the pond with his bare hands. He was the only kid in the neighborhood that could keep up with me in a race down Oak Root Alley to Creel's Creek. That was a three block path that wound through the largest oaks in the county down to a deep, cool pool in the creek. The overhanging limbs and thick moss provided the perfect canopy for a race to the finish and a dive headlong into the refreshing, crawfish-filled stream.

As the party at Reynolds's farm progressed, we laughed, traded barbs and continued drinking to excess, as only young men full of vim and vigor can do. I couldn't explain to them why I was casting all my fortunes in with an unknown school at the far edges of our known civilization. The more I had thought about it, the less sense even I could make of it. I was born and raised in Mississippi. I loved this state and just about everything about it. Standing by the lakeside at full moon, re-living old times with my best friends (a symphony of frogs and crickets providing background music), it was an easy place to love. But Lisa Rae had convinced me there was more out there to be experienced. But how would a simple country boy from southern Mississippi fit into the Ivy League?

Lisa Rae tried to drag me though the apprehensions I carried with me throughout that long summer. Sometimes on a warm Friday night we'd sneak out for pizza and end up sharing a bottle of wine with our feet hanging off the old train trestle over Winowee's Creek. She could point out every planet lit up in the sky and half the constellations. She had a sense of the misgivings in my head and she tried her best to bolster my spirit.

"It's cold," she said. We sat with the rusted steel beam tucked beneath our legs, leaning forward across the cable, looking down. The creek slipped by us quietly in the darkness far below.

"Should've worn some long pants," I counseled, "Or even some shorts."

"Oh. You're embarrassed now."

"Hey -- just cuz' my older sister walks into Pizza Hut with half her ass hanging out: no cause for alarm!"

"Well, it's so sweet that you're worried about my reputation." She threw her long brown hair back, letting the soft breeze toss it down her back, then she spit off the edge. "Though perhaps it's your infamous name that you're worried about."

"Nope. Too late for that. My virtue and virginity are well documented. I've been turned down by every high school age female in Lamar County."

She laughed, a mere whisper. "And now you have the whole of Connecticut to corrupt. I see your strategy now. Hey, pass the wine."

"Hmpf. I don't know about that. Seems like a bunch of spoiled rich kids to me."

"These girls are gonna be cultured, honey....sophisticated. They might even know how to behave in public. And unlike your current harem, most of them will speak English." Lisa Rae had an obsession with the proper use of the language. She used to drive all my friends crazy with her constant corrections of their natural southern slang.

"Well, as long as they can pronounce the answers to my favorite questions -- yes and more -- I'll be happy."

"Hah! Yes and less, you mean."

She passed me the bottle back just as a bullfrog lit up far below us on the far bank. The cacophony of crickets seemed to rise up to meet the challenge of song. There would be no old, abandoned train trestles in Lassiter, Connecticut, few warm nights to ride the breeze, and no Lisa Rae to guide me through the stars. She held my hand and told me how much I'd be missed. We were in this together, she said, and I couldn't help but cry a little when she gave me a kiss on the cheek. I smiled and looked toward the planet Venus, rising like a diamond over Crowder's farm. I pulled her to me with a firm hug and we looked out into the moonless night, our lives fixed on a precipice so thinly drawn only the fibers of our own mysterious love could guide our wild and roaring futures towards balance. Just then, we saw a shooting star blaze through the western sky. And we made a silent wish.

Chapter 3
Call Me Deacon Blues

The plane trip from Jackson, Mississippi to Hartford, Connecticut is a long one, with stopovers in Atlanta, Georgia and, usually, Newark, New Jersey. The trip takes you over the deepest of the Deep South, and then makes a long stretch run over the Appalachian Mountains from Atlanta to Newark. From Newark I'd usually catch Continental flight 310 to Bradley Airport, just north of Hartford. For a green cracker from the Deep South like me it was a trip filled with the most vibrant of scenes, people and interactions. You get a feel for people when you're traveling. For me, once we left the ground from Jackson International, all the sights were new.

For some reason, every time I made the trip and stepped foot onto the plane the emotions of my first trip would always come washing back over me. I remembered how I stared out the window childishly during that trip as each city and town came into view below us, and as each green mountain top rose into view. I remember in particular the view I caught one night. We had just left Atlanta and had about completed our climb through the clouds. Suddenly, there appeared below us a deep, wide valley, stretching as far as I could see. The only signs of civilization I could make out were the clusters of white lights shining up from some small, nameless town to the west and the speckling of a few yellow dots here and there throughout the broad valley, perhaps marking an isolated farm, or a quiet street corner. Pines clothed the valley like a rich, green cloak, holding in the secrets of the wilderness and homesteads. How empty the land looked. There seemed room enough here for all the uncultivated, all the frontiersmen that might be left among us, looking to carve out a better life. I began to wonder where I might eventually fall into this broad valley called America. Where sat my yellow light in the woods? I would pass over that valley many times before I finally stepped off the plane for good, and each time my memory would stir up the same old dreams and possibilities. The road led everywhere from here, but I could only claim one stop.

On my first arrival in Hartford, the mysterious Dr. Cannon had arranged for my new roommate to meet me at the airport. His name was Larry Jarvis. He played tight end and hailed from Boston, Massachusetts. I suppose they felt since were both receivers we would have a natural bond of interest. It was a ridiculous assumption, given all the circumstances, but for all I knew as good as any. Larry was a truly friendly fellow and came from a family where good manners and a pleasant disposition were taken for granted. Unfortunately, he couldn't block a tackle to save his life, nor make heads or tails out of macroeconomics, which happened to be his major. But that's another story.

On my first day in Connecticut he drove me through downtown Hartford, showed me a few sights and bought me a burger and a beer before helping me unload into the freshman dorm. Hartford had, at the time, about a million and a half people, while Jackson, the largest city in Mississippi, probably had half a million tops. I was immediately struck by the scale of the buildings and the beauty of the new mixed with the old. One got the impression of historic tradition coexisting awkwardly with a modern technological rush. A set of rules governed both these cultures and I understood neither. On the streets were people in a hurry, impatient to be somewhere that they weren't (whether a physical destination or one in the mind I couldn't necessarily determine). I was a foreigner and I felt foreign, but I received not even the merest glance of recognition. It was into such a world that a wiry and wide-eyed John Colton made his first impressions, green as all outdoors, but geared up for whatever might lay ahead.

Lassiter's campus sat just west of downtown Lassiter, Connecticut, right off 291 and within an afternoon's jog of the Connecticut River. The architecture was largely gothic, typically Ivy League, extending no more than ten blocks from one end to the other. It reminded me of home, how the buildings crouched in the trees, weighty but quiet, as if they harbored some half-revealed secret. Green and golden ivy crawled up the gray stones like an untamed beard. When the sun shone the mica and flint in the stones caught the light and glittered wildly around every turn; on a drizzly day the stones dripped solemnly, as if the buildings were a naturally risen formation. The stone steps leading into many of the buildings were worn to the white of the stone, carved out by the years of students busy to make the bell, busy to gather in the glitter and gold, busy to make the nearest bar. In that first month of college every doubt I'd ever had about myself as a football player (and as a person) circled around me like flies. The power of the campus, and Hartford, and all of New England -- and the ever-present pull of New York -- cast an allure that dwarfed the pine-sol-and-old-sock hallways of Jackson High and the simple laziness of Magnolia Lane on a humid Saturday night. Not even Lisa Rae suspected what shocks awaited me, nor the machinery I would find to smooth out the waves.

For me, this was as close to Big League football as I would get. I understood this, if not in outspoken terms, then intuitively, and so, I believe, did most of my teammates. At this level it was no longer possible to rely on God-given talent to succeed; we would have to work for it. The competition made the workouts strenuous and trying, and the demands of the coach did nothing to alleviate the stress. I liked Coach Kinney, the coach who, persuaded by Dr. Cannon's obscure endorsement, offered me the scholarship. He understood the game of football. He had once been a running quarterback at Dartmouth and he had an understated ability to gather the players into a cohesive unit. We responded largely from our common desire to win, but also out of respect for our leader. Perhaps his shortfall was recruiting. I wish he'd had more success my freshman year. I think Coach Kinney could have molded this collection of players into something great before my four years there were up.Not necessarily because of my own talents (though partially that is true) but simply because I could see a gelling force emerging late in the season, when his fate had already been decided. I would have liked to see him stay with us, not because he was a great coach, possessing some sort of extraordinary insight into strategy, but simply because he was fair and, where it mattered most -- in the heart -- he was a good man. Coach Kinney's record at Lassiter after four years was 12 and 36. He'd won enough games for a perfect season, but not enough in any one year to give him a single winning record. He knew the risks when he took on the challenge. Lassiter had a legacy of terrible football teams. The last time they'd won a league title was in 1948. Football at this university was an avocation engaged in for the intangible amenities cultured competition could bring to the alumni. After each trouncing they would gather in the Hoskins's Room and sip dry Manhattans in their tweed jackets and neckerchiefs, nodding their heads quietly as they gave quick strategic assessments of the contest, then awkwardly pushed the conversation toward Wall Street, or the America's Cup. After all, football was an awfully ill-mannered industry. Sophisticated adults should dwell well above its primal focus. This position was as much impetus as product of the legacy, but it was a position, I found, without genuine consensus.

It would be easy to say the folks I encountered in Connecticut were by and large snobbish and unfriendly, and to say that they never passed up on an opportunity to embarrass me in the subtle graces of eastern affluence. But that's not how it happened, overall. Perhaps because I spent so much of my time rolling around in the dry grass with a bunch of other poor souls in mutual states of distress, it was difficult to focus on the occasional infelicity which my cross my path. Football, like death, is no respecter of persons.

I wish the same were true of women. Easily the most painful transition for me revolved around courtship and romance. I had come from a small town where romantic value was often determined solely on the ability to look masculine in a pair of cleats, and once your reputation as a womanizer was established, no degree of loathsomeness could endanger it. Within a week I missed my girlfriend back home with a whole new invention of heartache. My first letter home must have made her nauseous with sentiment. I was new to this sort of thing.

Dear Susie,

I know you're probably at home now, sitting on your bed, leaning back against the headboard which squeaks so sweetly I lose my mind every time I hear it. You can see my picture on your table -- you know, the one where I'm covered in towels like a degenerate monk -- and outside Kelly and Tim are no doubt chasing each other around that big old oak. I miss you terribly, Susie. Everything here is weird--most of all the people. I haven't met anyone that I really get along with, though I guess my roommate is OK. He's from Boston and plays tight end. If he can make it then I feel my own chances are improved considerably. It's been hot, but I guess not quite as hot as in Lumberton. I bear the heat gracefully and try to keep my eye on the ball. That's the key, you know. Oh well! I know it's only been a week, but I'm ready for a trip back. Send me a picture so I can put it under my pillow and kiss it when my dreams get carried away. 'Bout time for chow. This place is a zoo. Oh well. Save me some, Honey.

In faithful, unrequited love,

John

That was the first of many such letters that semester. I found, even with the demands that football put on me, I had more time to myself than ever before. I had no car, of course, and the athletic dorm was beyond walking distance to the nearest bar or fraternity house. The unspent desires in me made me look at the girls in my classes with a distant, shaky longing. I watched them stare off into space as if their minds were overcrowded with philosophy, their brunette hair short and neat, roman noses as sharp as the cut of their teeth. I listened to them talk, slowly picking out the differences in the inflections, the short a's and o's, the common nasal tone. I missed the slow, drawn out expressions of the belles in Mississippi and the easy, simple gestures. I watched these coeds cross their legs, put a pencil behind their ear, and I wanted to hug the whole bunch. I wanted to jump on 'em! Yet I was afraid to make a peep. It was like being introduced for the first time to a steaming pot of Cajun shrimp and standing there with the succulent aroma fogging up your eyes, afraid to ask the chef for a serving.

There weren't too many good ole boys from the deep south in the over worn desks beside me, so when it did become necessary for me to interject a comment in class or answer the teacher's questions - or, God forbid, give a presentation -- I became painfully aware of a handicap I had never before even noticed: the dreaded Southern Accent. It was true that my own accent was slight compared to many of my friends back home, but in these environs it was enough. I heard giggles at every sentence, or so it seemed, in my growing linguistic paranoia, and it made me naturally reticent. I remember one of the football players, a tackle from Pennsylvania, introduced me to some gals in the library one afternoon. I nodded my head to them and said, "Hey, how ya doing?" a rather innocuous greeting, I thought. One of the girls smirked and, throwing a curl behind her ear, came back: "Hi yawl," which brought uproarious laughter from, it seemed, the entire library. Even my fellow jock got the joke. I smiled and acknowledged her wittiness, wishing to strangle her perfumed neck. Surely there was some lass in New England whose sense of dialect did not overwhelm her sense of affection. Surely there was. And I intended to find her.

As my freshman season played out my vistas slowly took on light. The team that year started two seniors at the wide receiver positions, two black fellows from New York City named Alfred Points and Alexander Mellon. Both of them could fly, but due to the weak arm of our quarterback their speed was difficult to utilize. There was another fellow, a sophomore from Connecticut, who was next in the rotation, and then me. With the exception of special teams play, I watched the games from the sideline. This was a new experience -- riding the bench -- and like my ineptitude with this new species of female it frustrated me to no end. Every time one of the Al's would catch a pass I waited anxiously for them to be slow getting up. But they knew the tricks. Hell, I never even saw one of 'em get a raspberry. So I waited.

It was the Seton Hall game, at home, when I got my chance. Our record at that point was 4 and 6, coach Kinney had a good suspicion that he was history (if he didn't know outright) and I think he liked my quiet and disciplined spirit in the midst of a largely minor drama. My father was a simple man, but he had taught me well the values of order and discipline, values that fit in well with a football team. Coach Kinney called me over before we went on the field in the second half. "Colton!" he yelled. I trotted over obediently, wondering what I'd done wrong. The Coach winked at me. "I'm gonna start you in the second half," he said. He didn't know I was playing to win.

We were down by two touchdowns and a field goal. Our first two possessions in the second half ended in punts, but the next time we got the ball they called my number. The quarterback tossed me a lazy spiral on a quick out. I had to slow down and turn back to pull it in and as I did the safety hammered me out of bounds. My chin strap came loose and my helmet bounced off my head and spun into the benches, but the ball stayed with me, good enough for a first down. Welcome to college football, cornpone! But now I was awake. We tried a few running plays. Nothing there. Third and long. "Split right, seven out, on two." That was me. Down ten yards and cut right. A timing pass. I sped up the field, then cut sharp to the right. This time the ball was there briskly and I pulled it in a good yard from the sideline. Then I made my move. I stopped dead still, freezing the cornerback. I made a shoulder fake to the right sideline, then I took a hard step to the left. He bought all of it. I slid by him to the sideline and took off. No one would catch me. I crossed the goal line into notoriety. I'd find my introductions easier from that moment on at Lassiter, but the game was not over. In the fourth quarter we recovered a fumble and on the next play our tailback broke off a twenty yard run for a score. We seemed to have the momentum and I felt an odd sense of predestination. Perhaps, indeed, I had the spark. When Seton Hall missed a field goal with three minutes left we set up for our final drive.

Coach Kinney wasted no time returning to his newfound tactics. After faking a quick trap, the quarterback threw me a wobbly lateral behind the scrimmage line. I took the ball and sprinted down the sideline. As the cornerback approached me, this time with caution, I slowed my step just perceptibly, then turned on the juice. His lunge just grazed a shoe as I stepped forward and flew toward the end zone. Where I came from this play was now over. I can't remember anyone ever catching Colton from behind. But times had changed. Their safety dragged me down at the twenty-two yard line like I was barely moving. Next, we tried a draw play. Then the coach called two passes to unsuccessful passes to the end zone. With forty-eight seconds left we sent our kicker out to tie the score. The spark lost its glow in the rush of Seton Hall's defensive line. A big nose tackle swatted the ball into the turf. My headlines were edited into a few laudatory comments. Nevertheless, the ballgame enlarged my credibility by a country mile. I imagined the alumni in the Hoskin's Room trading queries: "Who was that little white kid out there?" "Mississippi?" "You must be joking."

In the locker room following the game Alfred Points came over and offered a hand slap. "You got some moves, Colton. Not too bad." I shrugged modestly. "Well, thank ya. Need a little bit of your foot speed, I guess." "Naw, you got your own stuff, man." Behind Alfred, Randall Breimen, a big white tackle from a little town in western New York State, spoke up. "You going over to Kappa Sig, Colton?" Kappa Sigma was a fraternity that frequently hosted post-game parties. I'd never been invited, nor given the idea much thought.

I shrugged. "Well, I don't have a car."

"You can ride with me and Alexander," Alfred offered. I pulled off my socks, thinking. I'd heard rumors of dope smoking at Kappa Sig parties. I didn't know what to make of the stories, both because the reports were third hand and because I knew almost nothing about the substance in question. Marijuana had certainly made inroads in southern Mississippi, but it just never occurred to me as a possibility. I had seen the effects the drug had on kids at Jackson High, the ones who hung around the parking lot before school when it was warm enough, or at the end of the English hall during winter. They were radicals, I knew. Jeans, jean jackets, work shirts, boots; they'd passed petitions fighting the dress code and the hair code, and in the end they won. Even I could see the rules were ridiculous. But there was a limit to my empathy with the drugees. I could tell -- who couldn't -- the pot was gumming up their minds, dulling their thoughts, blanking out their sense of good reason, leaving empty husks for heads. They'd laugh -- "Huh, huh, huh, huh, huh, huh, huh" -- as void of humor and life as the gravel parking lot they stood in. I and my buddies would make fun of them some nights, driving around drunk, spying them gathered like gangsters outside an EZ-Shop, involved in some devious scheme. Growing up in Lumberton we were convinced that we would never even consider using THE DRUG. We had heard the horror stories: brain damage, hormone irregularities, loss of reality. It was downright unthinkable. But it was the first invitation to a real party that I'd had at Lassiter. The night seemed mine. How could I refuse?

It is common knowledge that there is an unusual euphoric state that often washes over a person after an extraordinary athletic performance. It can't be explained, really, or even described; at least not with any degree of accuracy. Athletic competition has too many angles and ambiguities for it to fit neatly into any paradigm. Just winning the game sometimes means nothing. You might have missed every pass, or struck out three times (or four, for that matter). And just playing well is not enough either, for if you don't win your personal achievements are a hollow victory. To really *get there* you have to win, you have to play well and you have to make *the play*. It is partly years of preparation, hard work and natural talent. But mostly it is pure luck. But when all those things come together for a moment in time you become *the star*. Everyone is on your side. No one ever thinks these things through. You do your thing, take your shower, then revel in the glory. There's no time for thought. Perhaps we know that too close an introspection may show up the giddiness for the fragile and transitory emotion that it is, a buoyancy that is subject to dissimilation at the mildest encroachment of reality. So I laughed modestly at the congratulations and walked quietly a foot and a half off the ground on my way to Alfred Point's Grand Prix. It was a weird and wild conclusion to what had been already an odd turn of events. If not for my airy state of mind I would had been suspicious of this journey. But it was the first invitation to a real party that I'd had at Lassiter. The night seemed mine. How could I refuse?

Still, it was a new and uncharted world. I imagined my name in the headlines of tomorrow's paper: "Flashy Redneck Trips on Acid and Dives off Delta Chi Roof". We stopped at Gosa's Kwick Mart and picked up some beer. The crisp, bitter liquid helped calm my anxiety. They asked if I'd ever been to Delta Chi before. When I said no, they laughed and made several jokes about The Roof and some gal named Katy, which amused them terribly. I chuckled, grew more nervous, took a long gulp, calmed down some. I had nothing in common with my new friends; that is, except for our exceptional abilities to catch a football, run like hell, and put up with the rigors of practice. I sat next to Reginald Lindsey, our knees touching, smelling his cologne. There is nothing like cheap cologne to link a redneck from the Deep South with a player from Deep Downtown. Reginald looked at me and smiled. "You've got some moves," he said, laughing. I looked at him, then at Alfred, who was delicately guiding the vehicle from the driver's seat with one eye focused on me from the rear view mirror. Oh my God!

Delta Chi. I could just make out two yellow windows through the waving limbs of a broad tree that rose up in the front yard of the fraternity house. What the hell, I thought. It was Saturday night. The stars were aligned. The music was loud. The house was rocking. The girls were tipsy. And I had the moves.

The Chi Delta fraternity house stood on Keaton Lane, at the edge of Keaton Park. Another fraternity, the Kappa Sigma Chi, had a house further up the street, but the remaining houses were several blocks away. This isolation, rather than being a sleight to the Chi Delts, became a source of distinction and added privacy, and they took full advantage. The exterior of the house was no marvel. White wood with black trim, the two-story structure resembled nearly every other building along Greek Row. The house took on greater dimensions as one stepped inside. Over the stairwell leading upstairs perched a stuffed Black Panther, poised for attack. Its teeth were lit up with yellow day glow and a blood red paint dripped from the eerie fangs. It made a startling and impressive figure piece. I saw Randall Breimen standing by the stairs and he toasted me with his beer.

"Colton!" he yelled out, a high, raspy voice. His eyes were bloodshot and half-closed, as if he'd been drinking all night. "Tightrope," he called out at me. It didn't occur to me for a moment that he was speaking to me. The two Al's echoed him: "Tightrope!" Hah! Just what I needed.

Breimen put his arm around my shoulder. "First time here?" I nodded yes."C'mon, I'll show you around." Randall Breimen was 6'3" and carried 265 pounds loosely on his frame.He had the type of face which is instantly familiar. His cheeks were always covered in red splotches and he had dimples, a childish expression cloaking a powerful offensive tackle. We walked through the den, filled with students partying, spilling beer on one another. I took notice of a blond in jeans near the wall, and she looked back curiously. The place had the same type of fraternity crap on the walls that I'd seen in the few other houses I'd visited. As we walked through the kitchen Breimen pulled a Schlitz out of the fridge and opened it for me."Shitz!" he said. He showed me up the back stairwell, lit up with black lights. Along the wallsthere were a series of posters -- Jimi Hendrix, black swans, exploding planets. I could hear from some hidden doorway the too-hip vocals and misty horns of Steely Dan sifting through the hallways.

I'll learn to work the saxophone
I'll play just what I feel
Drink Scotch whisky all night long
And die behind the wheel
They got a name for the winners in the world
I want a name when I lose
They call Alabama the Crimson Tide
Call me Deacon Blues

Breimen laughed: "How 'bout this shit?" I didn't know what to make of it. I was uneasy, like a child in a funhouse, unable to discern danger from illusion. I asked him where we were going. "The Roof, man," he answered, "The Roof."

We filed down a hallway, catching stares, it seemed, from every half-opened door. Then we entered a bedroom filled with throw pillows. Earth, Wind and Fire played vibrantly from a stereo. It seemed to surround us. A stale, spicy smoke hung in the room, mixed with strawberry incense. A voice called from a dark corner. I could not make out the features in the hazy light."Breimen! Suck me, honky!"

Breimen stopped, offered the voice his rear end. "French kiss, Klondike. French Kiss," he replied.

The voice called back: "Tell Koslowski I want to see him." Koslowski was the backup quarterback.

"Yo," Breimen acknowledged. He stopped at an open widow and peered out. "This way, tightrope," he said, then he led me out the window onto The Roof. I followed nervously. It was much too late to turn back. I put a hand on the peeling paint of the wall and looked out.

The Roof spread out around the southwest corner of the building, providing a full view of Pope Park and the southern end of the city. A pleasant breeze came through the trees, carrying the odors of the city streets and the seafood restaurant at the corner of Broad and Keaton. Koslowski sat with his back against the building, looking out into the night sky.His eyes, too, were half-closed. He spotted me. "Colton!" he shouted. "What you doin' up here? You ride out with Breimen?"

"Naw. I came with Al."

"Well, welcome to The Roof, man!"

Breimen walked to the corner of the ledge and spit off, then turned back to Koslowski."So where's the IVM, Koslo?"

"Shit man, don't look at me.It's hard enough just to keep up with my own ass.Hey Colton, that was a good game, man." He stuck out his hand and I reached down to shake it. "Is he cool, Breimen?"

"Shit. You kidding? He's from fuckin' Lumbertown, Mississippi. You ever met anybody from Lumbertown, Mississippi that wasn't cool?

"I never met anybody from Lumbertown, Mississippi." Breimen spotted the joint passing hands around the corner of the building. "There it is. How 'bout it?" Someone handed him the joint.

"Lumberton," I said.

"What?"

"It's Lumberton, not Lumbertown."

Koslowski laughed and shook his head at the correction. Meanwhile, beside me, Breimen took a long drag off the joint. It was rolled in blue rolling paper, twisted clumsily at both ends.Smoke streamed from it in rich curves as Breimen pulled in the smoke, held his breath, then handed it to me. I took the joint and shook my head in disbelief. They all looked at me as I eyed the preparation. I felt as if I had climbed onto some slippery cliff overlooking a green, washing surf, committing myself to a long and uncertain dive. I drew on the joint slowly. The smoke was rich and hot, much heavier than cigarette smoke and much more volatile. Almost immediately the smoke exploded in my lungs and I coughed violently, raising laughter from my audience. Embarrassed, I passed the joint on and sat down next to Koslowski and waited for the next pass. Alfred and Alexander came out, laughing and slapping everyone's hands. I took several more tokes -- with more caution -- and tried to appear at ease while my mind and heartbeat raced. It wasn't until about twenty minutes later that it first hit me. I had just taken the last gulp of my beer and had leaned back, feeling a little sick to my stomach. Suddenly the sound from the cheap stereo inside seemed to seep into my head as if the music emanated from some inner bandstand. I can still remember the song - Rhiannon, by Fleetwood Mac, the sultry voice of Stevie Nicks grabbing me by the heart and balls.

The bass guitar and churning drum beat seemed to fall out of the sound and overwhelm the other instruments. I was about to speak when suddenly I felt a tingling sensation run straight down my backbone, through my legs, and then out my toes, as if the Rush might be setting out a carpet for all of Lassiter, Connecticut, or the whole state, or this planet.

"Jesus!" I said, the exclamation always reserved for those events so startling and unusual they defy description. We call out to God, thinking He's the only one with a reasonable explanation when the world becomes crazy. Someone drove me home. I found out later it was Koslowski. He said we had a heavy conversation about God and the universe, but I remember little of it. That night I was introduced to the infinity of my mind and my own finite presence. I found something wild and new in my imagination, but I lost something too. This began my apprenticeship with hallucinogenics. I was too busy, most times at Lassiter, to get too curious, or too wild. I ran in unsophisticated circles and tuition was too expensive for most folks to waste much time stoned to the gills. But it wouldn't be the last time I visited The Roof. I am a curious cat, and unsatisfied.

I began, in my freshman year at Lassiter, to become aware of the expansiveness and peculiarity of my existence. It was a year of great introspection. I studied my past with the same verve I studied the world I came from, struggling with my current options and the implications of various modes of thought or action. I began to take in some of the common truths of our society while engaging a thousand less answerable queries, wondering at my own insignificant clock-piece in the cosmic machinery. My girlfriend in Mississippi, Susie, found another, more convenient partner, as I too made new friends in Connecticut and even came to enjoy their more cosmopolitan culture. I felt a strange link with the literary traditions this district had inherited, though still far from the qualifications necessary for admittance even as a visitor. I visited Mark Twain's old home and Noah Webster's and Hawthorne's. I spent three nights in Queens; saw half the sights of the Big Apple. During the second trimester I met Professor Strache, who heaped great helpings of the English Masters into my already brimming imagination, and who outshone for me every teacher I'd ever seen work their craft. The Professor would become a friend and, when things got craziest, a vital ally. It was a year of great pace, academically, socially and intellectually. When spring practice came around my thoughts could hardly be captivated by the rote demands of the scrimmage. New alchemy's were replacing the old faiths.

We had a new coach, Jack Rivers. In my metaphysical fog I found him simple-minded and distant, and I think he sensed my resistance. I went through the routines and rigors of practice and made my best case for a starting position, but my heart wasn't in it. He seemed to know the strategies, but he had a bad temper. He was a man who seemed always at war. I knew his kind. But I had already learned this game; I could see no obstacles to slow me down. My eyes were too full of stars. I grew up in the Dragon's Den, and besides, I had the moves.

Chapter 4
But why will you say that I am mad?

Things would get weird in the days, months and years that followed. As my star in the football sky began its ascent, the challenges of higher education and the realities of my shortcomings came into full bloom. Whoever these freaks were, they were much smarter than me. Had it not been for The Professor, I may have called it a day. I met Professor Strache in the second semester of my freshman year. I think the class was Early American Literature, but the subject matter of the class was eclipsed fully by the light The Professor brought to the exercise. He was a legend on campus. By the end of the first class he had held me captive to his genius.

The Professor had a unique style to his lectures. He was not a big pacer; he liked to sit and lean on stuff: all edges of the desk, the window sills, the desks of students, the sill of the chalkboard, a doorknob -- nothing was sacrosanct. I think he owned only two woolen coats -- one plaid brown, one gray -- and both were worn to the point of being frayed. He seldom wore a tie, but if he did, it would be gray, or sometimes a clip-on bow-tie. He always needed a haircut. His dark brown (though largely grayish now) hair seemed to sling out at all angles, in concert with his train of thought. He spoke a lot through his hands, curled over his mouth, covering it fully, or pulling at some part of his face. He literally formed the words he spoke. Occasionally he would stop and look off -- and even smile slightly -- struck by his own cleverness. He could be intimidating; he didn't condescend to fakery, would ask a student point blank if he had the slightest idea what he was talking about (either of them) but he did it with style. He had delicate blue eyes and he cared deeply about his subject and his subjects. He loved and he lived to teach, and he was the best I saw.

While many of my classmates found him eccentric, confusing at times, even unapproachable, I was always transfixed by his methods. I watched him lecture and it was like he was a child wandering through a toy store, or perhaps a grandfather re-telling vibrant memories which he couldn't fully recall, scribbling titles on the board, opening a window, later, closing it again, asking for our opinions on the deepest of philosophical constructs and listening as if we might truly shed some light on the matter. He taught literature, but he understood the importance of an author's time and culture. He asked for excellence, but was forgiving of mediocrity. I could not meet all the trials he set before me, but I battled in the cause. He turned my interest in literature into a passion, from a hobby to a craft. I sought out his advice and his approval and he carefully meted out both when they were both most needed. In my senior year his pale, yellow light shone like an old lighthouse on a windy point, sturdy and clear in all storms. The game of football had brought me across the nation to this small, old college. A small, old teacher made every mile of the journey a priceless endowment. I knew almost nothing about English when I entered Lassiter. Sure, Lisa Rae had introduced me to the richness of some of the great American writers, but all it did was give me an appreciation for the craft and, perhaps, an ear for the melodies. Before I would finally walk up to the podium to receive my diploma from Dean Tutley I would at least learn the basics of grammar…and how to use a thesaurus.

Two full years of college and life would pass before I made it to my senior year at Lassiter College. They were years of knowledge and confusion, confidence and awkwardness, triumph and disappointment, love and heartbreak. My sophomore and junior years, looking back now, the advantages of time on my side, were pretty much typical of all college students in my time, or in times previous. College students are, for the most part, kids. I was no different. I thought I knew more than I did and pretended to be more than I was. College is the last warm swamp of youth. For the enlightened and the bold, it is a briar patch filled with honeysuckles. As an athlete from southern Mississippi, I expected to be spit out. Had it not been for Lisa Rae, I would've been. Unlike my experiences at Jefferson High, academics at Lassiter were not a joke. The faculty was nice enough, on the whole, but they didn't really care where you came from or why you were there. They desired students who would listen to their every word like it was handed down from the heights of Sinai. They looked for students who turned in their assignments on time and for students who could write. I could fake the first requirement, barely meet the second, and smoke the last.

It was Lisa Rae who turned me on to the images, sounds and meter of great writing. "We're from Mississippi," she'd whisper to me, reading a long passage from Pride and Prejudice, "just like Faulkner." "You should read with your ears," she'd say, "and listen with your eyes." I thought she was crazy. But she was my older sister. What could I do?

In all my life I'll never forget those times when Lisa Rae would drag me off to the edges of James' Creek, where she'd pull out a copy of Huck Finn. In her velvet southern voice she would read to me like I was a three-year old, while she finished some of Twain's classic passages. Had anyone else tried such a thing I would've quickly given them the slip, but she was my older sister, and always had a hold on me. So I let her finish, and took it all in. For some reason, Lisa Rae loved the English language, and its proper usage, like some sort of inheritance. I've given it a lot of thought, but I still haven't figured out where her writing abilities came from. No one in our family, including our parents, grandparents and direct relatives, were respectable in the least in the written word. She must've had a gift. When she was still in high school she had published two short stories and finished a volume of poems. I was a poor speller, with a limited vocabulary. This story, in a sense, is dedicated to Lisa Rae, because she is my older sister, who I will always love, and because she taught me how to write.

I returned to Lumberton for the summer of each year following my freshman, sophomore and junior years at Lassiter. Lumberton was at once a gentle refuge and a stormy harbor from the swirl of winds that made up my past, my present and my uncertain future. I was never so naive to believe Lumberton was a clear representation of the larger world, however, the substance of such concepts is always best understood with firsthand experience, seeing the variety close-up, touching it with both hands. Watching the familiar sights of home from the bus that carried me from the Oxford airport to Lumberton after my first year of school brought back an irresistible nostalgia. Every summer that I returned to Lumberton I re-entered the past and fell back into a quiet and wonderful world. The joys of childhood were paved into these dusty streets and storefronts: afternoon dips in Ocoee Spring, fish fry's on McSwain's farm, all the adventures of danger and lust: everything seemed wrapped up in the simplest of images -- the gray water tower, the huge sprawling oak in the middle of the town square. I'd once carved my initials there. But in this warm, immutable scenery I felt now other emotions, barrenness as though time were slipping away from me down some deep creek. I was torn between two worlds. In the summer after my first year of college my sister would get pregnant and then run off and get married in the midst of my father's first run for city councilman. With my head already full of the confusion and dreams spawned at Lassiter, these shenanigans made the summer frantic. I wanted to escape from all of it, either to a more promising future or to a simpler past; but these options were out of reach.

Much of my time during the summer (but little of my attention) I spent working at Dad's hardware store, lazing around behind the counter watching ballgames and doing the occasional stock work, or cleaning. Sarge took the business seriously, as he did almost everything, but during his campaign he left many of the minor details of the operation to me. Though I found the job unglamorous I was in no position to object. I began to sneak off up the block to Crowder's Bookstore and hunt through his used section for whatever book caught my eye or curiosity. Since Crowder let you trade them back in three for one, it was an affordable treasure. I began to devour books like Bar-B-Que: I fell in love with Twain, worked my way through a good part of Chaucer and Shakespeare, fretted over the intricacies of Joyce, then drowned myself in Poe's madness and genius. Business was slow for the most part, I had time on my hands, and I found the perfect medicine for such times. Lisa Rae had given me a collection of Mark Twain's short stories, along with copies of Huckleberry Finn and Tom Sawyer that were 3 years overdue. I'll never forget those afternoons reading with Lisa Rae, discussing Twain's magic, or reciting Poe's lyrics. Poe, Lisa Rae, explained, was a tortured genius:

> *TRUE! - nervous - very, very dreadfully nervous I had been and am; but why will you say that I am mad? The disease had sharpened my senses - not destroyed - not dulled them. Above*

> *all was the sense of hearing acute. I heard all things in the heaven and in the earth. I heard many things in hell. How, then, am I mad? Hearken! and observe how healthily - how calmly I can tell you the whole story.*

Many afternoons, when Dad was minding the store and I could get away for a while, I'd grab a book or two and my cheap rod and reel, pick up a can of worms from Smiley's bait shop and lay back along the banks of Winowee's Creek and fish for catfish and drum. A big willow tree hung over the creek near one of the quiet turns and it made a peaceful and comfortable resting spot. Sometimes Red Simpson would join me, or Tommy Dickenson (whose father owned the land I fished on). Even Lisa Rae would sit with me on the grassy banks, when the mood struck her, and we'd read poetry to each other, or make stupid jokes, or sit and listen to the Mississippi wind whispering a warm summer welcome. You'd never catch much and what you did catch wasn't much worth keeping, but the scenery alone made the afternoon pleasant and nothing can match a quiet creek-bank for enjoying the likes of Mark Twain or the winding subtleties of a long conversation. When it was hot in Lumberton, as it was during the summer, the sky turned almost white. The only clouds you'd see would be strays, picking up their moisture from some deep lake perhaps, only to drift a mile or two before the summer sun tamed them into haze. A half-bent pine and a restless willow sheltered my lonely settlement. You could smell, with a strong breeze, the sour saw grass Dickenson fed his cattle, or the pungent aroma of dung. From the creek, other rich odors: gray, thick mud, cool water carrying off crayfish and minnows, biting at the surface like they were catching breaths. The soft bank was full of life: rising, swaying, feeding, sliding silently into the final decline and then final decay. I used to drag my bare feet in the cool, sweeping current and lay back along the shady banks, reading and resting without a care in the world.

Most of my old running mates were still in town -- Kerry Stahls, Pete Kaufman, Red Simpson -- and we were able to dig up some excitement from time to time on Saturday nights. I found that my experiences with pot were not unique and before long we were passing joints on our excursions to Hattiesburg or behind the bowling alley on a boring Sunday night. They couldn't resist digging at me about the ambitious course I'd charted.

"Ain't no women like Patricia Hicks up there!"

Red said it as if it were a fact; there was no debate about the idea. He was probably right. She had about a forty inch chest.

"That's true enough," I said. "Hard enough to fit one of her in this land."

Red went on."Kerry's been going out with Hallie Matson."

"No!" I objected.

Kerry looked away, kicked at a rock.I was leaning against his red Camaro, parked beneath a tree in front of Red's old home. A squirrel crouched in the shade working on a nut. Even the squirrel seemed to be sweating from the moist air.

"Ch'yea," Red continued. "Took her to Hattiesburg last Saturday. Got a motel room!" Red gave me an elbow in the side. He loved to be hitting at you when he talked. Red had the kind've freckles that were so dense they almost blended together. He had an eye for adventure and a wicked curveball.

"Sounds pretty serious," I said.

Jimmy fessed up. "Aw, it ain't nothing. I'm just seeing her some. That's all."

I hardly remembered who Hallie Matson was. Seems she was awfully shy.

Pete prodded me. "What about you, Colton?"

Pete had a deep, quiet voice and wore his black hair in a flat top. He had dark, blue eyes and could appear serious doing anything: wearing women's underwear say, or discussing the implications of a fart. He seemed out of place everywhere, but didn't care, and perhaps that's why I liked him so much. He was a weird athlete, for he had the odd talent of being ambidextrous. He thought nothing of the fact he could throw a football left handed, while he wrote with his right. I had few stories to tell them.

"Well. I met a few girls. None that could really stand me. They think I'm a farmer. Can you imagine that?"

"Well y'are," Red said.

"Well, I guess you'd know." I grabbed Red by the neck, put him in a headlock and rubbed his tangled scalp. He struggled and yelled. Jimmy picked up a nut and threw it at the squirrel. Pete pulled out a Marlboro, lit it and looked at the hazy sky. There were certainly worse places to be for a college kid on break than Lumberton in the summertime. If it hadn't been for Sarge's obsessive campaign and my sister's carelessness I would have been happy to be home.

My father should never have gotten involved in politics. They say the secret to successful political careers is the ability to satisfy many disparate factions simultaneously, to know where to make a stand and where to walk the fence like an alley cat in the moonlight. The best politicians, it always seemed to me, were the ones who could handle every issue with kid gloves, seizing on the publicity while remaining essentially vague on the substance of their position. My father had none of the tact necessary for this approach. He was a hip shooter. He believed he'd been around long enough to know what was going down and his opinion was as good or better than anyone else's. He saw no gray areas. A thing was either right, or it was not right, and he was ready to spread the word. There were two problems to his strategy: 1. Nothing is absolute. 2. The constituency of Lumberton didn't really give much of a hoot one way or the other. He ran a campaign full of passion and zeal and courage amongst a community addicted to the status quo. Add all this to his almost total lack of skill in public speaking and the whole damn thing began to get embarrassing.

My father ran against Jim Highfield, who was a manager at the sawmill and a quiet Republican. Highfield was never without his blue pin-stripe suit and red tie, but at the same time it seemed he could never get a decent haircut. He was clever enough to realize that my father, however sincere, was unskilled in this arena where he'd been tinkering for years. He had friends all over town in business (because they nearly all were connected, in one way or another, to the mill) and he ran a low profile, high-pressure campaign. Meanwhile, Sarge canvassed the black communities, which probably wouldn't vote anyway, and talked about his honesty and the need for integrity. He dragged me up on the podium with him for a speech he gave before the Rotary Club in the Jackson High auditorium. The larger debate occurred earlier in the evening, when he informed me of his intention to bring me along. I was pissed.

"This is ridiculous!"

"What?" he said.

"I said, 'this is ridiculous.' I don't see why I have to spend Saturday night sitting at some boring rotisserie club meeting."

"Rotary! It will do you good. This'll be educational for you. I think you can survive one night without riding around town seeing who can drink the most beer."

My mother stuck her head in. "John? What's this?"

"Johnnie says he got better things to do than support his own family. Be sure you wear your suit."

"I've got plenty of support for this family. It's just I'm not running for anything and I don't see why I've got to be displayed like some sort of trophy or something."

Now my father was pissed.His face turned red. You could tell he was debating some course of action, but now I was the quicker one, and he knew it. I kept an angle on the door.

"If I'm running, you're running! What do you think you're some kind've hot shot now? You've been to Connecticut and now you know what the world is about? You don't know diddlysquat, Junior." He shook his head and walked into the bedroom, as if he'd settled the matter conclusively. It was left to my mother to convince me. She saw my point, but, after all, it meant a lot to him. I didn't tell him the real reason for my reluctance. I knew he'd make an ass of himself and me, by implication.

I sat behind him, with my mother, on the stage, looking off disjointedly, trying to appear as removed from the immediate events as possible. There were hardly 45 people in the auditorium and they seemed restless to be about other chores. Blanton Thales made the introduction, playing up my father's war record, patriotism and honesty.Then my dad stepped up. As always, he was noticeably nervous, even before minor crowds. A drop of sweat had already appeared on the right side of his forehead. He still sported a traditional Marine Corp haircut. He looked out over the crowd without seeing a single face. This was from a man who had charged across rice paddies in a hail of gunfire and single-handedly taken out machine gun posts; a man who had spent many a night deep in foreign jungles, knowledgeable that death could stalk him from every leafy shadow, a man who preached the power of discipline to overcome all obstacles.

He fumbled with his papers, and began reading verbatim, looking up at the end of every other sentence toward the back of the room, toward some dark sense of security.

"Thank you Blanton," he began. "It is certainly a pleasure to be here with the proud members of the Lumberton Rotary Club. My name is John Colton and I'm running for the seat of city councilman."He looked glassy-eyed. "I have been a resident here in Lumberton almost since my birth. I was away for a few years with the Marine Corps, but even then my heart was always here. My children have both grown up here, Lisa Rae, who couldn't be with us tonight, and John Jr." (He turned and smiled at me insincerely.) "Many of you are here tonight, I know, have spent much your life here. Many of you are perhaps new to our community. All of us, however, are interested in the quantity, uh, quality, uh, quality of life here, in Lumberton." He took a deep breath. "I believe, in order to make this town the same great place to live in that it has always been will require a commitment to excellence on the part of our city leaders. I think we need people willing to make a stand." The words were coming out like teeth being pulled now. He licked his lips and looked down at his notes as if he'd lost his place, or was unsure whether to continue with his next statement.

"We need to be able to trust our leaders that they will make the best decisions which have our best interests at heart. Our world is going through many changes. One cannot underestimate our, that is, the importance of each and every individual in our society. It will take the efforts of all of us here to make Lumberton be the same great place it has always been." (The perspiration was now beaded on his face and a drop fell onto his papers. He wiped at his nose hurriedly, and went on.) "And this is why I'm running for city councilman. I think I can bring to Lumberton much experience from my travels around this world and from my background as a leader in the armed service. Thank you and I look forward to your support."

Sarge breathed a heavy sigh of relief and looked back to mom and me with another half-cocked smile. It was clear that he didn't enjoy a bit of what he was up to. He took my mother's hand and walked into the crowd to make the rounds. I nodded to a few familiar faces and tried to slip away to an inconspicuous corner, but everywhere I turned some Lumberton Alumni cornered me. 'Yes, I am still playing football, and yes, Connecticut is sure a lot different; You have an uncle in New Haven? Sure, give me his address; I'll run down to see him first thing!'

Meanwhile Sarge talked issues, pressed the flesh and asked for votes to a series of blank expressions. My mother was the only one who seemed to fit in with the mob. She and Ginny Cone were laughing over a whispered joke. By the time the evening was over I was smiled out and ready for a cold beer.

My father would not win this election. He no longer represented Lumberton. Right or wrong, his had a larger agenda than these folks could swallow. I would have admired his idealism if he hadn't been such a lousy loser. When the results were in and it finally sunk home how overwhelmingly he'd been rejected, he blamed every cause except the real one. Politics was not a brick wall to be smashed down with a thick head and a run. The subtlety of the game had my father baffled and his frustration drew our family farther apart. I sought shelter in silence and watched helplessly as my sister drew back her forces.

It didn't take long for my father's frustration to come to the fore. We were driving home from church on a warm, humid Sunday afternoon, the air full of clouds, when the first hints of his anger came out. Lisa Rae was feeling lousy also, for undetermined reasons, and to tell the truth I was still half hung over from yesterday. We sat in the back seat looking solemnly at each other as Sarge missed Terrapin Road, which led to our subdivision. He rolled the window down and spit out thickly.

"Looks like the Ogleby's are holding out their sorghum." Mom looked his way disconcertedly. Sarge went on. "Ain't been that hot a summer." He looked back at me and frowned. "Hell, this ain't nothing next to the summer or 69. You remember that, mom?"

Mom nodded yes and rolled down her window. Dad had turned off the air conditioner. Lisa Rae punched me in the leg and we both followed, rolling down our own vents to the hot, dusty air. We were driving slowly past the entrance to The Winston's pecan farm. Old man Winston had bought out the last of Grandpa Justin's seedlings.

Sarge continued, raising his chin and looking down his nose toward the full, dark pecan groves and the rich, green lawn beneath them. Squirrels hopped everywhere and a truck sped towards the Winston's big, old house up their dusty driveway.

"I asked your Momma to tell you 'bout that dress Lisa Rae. Apparently she didn't think it 'portant enough. Ya shouldn't wear an outfit like that for any reason. Least of all to Sunday church!" He shook his head and frowned like he was tasting some vile substance. His eyes, like all of us in the car, were watering from the heat and dust. He turned slowly onto Cooper's Trail, which wound along towards Ocoee River and eventually, with any luck, back towards home.

Lisa Rae threw her head back. "Well Dad, it ain't like I got a closet full of gowns, or nothing! I mean, I'm lucky I got one dress that looks half presentable." She knew how to talk his language and only too well where to hurt him most.

"Hush!" he turned back towards her with a scowl, raising his voice. "Now, you're my daughter and John there, like it or not sonny, you're my son. N' its time y'all started acting like a family here. Your Momma off protecting you from me like I'm some ogre or something, it ain't right and it's gonna stop. You know they said us Colton's weren't right to be involved in the government -- weren't slick enough, too country. You're gonna find out one day what a family means to you. You're getting old enough now, one day you're gonna be on your own and then you'll know." The car was gradually accelerating as his speech gained force. The dust picked up and swirled behind us like a storm as we sped through the flat river valley and crept up on Oak Tree Lane. A two hundred year old oak tree spread out on the corner there, thick as a truck, gnarled and twisted with age and time, moss-covered branches reaching clear across the road like the arms of a grandmother in a worn shawl.

Lisa Rae couldn't let it lie. Something was bothering her. "Well, what are you saying? That me and John are the reason you lost that stupid election?" Tears were in her eyes. "Gimme a break. Highfield bought off every official in the county. Wudn't nothing any of us was gonna do make a damn bit of difference. Can't you see that?" I grabbed her leg, pleading for some peace. She slapped my hand away. "Quit it!" she said.

Sarge slowed down as we neared the entrance to our subdivision and he looked back at Lisa Rae, the tears streaming down her face. "Naw. I can't see that. But I can see a little girl that ain't near as smart as she thinks she is. One day you'll grow up. They all do, someday."

Lisa Rae confided her little problem to me a week before she told the folks. I stood stocking paint supplies in the back of the store when she slunk in. The bell over the door made almost no sound. "Hey," she called. I peered over the shelf. "Hey!"

"Jeez, it's hot in here!"

"Yeah." I wiped the dust from my hands onto my jeans and gave Lisa Rae a small hug. "It's a wonder we get a single customer."

"You'd think you could get a little air conditioner in that back window."

"Yeah. Sarge's not too keen on creature comforts."

"Well, you, being the creature, should know."

"Like sister, like son." She walked toward the cashier area and picked up the paperback laying there face down.

"Castenada?"

"Yeah. It's pretty wild."

She sat in the stained pinewood chair and propped her tennis shoes on the desk. The fan in the corner above her blew the hot air back and forth above our heads. Two flies chased each other on the window behind her, buzzing steadily. She read some to herself from the book.

"He's the one who does the peyote, right?" Before I could answer she went on. (I cleared a seat for myself on the desk beside her feet.) "You know, I heard a disturbing rumor."

"Uh-huh."

"Something about hallucinogenic substances and young southern gentlemen behind the Fairlanes Bowling Alley." I tried unsuccessfully to feign surprise.

"What's this?"

"Just a rumor. Imagine it. Shocks the sensibilities. Boggles the mind. What has Lumberton come to? Tsk, Tsk. Next thing you know they'll be hippies congregating in the park. Sit-ins. Peace marches.Wild animalistic orgies of sex and drugs and perverted music."

"One can only hope."

"Don't fret. I'm not so naive as I appear, you know." She smiled devilishly and tossed the book back on the desk. "But you, on the other hand. Oh, little John. Johnny Junior. You're outgrowing your britches. 'Fore ya know it, you'll be running for office."

"It's in the blood. . . .I guess." She laughed, then looked at the floor somberly.

"Well, I've got a problem." She reached out for my hand and looked at my face, her expression distant, disconnected. "I'm pregnant, son."

"No!"

Her tongue licked her upper lips. There was a sweat drop on her cheek.

"I need your help, John."

"I'm... I," was all I said. I was hopeless. I could not move through the implications and depth of the situation."I can do . . . what?" I asked, stupidly. Even at her most vulnerable she stumped my perceptions.

She smiled and blinked back a tear.She let go of my hands and stood, then turned to look out the dusty window. There was almost no breeze outside. A black fellow was filling his station wagon at the E-Z-GO across the street, halfway down the block. Another, older black fellow walked our way, in overalls, rolling slowly, in no hurry to get anywhere. The flies still buzzed, now in the corner of the window.

"I don't know," she said. "Your help is all."

"Whatever I can do Lisa Rae. You know I'd do anything." You could see from the store window the front of Rexall's Drug Store, where a 25 cent pony ride sat motionless. The Laundromat door was open, and you could see three black ladies sitting together on a bench, one of them working a fan, all of them looking off in boredom. A black and white mutt came trotting up the sidewalk, catching up with the old man, panting heavily, swishing its tail to keep away the gnats. The sidewalk was half-covered in white sand, as was the road. This town was full of dirt. It was dirt that made it country; dirt that kept it fresh; dirt, somehow, that made it home.

I was upstairs in my room when Lisa Rae told Sarge the news. He was incensed, out of control. He struck my sister with the back of his hand. She whirled, stumbled backward and fell into our dumpy, living room chair. My mother barked at him: "John!" then turned and knelt to my sister's side.

As I came down the stairs I was struck -- as if by another blow -- by that strange fierceness in my father's eyes. One eye seemed to quiver with anger. My heart fell.

I held the staircase, both hands on its last rounded pole, motionless, looking on. Sarge turned and headed out the door toward the car.

Lisa Rae moved out the next day. She planned to live with Roger's family in Biloxi until she could get up enough money for her own place. I helped her get her clothes into Mom's Buick Skylark that evening and we took off down Highway 49 at morning's first light. The morning air was filled with the ripeness of corn and sorghum. Peanuts hid beneath green weaves to both sides. An occasional tractor lumbered along the shoulder, slowing everyone, but all were patient here; no one seemed in a hurry. I spit out the window and took a long gulp from my root beer.

"You know, you didn't have to speak up. Not right away, you know?"

Lisa Rae laughed. She let the air blow her long brunette hair across her face, catching the gold of the sun, as wild and carefree as her mood.

"He's fuckin' crazy." Then: "So is mom, y'know? They live in some weird time and space. It's not even part of the past.They've invented this weird niche not even they understand."

I slowed through a four-way stop. The brakes squeaked lightly.

"Well, there's a lot of weird folks out there. I mean, think of Allyson's folks. Remember the time Mr. Harris took 'em all camping 'cause he was sick of their TV--"

"Yeah, and they ran out of food and he gave 'em a bunch of berries and shit. Made 'em sick for a week."

"What an idiot."

"Well, they're all crazy. All the fuckers in that town. And we're probably just as bad off. At least you."

I gave her an elbow to the arm, pushing her against the door.

"So what are you gonna do, huh?"

I motioned to the row of live oaks off to my left, and smiled.

"Roger is quite a guy, you know?"

"Yeah."

"Yeah. He ain't no jock or nothing. They can't all be specimens. Like you. But he's book smart. His folks are gorgeous. You should see their house."

"So that's the deal. When are you gonna get married then?"

"Hmmmm. I don't know. It's all so dreary now. Like I'm walking onto some old theater stage, looking for a prop, an old chest I might rummage through."

"You're the one, you know." "What's that?"

"You're the gorgeous one," I told her.

"Oh Johnnie. Johnnie," she said, and she put her head against my shoulder and shed a tear. So ended my first summer home from school.

In my next two years at Lassiter our sense of family would become more and more tangled up. Now that my sister and I were practically out of the house there was little glue left to hold my folks together. It was the nature of their relationship. They had married in a time when people married for life and personal happiness was not something you let get in the way. My mother -- open and gracious, musical, even funny at times -- was so different from my father, who could be so serious about even minor situations that it tried one's patience. They had little in common. Only the allure of The Family kept them close. Now they saw it dissolving. Lisa Rae had given up on trying to make it work. Neither Mom nor Dad had ever understood her glowing mind and the winds which gave life to her ideals. Not to say that I entirely understood her either. Often, at family reunions, you'd overhear an aunt or cousin gossiping about my sister's unique and formless personality, and to watch her behavior from across the yard you'd have to agree with them. But I knew how she'd come to hear her breezes, and I admired her innocent embrace of every storm.

She had finally taken in too much of these waves. She would head for calmer seas now, and clearer skies, and she would cut my father's anger from her heart. Sarge's pride kept him from making the hard journey back into her life. Lisa Rae had learned to be alone. For Sarge, the lesson would be more costly.

By the time my senior year arrived Lisa Rae was living happily with Roger and their son Jaimie down in Biloxi. She taught high school English and hated half the kids at Gulf High and wanted the other half legally adopted. She would talk to mom occasionally on the phone, or would write, but she refused to approach Sarge. He was similarly resistant. I always tried to visit her at least once during the summer.

"Where're you going?" Dad once called out. I was just opening the door to the Buick.

"I thought Mom told you."

He looked at me, disturbed; trying to make me feel guilty, perhaps change my plans.

"I was planning on driving to Biloxi. Y'know I haven't seen Lisa Rae all summer."

He kicked a caterpillar off the driveway, spit into the grass. "She's, uh, she's still living in an apartment, huh?"

"Yeah." I slowly pushed the car door closed and leaned back against it. "They've got a little place not too far from the beach. It's alright, I guess. They bought a piano. Takes up half the room."

He almost grinned, then squinted and looked across the road, as if he'd heard someone yelling. He shook his head slightly, slowly. "Well, I don't know. I don't think she. . . . just cares about anything anymore."

I scoffed at the remark, thinking of how she fretted over the poor souls in her classes, struggling to spell and read.

"I don't. Have you seen little Jaimie?"

"Neaw."

"He looks like you. Only taller."

Now the grin broke loose. He kicked again at the dirt. Spit once more. Spittle landed on his lip.

"Well. Who knows? Probably be a surfer."

I was tired, though I'd done nothing all day. Sarge had cut the grass in the back yard before church and had just finished the front. His face and arms were red from the sun. Grass stuck to his shirt and arms. He liked being dirty. You could tell.

Why don't'cha come with me? Be a helluva surprise."

He looked at me slyly. I had learned over the years how to sweep through his tackles, reversing the ball, attacking, dropping back for the pass.

"Neaw." He shook his head, sucked at his back teeth. "You better get on," and he turned and walked toward the front porch, brushing off his pants.

Nothing I could say or do could seam this rift. Through my sophomore and junior years all I could do was keep my eyes on the ball and my thoughts focused on the challenges of schoolwork. I couldn't solve the puzzles of my family so I turned to less puzzling tasks. I mastered the art of utilizing every spare moment to study and work on assignments: a quick lunch could offer an extra thirty minutes to draw up an outline, a long ride to a friend's house (or a party even) might give me time to finish a chapter. Every moment between classes was golden -- you just needed a spot to sit and spread out. Thus I came to know every nook and cranny of the library and half the other quiet corners on campus. No one likes the tedium of bookwork so I forced ever hour of it into fifteen minutes and managed somehow to keep my head above water. Perhaps picking English as a major, a subject full of the deepest treasures, helped me stay on track.

No one thought a goofball like me could make it through three years at Lassiter.I didn't fit the profile, but I kept my cards close to the vest. All I wanted to do was finish up two more semesters at this fertile yet toilsome academy. It wasn't much of a thing. It wasn't like being a war hero or anything, but given the profile, it was enough for me.

Chapter 5

What is that makes a man genius?

What is it that makes a man genius?
Bottomless vales and boundless floods,
And chasms, and caves, and Titan woods,
With forms that no man can discover
For the dews that drip all over;
Mountains toppling evermore
Into seas without a shore;
Seas that restlessly aspire,
Surging, unto skies of fire;
Lakes that endlessly outspread
Their lone waters--lone and dead,
Their still waters--still and chilly
With the snows of the lolling lily. -- Edgar Allan Poe

Poe is a poet of waters. His language flows. His images ebb. He is deep, often dark, often un-forded. He laps at the edges of existence and will engulf and submerge the innocent, cloud reality with the unreal, and, in the end, tide all away towards nothingness. I sat in a window seat of the 747 sailing toward Connecticut in August of my senior year, looking out the window through the clouds and the sunlight like I was looking into a dream. Poe has a story called The Maelstrom in which the narrator gives a vivid account of his experience at sea, in the most violent of storms, actually finding himself and his companions being engulfed by a gigantic whirlpool. One assumes that the swirl will finally be the end of these poor souls, but the forces of nature drive the small boat down into the depths of the vortex and then back up the other end of the spiral, depositing them eventually into a calm and secure sea. There are theories of history and human life which hold that for all times and peoples there are critical moments which can turn the course of events unalterably in one direction. We cannot prepare for such times (or perhaps our whole life is one long preparation -- who knows?). We can only shield ourselves from the storm when it lands and step toward our destiny when it appears unshielded. There are no winners in the heart of the tempests, only survivors.

This I think I know, however: simple games can change your life. After three years on the Lassiter football team I had the earned the place of a leader on our team, obtained the stature that comes only with experience, having dragged my will through the grit and the cold, having felt the bite of the pain and yet: I kept showing up. Every inch of the facility was familiar now: I knew every smell, every faucet that barely worked, every shower that ran too hot, every patch of over worn grass. I'd be first in line for taping and the freshmen would look at me as I had once looked at others in my first year, nervous and impressionable. I was bigger, faster and tougher than when I first suited up in Lassiter's mildewed benches. I had earned a starting slot and made some big plays. We had won six games the year previous and lost only five starters to graduation. The team seemed on the brink of real success.

I looked forward to mixing it up with my teammates once more, for athletes have a propensity towards character and this team was no exception. There was Jerry Lupestein, a smallish running back whose wit was as sharp as his cuts on the field; Kip O' Neil, a defensive nose tackle, half-bald, half-crazy, thick and lumpy as an old, stuffed chair, and half-nephew of The Speaker; Reggie Pace, from Scotland originally, our place-kicker and woman killer (wore the wildest scarves on campus); and Chip Lowell, who would drag me into a corner as soon as he saw me, tell me the details of his latest romantic conquest, eyes wide open -- and I would shake my head like I believed every word of it. And, of course, there were my buds, Jimmy Piehler, our punter, and Fred Cole, a tight end. We spent many a night in deep collocution, inebriation, and comradeship. How could such fun-loving boys play so hard, attack so viciously, take a game so seriously? It is a game of violence, and I was a part of the game.

Coach Rivers understood that the integral foci of pain, violence, and intimidation played in winning football. He knew that once you got the opponent thinking about the next hit, you were halfway home. He called it knockin' the fire out of 'em, and it worked. He tried hard to make sure we also understood his philosophy. He nearly always wore a Lassiter cap, hiding his bald, red scalp, so that his eyes peered out from beneath the shadow of the bill like two black pellets. His lips were thin, matching the flow of his cheeks toward his shoulders, arms and legs. He seemed always on the verge of eruption, though he seldom even raised his voice. I'd hardly ever seen a man so bottled up and hard to read. He was not one of the characters I missed.

By the time I arrived back in Hartford for my senior year I had become close friends with a little coed from South Windsor. I had fooled her into thinking there was more to me than quick legs and a goofy smile and somehow the romance had survived almost two years at Lassiter. It was a strange mix of backgrounds. Her old man had made a bundle in the insurance biz, mortgaged himself into a beautiful and expensive home and had raised a beautiful daughter. He was a nice enough guy, but eccentric. Jim McIntyre would wear a tie when he blew the snow from the sidewalk. When I stepped down from the bus I saw Karen coming my way from the station. We hugged and kissed, then hugged again.

"How was Mississippi?" she whispered. Her face was as small and delicate as a rose.

"Hah! How was South Windsor?"

"C'mon, let's get your bags. I gotta show you the new car." When I put my arm around her I could almost carry her on my hip.

"What'd you say it was? A Rambler?"

"Oh, please!" We gathered my luggage and made our way to the lot. Her red Audi convertible was parked close. She had the top down. I pointed towards a truck.

"It's a truck?" I prodded her.

"Oh, please. Isn't it gorgeous?" She beamed, dropped my bag and hugged me again. It was. She was. And so was the New England sky.

You don't have to be a poet to fall in love with New England in the fall. Karen, being a native, knew the most scenic routes in the area. She delighted in showing off the colors of her home, breathing in the crisp September air and filling up with pride like she'd had some part in creating this beauty. We'd drive out to her folk's home in Simsbury, a place she maintained as the first colony in Connecticut (though some dispute it) then head west, through Stratford Brook and Canton, Karen driving without hardly watching the road, missing every other turn.

We'd come over the big hill by Unionville into a rolling valley full of colors. Farmlands stretched out everywhere into the hills, maples glowing their autumn crimson, birches, tan and peeling, washed by our wind. This was the land our country was founded on. We visited the old homes -- museums now -- and you could almost hear the whispers of patriots float by in a suddenly opened door, ruffling our clothes. "Liberty!" the wind whispered, "Freedom." I held Karen's hand as we looked over the Royal Charter, yellowed and flaking, slowly making its transition from substance to dust: such rich, iron words, now powdered, so easily pushed towards powerlessness by the warm winds.

These were lovely hills and times. I fell in love with Karen's easy laugh and her ivory shoulders. She had a way of reaching to a person and yet not reaching, so that she drew you in, made you a momentary captive; I saw it over and over. I was a stranger in a strange land and she made me feel, at times, at home. This was her gift.

Karen was really an adorable creature, but she had been sheltered. I loved her because she was early to reach out for me, guide me through the storms and she was sexy. She never really understood the deeper questions circling within me, never really took the deep step which is needed to feel a person's soul. It's funny how you can make love, tell deep secrets, share your life in the deepest ways and still not be allies. Her eyes: green -- or hazel -- depending on the moment! How wide at times, open to everything around us, ready to take in the world over and over. She played the flute (or had in high school) and her voice at times could be melodious. I'd seen her talk poor men into silence in the course of a few sentences. I'd have to drag her out of the room to give them some peace.

College kids are a real pain in the ass. Someone once said: A little knowledge is a dangerous thing. Karen and I had just enough knowledge to think we knew where we going, and how the road was formed. But we were fools, of course, piles of seasons removed from the understanding of life's complexities. Karen had shoulders as white and soft as snow. Cheeks like frozen cherries.

As for Connecticut: God, it got cold! Jesus! I was from southern Mississippi. We thought it was cold when a sudden frost crept in and made the pumpkins hard. These guys didn't play. I remember a few times walking around the corner of a building (I was bundled up with everything I had) and the wind would just whip right through you. Man, your bones would be cold! I'd trudge on to class and walk into the heat like I'd survived the artic. And the snow would start -- I'd stand by the window at the dorm watching it -- and it was like dove's feathers. This was the first I'd seen of this. It took a few seasons for me not stand cloddishly watching the spectacle. We used to play in the stuff: that was a deal!

I remember the Princeton game, at Princeton. The ground was frozen and we were crouched in that locker room like a bunch of vagrants. The snow began falling just before kick-off and continued at a flurry throughout the affair. It was a challenge to see the ball clearly, much less catch it. By the end of the game the field and the stadium and the seats were covered in white, our hands were frozen; snow melted on our eyebrows. It was a struggle of wills. We would not let the elements defeat us. I caught only two passes. When I turned them up field I was blinded and got tripped up by my own men. My game depended on vision. I think we beat 'em by 6. The bigger victory occurred in the warm showers when we looked at each other and said: "Jesus! It was cold out there!" It took a good half hour for my hands to warm up. When you got hit in those temperatures your teeth rattled. Real Men live in Minnesota. I was not yet a real man.

My senior season at Lassiter Coach Rivers pushed us hard. He knew this was his chance to make a big mark. Coaches are plagued by their records, players by their stats. I disliked his harsh and intimidating methods. He had little feeling for the injured, no respect for those who tried and failed. I don't know who he trusted. He would huddle with his assistants in his office or on the field, giving them the latest gospel like they were words handed down from on high, and they would scatter like geese, squawking out the latest of the commandments. He was married, had a kid. What a lifestyle, I thought. Did he treat his family like he treated the rest of us? Was everyone a mere tool to be manipulated and bent so his own plans could reach fruition?

Every society has its culture, you know. In the society of the football player the culture is crude. It is a game of violence and pain and the language is one of wars and battle: "Attack," "Fire," "Enemy Territory," "The Bomb;" these were the words of our mission and in "The Trenches" few had respect for the language of gentlemen. We cursed as if our lives depended on it. On the football field no one's lineage was sacred. Every vicious collision was followed by a fierce howl to one of the God's. If any of the Methodist creed was true, then we were all sinners, doomed to some sort of football purgatory, or worse, a hell made up of sweaty, overweight linemen, elbowing their way through hell's soup kitchens throughout eternity. And yet it was a culture of survival. We would smash heads together for two and a half hours then retire to the showers where the slapping of naked butts was a common ritual and the shaking of one's genitals towards whoever drew your latest ire was nothing more than proper etiquette. A man who ten minutes earlier had spun you to the ground as if to remove one or more of your limbs would assist you in the locker room when applying medicine to your wounds, or unsnap a stubborn catch at the back of your shoulder pads. The contests strengthened our mutual respect. In the heat of conflict, each of us would rise to moments of courage, fall into the abyss of fear, improvise a plan of action which led to victory, or stand dumbly watching when the moment called most for action. Your success and safety depended on these men. You saw them at their most vulnerable. You saw the glares of absolute will inches from the narrowed eyes. You saw the sadness and the disappointment when the effort fell short. How much more could you know about a person than what you saw here, everyday, in a simple game?

My closest friends on the team were Jimmy Peihler, our punter, and Fred Cole, who played tight end. Jimmy had a devastating wit which could make and lose enemies in seconds, though he never meant a soul any harm as far as I could tell. Fred was just cool. He reminded me of Pete Kaufman, back in Lumberton, always watching the action from the shadows, always ready with the right analysis if you could pull if out of him. He would be a financial consultant one day, or a politician. But on a team surprising alliances are formed. A face you don't even know will watch you from the benches and emulate your style without hardly looking you in the eye. A few loudmouths will get on everybody's nerves at times and provide the vital soothing perspective at others. In the course of four seasons I had gravitated towards those whose minds that worked with the same crazy logic as my own. We were all second-class athletes; this was for sure. There was no point in The Game if you didn't play to win, but The Game was not everything that it was cracked up to be. Vince Lombardi, the legendary coach of the Green Bay Packers, once told his team: "Winning is not everything. It is the only thing." I always wondered what he meant by that. And what type of competitor really believed that? How do you regain your faith when, despite all your will, you finally lose? I was a football player, but I had come here to learn other games, to master new moves.

Chapter 6
It was Saturday night and the beer was flowing.

Learning is half the story of my days at Lassiter, but it was the half that didn't come naturally. Lassiter was foremost an educational institution with a deep tradition of excellence. So many of the kids I watched resolutely wandering from class to class had the look of brilliance on their faces it came to me to be accepted as a feature of the school. Some of these folks were smarter than I'd ever be the moment they finished high school. Intelligence is a quality that few can hide.

But to play a sport and make it through this school required another kind of discipline. One had to pay attention to your schoolwork and spend the time studying or you'd be swallowed up in a week. I tried to counsel many of the new recruits on this fine point, but I saw great talents come and go with an amazing rapidity, buried in the latticework of Set Theory and Freshman English. We had practice every afternoon, rain or shine, at 3:30, and a ballgame, starting the second week in September, every Saturday afternoon, except for a week off around Thanksgiving. Even a second-class athlete could lose his perspective on game day.

The coaching staff had developed over the past three years a fairly intricate offense. We ran a bunch of different sets, from which the same general plays could be worked from one side to the other. Our quarterback, a lanky junior named Bucky Shoals, was pretty good on the sprint out pass and, while not real deceptive in the backfield, could play-fake well enough. His biggest strength was the long pass and I caught enough of these myself to open up the offense for less obvious strategies. Having to rely largely on slow white boys to carry the ball, we didn't break too many running plays, but we could pound the ball up field behind a well disciplined line, then catch them unawares with a counter or a trap, or even a reverse. When things were going right we seemed unstoppable. We scored 31 points our first game my senior season, beat Harvard 28 to 0, then erupted for 45 points in the next game, against Brown. Bucky was sharp and he hit me twice with perfect throws for touchdowns of 25 and 40 yards. He had a good arm, but I'd never seen a quarterback so nervous. He'd look up at us in the huddle like a rat in a cage, unsure if even he recognized the play he was calling. Countless times we had to re-call the play he'd called wrong from the relay man. I always tried to listen in to the exchange between the two, so at least one of us would know what was going on.

On defense, we started out equally as tough. Here, Coach Rivers' personality found a ready vessel. The Coach had played defense and you could see a natural connection to this half of the squad. I feared playing against them in practice much more than I feared our opponents on game day. The Coach enjoyed the fireworks of contact so much that he made routine workouts dangerous for everybody. Though his expression was stone-like during the practices, you sensed delight in his eyes every time someone got nailed on a crossing route, or blindsided from behind. You had to be tough and lucky to get through a day without a nagging bruise or even a more serious injury. The Team loved our defense when they took the field fired up after we'd turned the ball over or were forced to punt, but we had trouble embracing them when there was no common enemy to unite us. I tried to keep my feet moving, my head down and my eyes unfocused on any potentially threatening glare.

Karen never quite understood the fascination of the game. She tolerated it, at best. But I was used to explaining my methods. Lisa Rae had always thought the whole thing barbaric and Neanderthal, though she'd been a cheerleader half her life. Each week I mailed clippings home to the folks and I kept sis updated with letters here and there. Mom would write back that Dad awaited each letter anxiously and became nervous when the mail arrived a day late. It was a frail link to my family. Any sudden wind could break such a flimsy hold, and shred all notions of home. Lisa Rae understood The Balance. Only cats can walk a fence gracefully.

Dearest John,

Greetings from the Emerald Coast. Yesterday Roger and I took Jaimie down to the beach. Roger planted a sand dollar at Jaimie's feet and you should have seen the little boy's eyes. The water has been so gorgeous lately, it's like our Momma's eyes.

They'll only be a few warm weeks left for beach fun and all the T-shirts are on sale as usual. I swear there's more air brush shops every year. Soon, even my pharmacist will have a gun going in the back room.

Sounds like you boys are kickin' that ass. You don't let them bite you or pull your hair. Us Colton's won't stand for cheating, regardless of the insignificance of the affair. I just finished another one of Faulkner's masterpieces. I know you find him too homespun, but he is, after all, from Mississippi. We're talking about taking a trip to New Orleans next Mardi Gras. Won't that be a hoot! Perhaps if you flunk out in time you can be our chaperone.

Glad to hear you and Karen are still talking. She seems like a real gem. (Safety note: Don't let your momentary passions bludgeon your grasp on the laws of elementary physics.) 'Nuff said Jr.

Heard from Mom yesterday. We live in different worlds, but I love her to death. Seems Sarge is still one big pain in the ass. They hardly talk anymore and he skips out on church whenever he can. Is he paranoid just because he thinks everyone's against him? Sometimes a cigar is just a cigar. (Though not in my case, of course.)

I must go. Please write. And keep your eyes on the ball.

Love,

Lisa Rae

Sundays in Lassiter, Connecticut were reserved for class work and Karen. Saturday nights' for The Boys. We'd ride through the streets of Hartford in Fred's Pontiac of Jimmy's Mustang, sipping from the bottles of beer in our laps (it would be Budweiser most often, or Molson Golden if the mood was right). Seldom could I afford to pitch in my share. It was an unspoken credo: they looked out for me. Best I could return was my naturally good humor and an introduction or two. Occasionally, Jimmy would bring some dope. Jimmy's folks had split up twice by the time he got out of high school. He liked to brag that he was a musician of sorts but he couldn't prove it by us. We were no judge of the wailing of a jazz saxophone.

"My mom is a nut!" Jimmy'd say, turning up the radio, changing lanes to maneuver by slower traffic on Wethersfield Avenue. It was a pleasant October evening and the air had the feel of romance in it. "Attractive, but a nut. She drives men off. She's like a black widow -- is that an appropriate analogy: I don't know, perhaps a Venus Fly Trap, yeah, that's better -- pulling guys in to lick her sweet nectar, or, in this case, sweet neckline, only to find they've been poisoned and digested. I'd say pretty much the typical female type."

You couldn't top that.Well, only Fred could. At times. Fred's folks were so normal it was scary. He grew up in a New Haven suburb, playing chess and crushing defensive linemen. Fred had the stern look of a TV Dad from the sixties (before color, of course) a face as square and perfectly measured as his shoulders. He was an All-State wrestler in High School and I'd heard rumors that he could dead press over three hundred pounds. The more time I spent with Fred Cole the more I puzzled at the disparity between his overwhelming physical presence and his gentle nature. He reminded a little of Pete Kaufman, in Lumberton, though with talent and an education.

"She is attractive," Fred added. "If she weren't your mother I'd ask her out myself."

"Go for it. Only problem is, she'd turn you into a homosexual and you'd have to shower in a separate stall."

"Well, there are hazards to everything."

"Indeed. Shall we stop in at Mrs. Johnson's?"

I was not in the mood for Mrs. Johnson's Bar and Grill just yet. "Neaw. I'd rather enjoy the night air for a spell."

"Yeah, particularly since I'm doing the driving and it's my gas."

"Hey. I'll drive. I'd like to see what this baby'll do through downtown Hartford. Though the tractor's back home didn't have no steering wheels -- just used a knob -- I'm sure I could get the hang of it."

Fred turned back to accuse me from the front seat. "Hell, Colton, you probably wouldn't know a pig if you slept with it."

"Yeah? Back home, that's how we identify things. We fuck it and see what kind of noise it makes. Throw me a beer, Goob."

Fred continued his assault. "D'you guys have eleven men on a team in Mississippi?"

"Well, we weren't against using women, you know, with injuries and all. Speaking of which, how's your leg Jimmy?"

"It only hurts when I drive."

Fred looked over, unsure if it was a joke. Jimmy looked back, a totally honest expression. His straw blonde hair and light eyes gave him a naturally innocent face. He never could seem to get a haircut that covered up his many cowlicks, so he finally went to letting his hair stick out wherever it wanted, further accentuating his childlike appearance. Only a few of us could tell when he was serious or making a joke, and we were often fooled.

"I think it will be fine. Have you ever had a groin pull?"

Fred shook his head yes, stoically. "Fortunately, I don't do much kicking."

"Yeah. It's not real comfortable. Our inimitable trainer, Bobby, has drawn out an entire recovery regimen. He gave it to me in writing. Actually, I was hoping you guys would give me a massage treatment later. What about Kyle? He looked like he was really fucked up today."

Kyle McClary was our best linebacker. He was an animal, but he'd let some fat guy roll on his bad knee.

"You know Kyle," I said, "He won't let a little thing like one of his limbs slow him down. I almost wish he'd be out so I wouldn't have to worry about him in practice. He really gets out of hand, you know."

Jimmy pounded on the dash. "It's that bastard, Rivers!"

Fred smiled. "I'm getting the impression you don't like him, Jimmy?"

I tried to soothe him. "Jimmy, you should meet my dad."

"You should meet my dad."

"Why?"

"I don't know. Cause he's a regular guy. Kind of funny. Wish I had an excuse for being an idiot. I don't. You guys should feel lucky. At least Colton."

There was perhaps some truth in his joke. I looked out the window at the sprawling office buildings and storefronts. They stood over the streets like immense glass tombstones. They seemed to have eyes -- dark, unemotive eyes -- watching the scrambling spectacle in the streets silently, confident of their own security and value, removed from the challenges of fashion and culture. They had purpose, but no will; personality, but no voice. Not even the screams of traffic could give these towers the breath of life. A white BMW pulled up beside us, the two black fellows inside rocking to booming disco music. How different would my life have been growing up in these streets, rather than the shaded dirt roads of Lumberton? There are hazards to everything.

Jimmy took a left onto Tower Avenue and sped by a Volkswagen loaded with coeds. They could've been from any of the local colleges. We all seemed to gravitate towards the same areas of Hartford on Saturday nights. That was the luxury of wheels. They honked and I turned and smiled as Jimmy applied the gas and kept going. Mrs. Johnson's Bar and Grill stood near the corner of Tower and North, an old brick building back off the street, its pink and blue neon half-concealed in the overhanging trees. Usually, by about 8:30 on a Saturday night, the place would be packed with glassy-eyed college kids (half of them too young to drink) all of them tossing back draft beers, making eyes at everyone and trying to look cool. Jimmy had gone to high school with the kid who took the door money so we generally could slip to the front of the line and avoid the wait. That was the luxury of connections.

You could barely make your way through the crowd toward the bar the place was so tight that Saturday night. Once we managed to grab a beer we made our way toward the back booths. We saw Reggie Pace, the place-kicker from Scotland. He sat between two beautiful brunettes, his arms around both their shoulders. He looked up as we caught his eye and he gave his dimpled smile, soaking in the glory. He was in a class all his own, but he had enough humility about him to keep me, at least, on his side. Two other girls sat across from him. We stopped briefly and he introduced the two he ' held.

"My men," he said, his Scottish accent as thick as the plaid wool scarf around his neck, "Meet Rebecca and Stacy." They both ran a hand through their own hair and looked up shyly, as if Reggie might be their uncle visiting from overseas. "They're from U Conn," he smiled broadly, "And we know what that means."

We laughed stupidly, not really sure what it meant. Jimmy prodded him. "Well it means they're women of taste and wisdom. Why are they sitting there? You girls should know: he kicks footballs with his bare feet. And he's likely to graduate. Unlike the rest of the team."

I spotted Kyle McClary, sitting with Scoop Thompson, draining a foamy mug and spilling it down his chin. He wore a Lassiter sweatshirt and his eyes looked dark, probably from the combination of alcohol and painkillers. He looked at me and squinted to make out the crowd I stood with, but made no effort to signal a greeting. In the very back I could hear the giggles of Janie Sauer, one of our cheerleaders. She was telling a goofy story to a booth full of gals, including a couple other cheer mates. The crystal blonde hair of Michelle Pucket caught the smoky light and lit a circuit in my own dizzy wiring. I always got along well with the cheerleaders (even in high school) but Mrs. Johnson's offered too many attractions to be distracted by a familiar face.

Jimmy had weaseled the names of the two other girls at Reggie's booth before he'd finished his second train of thought. He flipped the collar of my coat up as he made my introduction. "And this huckleberry here -- I couldn't help but notice your wandering eyes -- is the inimitable John Colton, the slippery but able, number 23." Reggie called out at me: "Tightropes!" And raised his mug in salute. I was just drunk enough to enjoy the show.

"I'm retiring this year, you know. I like the sport, it's the morons I'm forced to play with that drive me to drink. This is Fred Cole, by the way." Fred nodded down to our new friends with his most intriguing, non-plus expression. They looked at us like we were unidentifiable zoo animals.

I turned to watch Michelle Puckett walk our way, undoubtedly towards the bathroom. She was a true blonde, with a cute, up-turned nose and almost perfect teeth. She was so cute no one took her seriously; including herself. She had a weird habit of laughing at herself regardless of her comments. It was hard, nevertheless, for any red-blooded American Male not to be attracted to her. She had light blue eyes; they almost made her look like a cat when she looked at you for more than a few moments. I nodded as she came closer. She smiled and touched my arm.

"Hey John," she spoke, softly, stopping for a moment, testing my wits.

"Michelle," I countered, "you're not leaving?"

"Oh no. I'm going to the bathroom. This beer, you know." She had come to Lassiter from Pennsylvania and her voice squeaked as she spoke. It had a liquid quality to it.

"Did you bring the whole squad with you?"

She laughed, looking at Reggie, throwing her golden, shoulder-length hair down the back of her blue sweater.

You see 'em," she answered me, We've been here since six. Hey! I've gotta go. See ya in a little bit." And she took off. The whole bar watched her stride rhythmically toward her destination. Jimmy squeezed himself and Fred into the booth with the two U Conn babes, leaving me to stand unclaimed. He ordered some beer (which I had no money for) and we continued the drunk. Jimmy was doing well, of course Reggie was set, and even Fred seemed to be on the verge of making Real Contact with the brunette stuffed under his huge bicep. I tried my best to get their jokes and appear sober while I looked away every other minute into the corner, looking for a glimpse of Michelle. Trying to catch her eyes. Trying to catch a slow wink. We were laughing, running on some joke about high school and beer, when my attention was drawn suddenly back down the aisle. There was Michelle -- she had slipped by me -- and Kyle McClary was puffing up over some kid in a flashy sweater. He was really drunk, and I feared for the worst. I knocked at Fred casually to turn his gaze.

"What?" Kyle screamed, suddenly.

Michelle fled and the other student flinched, but both were too late. McClary snapped a right hook across the young man's jaw and sent him spinning backwards into the crowd behind him. Kyle barred his teeth and jutted out his pimpled, un-shaved chin. Another, larger student stepped forward, too drunk and incensed to know any better. He ran head first at our middle linebacker and it was like he hit the side of a building. Kyle grabbed him by the hair and pounded his fist into the poor fellow's face. No one else dared intervene in the spectacle. I saw Scoop Thompson throw off his jacket and kick the first victim as he let out a howl. Beside me, Fred stood and looked fiercely at the fight, tempted to put it to an end, but hesitant. You could see the blood running down the chest of the kid in McClary's grip. Michelle Puckett was crying and ducking away through the crowd. A bouncer appeared and even he seemed unsure how to bounce this patron. Only the whistle of an Officer quieted the fight. McClary and Thompson laughed as they were escorted to the door.Kyle looked back and yelled at Michelle, then he gave me a wink. It was Saturday night and the beer was flowing. We shook our heads disgustedly and tried to cover any markings on our clothing that might connect us to Lassiter and our pitiful middle linebacker.

Michelle was crying as she approached us. She came to my side and put her head to my shoulder. I held her providently.

"He's a brute," she got out, through her tears. The mascara was running down her face something horrible.

"What happened?" I asked.

"The guy," she stuttered, "The guy was just talking to me. He was just flirting. Kyle told him to leave me alone. I didn't. I don't know him. This is so awful." She looked at me and licked the tears from her lips. "I've gotta go," she said. "Can you?" she stopped. "I don't have a car."

I looked at Jimmy, trying to sort out some way to help the poor girl, but I didn't see much I could do.

"I . . . I don't have a car, Michelle. I . . . Can one of the other girls give you a ride?" She sniffled and began to collect herself.

"Oh. I never.Yea. I suppose." She gave me a hug. "Thanks," she said, and she made her way back to her friends. Fred looked at me suspiciously and I looked back him with my own puzzled expression. I didn't realize she'd left a trail of mascara on my cheek.

Chapter 7
Not to-day is to justify me and answer what I am for

The next day I read from a collection of Poe's short stories on the way to The Professor's home. It was a golden day, chilly but not yet cold. October's frost had not yet locked in, but it was the time of year when each southern breeze carrying the warm New England sun might be the last you'd feel until the next springtime. Karen drove nervously. We had been invited over for Sunday brunch and Karen and the Professor had never really hit it off. His directness didn't mix well with her subtle mystery. Meanwhile, Poe described his approach to the House of Usher. How he took such seemingly ordinary scenes and made them sing, caught you by the shirt collar and carried you through the story, the words: a poem, the poem: a song. The sun fell behind a cloud as we topped the last hill towards North Coventry, lending shadow to the page. Karen spoke and I could not answer, having barely heard her voice. Another voice filled my head, quiet and solemn. I wished for the road to go on for another 100 miles.

"John!" She grabbed my leg.

The dream shattered, faded from view.

"What, dear?"

"This place always gives me the creeps."

"What do you mean, creeps? It's a beautiful, old home. I love his back porch. And how 'bout his library?"

"Yeah, but it smells funny."

I looked down the road, exasperated.I looked at my reflection in the side mirror. I was scowling like Sarge in one of his moods. I tried to shake it free. Professor Strache's wife, Carolyn, saw us in the door. Bob Leahy and his wife Judy were seated in the den. Professor Leahy taught English at Connecticut. He was an avid football fan. He knew a heckuva lot more about what was going on in college ball than I did, but he was only occasionally overbearing. Carolyn poured us tea. She was as petite as Karen, hands as delicate and small as the china saucer she held.

"Gerald has roasted some brisket," Carolyn announced, loosening the catch at a window and quietly pulling it open. You could almost taste the fresh air. She moved so much more gracefully than her husband, her countenance unassuming yet confident. She stood by the window and the light made her silver hair shine like a halo.

Dr. Leahy began repacking his pipe. I could see him musing over some thought, probably concerning the current Ivy League standings, but he held mute, for the moment. His wife broke the silence.

"Oh, it smells lovely! I wish Bob could cook a little." I guided Karen to the love seat and she sat carefully, then crossed her legs. I stood behind her, my hand in her golden hair. Judy went on.

"No," she put her hand to her husband's leg, "I kid him. He actually is quite the chef." Dr. Leahy dismissed the idea with a wave of his free hand, separating the fresh billow of smoke from his pipe. The room seemed overwhelmed with scents: the rich beef juices that rolled from the kitchen, the sulfur of the match, the almost cinnamon smoke of Dr. Leahy's pipe, Karen's hair, her perfume, the olive scent of the sitting room, the crisp October breeze (full of syrup and wine) -- even the delicate perfume from The Professor's wife -- I sensed them all, somehow removed from the scene, somehow in the center of the swirl. I ran my hand to Karen's ear.

"It's just a brisket," Carolyn intoned, putting the room back into focus. We all smiled, knowing the morsel would be our delight in minutes.

The Professor cared little about the formalities, but he moved through them well enough. He seemed always on the edge of a faux paus, always a second from losing his train of thought. You couldn't be sure if it was real or act. Out here in North Coventry, after two glasses of Merlot, reality and illusion were slippery comrades. Professor Strache served up the brisket and I dug in ravenously. Karen ate, as always, like a bird. We must've made quite a contrast. I mentioned the story I was reading on our drive out.

"I almost wish the road went on another few miles so I could finish the story." Mrs. Strache passed me some cornbread. Dr. Leahy spoke up.

"Poe believed strongly that a story should be short enough to finish in one sitting. He felt the maximum emotional and intellectual effect could be achieved with the short story or short poem. He had no patience for novels and epic poems. Strange attitude for such a calculated writer."

"Unique indeed,"Professor Strache added, running a napkin across his mouth. "Though it's a point not without some validity. However, who would forego the joys of the contemporary novel simply because you can't get through it in one sitting?"

A sudden draft made the candle flames dance in the center of the table. Karen added her view.

"Poe is just so creepy."

The Professors looked at her and smiled. Mrs. Leahy reached to Karen's arm and agreed wholeheartedly.

"Oh, goodness yes, honey. The wildest of ideas in that poor head. You know he was an alcoholic and opium addict." She spoke as if gossiping about a neighbor. Professor Strache came to Poe's defense, talking through the cabbage and cornbread in his mouth.

"Lovers and madmen have such seething brains, Such shaping fantasies that apprehend More than cool reason ever comprehends."

Dr. Leahy laughed, "And what is next?" "The lunatic, the lover, and the poet Are of imagination all compact:-- Oh, it goes on well enough. All geniuses are haunted by their private demons. I've forsaken brilliance for a sturdy family life."

Dr. Leahy added a thought: "There is more brilliance to that than is commonly conceded. But enough about our mediocrity. I must press John on a more vital matter. How are the Cougars looking going into the Pennsylvania game?"

I smiled. "Well, we're okay, I guess. I hope you don't depend on my analysis for wagers with the dean at U Conn."

The Dr. looked slyly at The Professor. "Hah! Betting on Ivy League football. That'll be the day." He winked.

"Well, our middle linebacker got hurt yesterday. Extended a ligament in his knee." The wine was making me dizzy. "Penn's won two games, right."

"Yeah," Dr. Leahy answered, "Beat Columbia and Dartmouth. Hardly good competition."

"I like our chances. I'd take the seven points."

"Try twenty!"

Professor Strache broke in and reminded everyone that I saw enough of this poor game throughout the week. As this was my one day for rest, I deserved a respite. I didn't mind talking shop with Dr. Leahy, but The Professor knew me well, knew how little importance I put on The Game. We retired to the library and sipped cappuccino. The room hung over us with the weight of The Professor's scholarship. A broad window gave a view of the sun slipping through the clouds toward the horizon. Two standing lamps lit the corners of the room with yellow light. The gold leaf printing on the books shimmered with each pass of sunlight through the sky. We talked more about Poe and the theory of the intellectual moment in literature. The Professor complimented my meager attempts at prose. It was the least he could say for someone who hung on his every word of criticism and guidance. I tried to keep up with the conversation, ask a pertinent question here and there, laugh when it seemed appropriate, but the pace of the vernacular was stultifying. I was becoming hooked on parlor talk. While me and The Boys had occasional philosophical insights and conjectures, our ideas were generally left to lie uncompleted, or cut off by the urgency of the next good pun. I sat forward on the couch at The Professor's home in North Coventry, watching ideas being developed like we were framing a home, or a church, careful that each joist held its place firmly and would support the next hefty consideration. You could drink it in like wine. Karen was restless on the drive back. I pulled back my seat, watched the bony trees reach out like the hands of ghosts in the night, and I fell to sleep.

The next day I clipped out the accounts of our victory from both the Lassiter Beacon and the Hartford Times. I was a day late getting them in the mail, but it had been a busy weekend. The enclosed note was short, as usual.

> *Dear Mom and Dad,*
>
> *Won another one! How about that! Didn't score any this game, but you see I caught five passes for fifty yards. (That's ten yards a catch if you've forgotten your high school math.) Didn't drop a throw. Starting to get cold up here. It was 40 degrees today and windy. Big week for me. I've got a test in one*

class, an essay due in another and Coach is all worried about the Penn game next week. You should meet The Coach, Dad, y'all would have a lot not to talk about. Well, time for class.

All my love,

Jr.

It was one of those weeks. Whenever I turned in an assignment for Professor Strache it took on great importance, but this one was particularly captivating. Perhaps it was the time of year, or the time of my life. I wanted my paper to be more than merely competent, merely sufficient for his highest grade; I wanted to create a work of art. The theme compared and contrasted the Romantic Ideal with Existential Philosophy. The ideas obsessed me. I found myself running through drills at football practice while working out paragraph transitions in my head, barely cognizant of the action on the field. It rained hard on Wednesday, but we had a full scrimmage anyway, until our uniforms were covered in mud. I would have found it comical if my mind weren't preoccupied with the essay and it wasn't so damn cold.

I remember Coach Rivers sending Willie Paterson through the mill for missing a downfield block. Willie was a skinny black kid from south Hartford, a freshman who likely would be the next John Colton. He was slick and smooth and he had maturity beyond his years. He watched every move I put on and tried his best to top it. I don't think he'd ever seen a white boy who could dance. He'd get it right one day. You could see it in his eyes. But this day belonged to The Coach. He had him racing downfield to throw a flying roll block at a blocking dummy smack in the middle of a mud hole. It was true, Willie was not much of a downfield blocker, but I didn't see this exercise being the solution. When Coach finally blew the whistle Willie came back to the huddle and stood beside me. Black mud dripped from his facemask. His eyes were about the only white thing left to see and he peered out with a rage and determination that made me shudder. Scoop Thompson, a second string cornerback, yelled over to salt the wounds.

"Come on Willie, I'm still standing here!"

I patted Willie on the butt. On the next play I snuck across the field and laid Scoop Thompson out, nearly knocking the breath out of him. He was slow getting up. I got Willie's attention as I trotted back to the huddle. "That's . . . . How you do it!"

Willie smiled. I knew then that Willie Paterson would make it.

Coach Rivers blew his whistle. "Colton! That's enough!" That night while I was up studying late I heard a knock at the door. T.S. Eliot had me confused and mesmerized and I pulled the door open in a daze. In the hallway stood Willie Patterson in a loose fitting South High T-shirt and knee length sweat pants. I was one of the few seniors who still lived in the athletic dorm.

"What are you doing?" I asked. "It's after midnight."

"I know," he said. He had a deep, clear voice, an intonation twice as large as his physical frame. "I saw your light on. I just wanted to say thanks."

"Hey," I said, "my pleasure." As I reached out my hand to invite him in for a coke he promptly turned and left. I heard his door close across the hall. I shook my head, fell back to my desk and turned the page.

The more I studied the question the more I came back to the same conclusion: Romanticism and Existentialism were precise opposites. Was it that simple? Would The Professor provide such a clean puzzle? Or was I missing something? The Romantics believed that art should elevate beauty (one's subjective sense of beauty -- however one saw it) and love, while perhaps not something you could put your hands on -- like the pencil you held, or the coffee cup you had just knocked off the table -- was nevertheless an entity with Real Energy. It was not important to give love a scientific definition as long as you knew in your soul it was there, as long as it made your heart sing. Einstein had blown apart every notion of 'The Real.' But it was 'the real', with a small 'r' that the Romantics were after. The tree outside my window suddenly shook and a limb touched my window, momentarily drawing my attention. I forced my way back to the problem at hand. There was a battle raging here over beauty and love.The conflict had led both camps to pick through the rubbish of their existence, looking for that rare glint of brass in the heap, searching for the final arbiter: Truth. My mother believed with all her heart that God will answer a righteous prayer. It is this sense of hope that gives our dreams color, allows us, in the end, to believe. It is the cold clang of mortality that sharpens our reflexes and keeps us alive.

Willie Patterson understood the sharp edges of survival, but there were dreams in his eyes. As for me, I was just a poor kid from Mississippi, trying to keep my feet moving and my eye on the ball. I'd seen the hazards of the sharp edges, but in my heart I kept watch on the dream.

I borrowed Fred's typewriter the next night and stayed up till three to finish the paper. I brought it to class the next day like I was carrying a loaded weapon. I tried to be inconspicuous as I dropped it carefully on the corner of Professor Strache's desk. The paper was not as polished as I would have wanted. My transitions were often forced. I worried that I quoted when I should have paraphrased. The more I re-read it the less the arguments held together. But time had run out. It would be left to the judgment of The Gods.

The papers lay in a sloppy pile throughout the class, and I know everyone kept watch on the disorganized scholarship from the corner of their eyes throughout the class, worried perhaps that The Professor might knock them off in a moment of absentmindedness. On this day The Professor introduced the concept of Artistic Morality. Much of the class seemed confused by the idea, too caught up in their traditional religious view of morality. We sighed, and groped in the darkness for a few snatches of light. He wrote on the board: Truth, Beauty, The Good, The Right, The Moral. He ran a chalk-dusted hand through his hair as he walked toward a corner of the room and leaned back against the wall. He wore his gray sport jacket today, with a beige shirt, dark pants and hushpuppies. He picked up a book from the desk, cleared his throat and began reading.

"Poets to comet orators, singers, musicians to comes
Not to-day is to justify me and answer what I am for,
But you, a new brood, native, athletic, continental, greater than before known,
Arouse! for you must justify me.
I myself but write one or two indicative words for the future,
I but advance a moment only to wheel and hurry back in the darkness.

I am a man who, sauntering along without fully stopping, turns a casual look upon you and then averts his face,
Leaving it to you to prove and define it,
Expecting the main things from you.
Walt Whitman, Poets To Come."

The Professor paused, then asked us to consider, "What is Whitman hinting at here? Anyone have a guess?" He looked down, musing on the words before him, perhaps momentarily lost in thought, perhaps waiting for a reply from the class. I jumped in." Is he talking about interpretation and subjectivity?"

The Professor looked up, as if startled. "Hah!" he chortled. "Colton!" He shook his head, ran another chalk-dusted hand through his hair, shading his gray hair to even lighter shades of silver, moving slowly toward the board where he underlined the word: Moral. I stuttered, unsure where he was leading me. The class looked on anxiously. The Professor asked another question. "What about the power of the artist? What kind of power does the artist possess? Anyone?"

"I . . . Perhaps." I smiled.

He turned back to the chalkboard, stared at it for a moment intensely, then turned and sat on the chalk-sill. Another student joined the fray -- Shelley Fogle -- who was overweight and always wore sweatshirts, further accentuating her obesity."They have power because people read them. They take in their ideas.They decide if they believe what they read, but they read it nevertheless."

"One item:" The Professor broke in, "Art is not limited to literature; but continue."

"I don't know," she said, "That's all. We have to be careful what we say. That's all."

The Professor underlined the word Moral once more, then pulled out his handkerchief to blow his nose. He motioned to the lights above us. "Yet all art is fiction. These are dreams and illusions, mere smoke, the dust-trails of time's wagon. How can we hold the artist up to a stronger light than the ordinary craftsman, struggling to make a living?" He pulled at his bottom lip, rubbed his brow. "Perhaps we shouldn't. You know we jumped to Morality, forgetting about our old friend Truth. See what I mean?"

I ran my fingers through my hair, once more drawn in to The Professor's easy pool. He left the ends loose. This was his gift. This kept the teaching alive, gave it breath long after the bell sounded. We cursed and threw his floating challenges around the light echo of Lassiter's dark halls, bounced them off our intellect and laughed at his riddles, our own naiveté and the mysteries of The Trip. He turned brusquely and circled the word Truth, breaking his chalk in half. A piece of the chalk rolled across the floor right between my feet.

"Let's examine this," he began. "What responsibility does the artist have to Truth? And: Can we, in fact, determine Truth? Is it really knowable? Is it, in the end, subjective?"

Kyle Parish raised his hand, a bright kid, who could really write. "I would say Truth has to be subjective." Professor Strache looked at him intently. "So what does that mean to the artist? Does he forget about any sense of Truth, or just flirt with reality, do circus tricks for a buck?" We were lost. He went on. "It is true, we can't know anything absolutely. The fact that every time I lean against this wall it holds me up, does not prove that the next time I lean here it may not crumble to dust. To use an old cliché: What looks red to you may be green to me. We live in a world of assumptions. Anyone's parents here ever told you: don't assume, it makes an ass of you and me?" Several of us chuckled at the all-too-familiar phrase. "Well, we make an assumption every time we take a breath: That we'll take in oxygen. Life is based on assumptions. And this is what makes great art: the ability to make assumptions about The Truth, about what it means to be alive, about the essence of the universe. We can't prove that what the artist says is true any more than we can prove this wall will hold me up, but we have a feeling about the work, it feels right, it has the ring of truth, despite all our doubts. Chekov said: 'Art tells the truth'. Tolstoy said: 'Art expresses the highest feelings of man'. Perhaps they both mean the same thing. For now, let's assume they do and move on." He smiled and looked out the frosted window. A single snowflake floated through the barren trees.

Few understood what these lessons meant to me, or how they captured my fascination. Jimmy was a writer, of sorts. He liked science fiction, could keep up with any crazy tale or spur of the moment connection. And Fred always nodded at you with quiet self-assurance, raising his eyebrows when I began to wax poetic. He had tried his hand at poetry, but he was a private person. As for Karen, well, she made an honest effort to appear interested in my rambling's, holding my arm, biting her lip, looking bright-eyed at my passionate pleas for logic and the Real Answers. I loved her for it, but it never was real, only the chores of love.

Of course Lisa Rae needed no syllabus. I could let loose in my notes to her and, often, I took it too far.

> *How cold is it? Cold enough to reach the ground. How crazy am I? Crazy enough to reach the ground. Where was I? Oh yeah, the professor. What a trip!*
>
> *The guy is brilliant, almost as smart as you. I bet you teach your disciples just like him, catching their interest and then pulling them on towards a rickety and unsafe ride.*
>
> *I think he likes me, though you can never be sure of anything with him. What's more, I think he likes my writing! Imagine that. Shocks the sensibilities. The professor is an anachronism. He dresses like our father would dress if he taught (or could teach). He cares little for computers, never cleans the board; he truly believes in the cleansing power of his theme. Others have caught the pull of his tide and sit hopelessly waiting for rescue, just like me: We're the lucky ones!*
>
> *What's in a phrase? Well to hear Professor Strache tell it you'd think the convolution of a phrase could make apples fall up! I've seen weirder things happen, but only in Mississippi.*
>
> *I'm sorry to hear about Mom and Pop not getting along. You know, they've always lived in a fragile balance. Dad does not deal well with boredom. He needs a fight. I hope he has not chosen our Mother to be his antagonist.*
>
> *One and a half more semesters and I will be done with college. I will have my own fights to take on; no more of the Easy Life of jock straps and study halls. Is The Real World as scary as they say, or can you still drop/add when you screw up? Like the rest of my life to this point, I have no clear plan what I will do when*

I get out, or where I should go. I'm not sure that Mississippi is home for me anymore. I'm not sure it every truly was.

Give Jaimie a big hug from his best and brightest uncle and give yourself a kiss from me.

Love,

Jr.

Chapter 8
"You're the best I saw!"

I awoke the morning before our eighth ballgame at 8:30 AM and rolled from my dirty sheets in a daze. I had been dreaming deeply. I was lost in a dark forest. It must have been in the south, for the trees were twisted and full of black eyes, limbs spread out over me like an impermeable roof. There was a voice in the woods; I couldn't make it out. I thought sure it was the voice of a girl. What was she saying? There was the whistle of an owl. I looked up and saw a ruffled and oily blackbird peering down at me with insistence. I shrugged my shoulders and felt my way on.

All light fell dreamily on the morning before a game. The air was filled with anticipation, excitement and a tinge of fear. Every motion was connected in some way to the contest which loomed in the approaching moments. We were playing Navy this day and we were expecting a battle. I saw Willie Patterson in the lobby and we walked together to the Administration Building where the team ate breakfast for all home games. The ground seemed frosted over. It must've been 20 degrees.

"Damn," I said, my words a vapor, pulling my collar up around my red earlobes, my cheap tennis shoes crunching in the icy grass. "It's gotta warm up today. There's laws against this. We have rights."

Willie looked at the sky. It was dotted with distant clouds.

"That was some catch last week against Brown." "On the five?"

"Yeah. That was some catch."

"Hey," I held my gloved hands out before me, like I was holding a baby, "the ball was there. He'd threaded the goddamn needle."

Willie held out a gloved paw and strutted like a cat feeling the moonlight, rounding out the last reverie. I caught the gesture and offered him a back-fingered five, threw my arm around his shoulder and pushed him onto the desolate avenue. Down the street, under a changing light, steam rose from a lonely manhole.

Willie and I were one of the first ones to make it to breakfast that morning. I saw our trainer, Bobby Dregorian, working over his scrambled eggs and picking through the Sporting News. We filled up our plates and sat down across from him. He barely acknowledged our presence. The food was not too bad: the eggs fresh, the bacon lean, the potatoes sliced and grilled with onions. It weren't no hash browns and grits, but it hit the spot nonetheless. Dregorian was a reservoir of sports' trivia; no one on our team could touch him when it came to current stats or obscure names, teams and critical events from the past. He was a year behind me, taking pre-med, and he took his job as trainer seriously. It's an American tradition for football teams to hurl as much abuse, both verbal and physical, as they feel their particular trainer can absorb. Being, generally, the smallest and least athletic figure in the locker room, the trainer makes an easy target.

"That was some catch last week against Brown."

"On the five?"

"Yeah. That was some catch."

"Hey," I held my gloved hands out before me, like I was holding a baby, "the ball was there. He'd threaded the goddam' needle."

Willie held out a gloved paw and strutted like a cat feeling the moonlight, rounding out the last reverie. I caught the gesture and offered him a back-fingered five, threw my arm around his shoulder and pushed him onto the desolate avenue. Down the street, under a changing light, steam rose from a lonely manhole.

Willie and I were one of the first ones to make it to breakfast that morning. I saw our trainer, Bobby Dregorian, working over his scrambled eggs and picking through the Sporting News. We filled up our plates and sat down across from him. He barely acknowledged our presence. The food was not too bad: the eggs fresh, the bacon lean, the potatoes sliced and grilled with onions.It weren't no hash browns and grits, but it hit the spot nonetheless. Dregorian was a reservoir of sports' trivia; no one on our team could touch him when it came to current stats or obscure names, teams and critical events from the past. He was a year behind me, taking pre-med, and he took his job as trainer seriously. It's an American tradition for football teams to hurl as much abuse, both verbal and physical, as they feel their particular trainer can absorb. Being, generally, the smallest and least athletic figure in the locker room, the trainer makes an easy target. After more 100 us, as always, adjusting the bill of his cap. He was never at a loss for a military cliché to get the essence of his thoughts into words. We shuffled begrudgingly down the hall to room 131 and fell into the plastic chairs with a collective grunt. We had been conditioned to sit in relative proximity to the other players at our position. After reviewing the films each group would huddle together and go over any new plays or strategies that might be used in the upcoming battle. Coach Rivers stood up front, playing with the videotape. Eventually, he'd call for the trainer to help him get the tracking right and assist him with the slow motion and pause. The Coach was not much on this modern gadgetry. We had a tape of Navy against Army and most of us had seen it more than once. With the lights down, you could almost hear snoring from the back of the room. I tried to appear attentive as he ran through the critical analysis.

"You can see here," (he held a pointer near Navy's offensive right tackle) "the quarterback, number 12, turns to his right. This gives the right tackle time to pull back to the left. The halfback takes a step right then receives the hand-off here and follows the tackle through the hole. Tim, you need to key on this. If you see number 12 turn to the right, don't assume they're running that way. Be ready for the counter trap right up your ass. You see here how Army's tackle gets pushed outside, opening up the lane. Step up, make contact, stink up the whole area." Scoop Thompson made a fart sound in the back of the room and The Coach turned sharply and gave him The Glare. His eyes, always mere slits and dark as night, could fix on you like a bat honing in on a moth. I'd seen him make a young man shake with premonitions of danger before The Coach had uttered a word. "Thompson," he growled, "That'll be twenty!" He turned to address the entire room. "This is the goddamn Naval Academy, gentlemen! You fuck-up, make a few mistakes, and they'll stuff that ball right up our assholes and make us shit pigskins!" The Coach had a real obsession with the word asshole. I and my buddies long ago came to the conclusion that he hid some deep homosexual longings in his anal-compulsive vocabulary. But his fears seemed ill-founded. In point of fact, Navy had only won three games to date, and none of the victories were in the least impressive. They'd have to pull a battleship up The Connecticut River and soften up our defensive line with some heavy artillery to even keep them in the first half.I drew on myplaybook -- feigning interest in Coach River's spiel -- a long spiraling line with an arrow pointing to the end zone. TD! I drew in, and circled it, and dreamed up the glorious spin and spike and the muffled roar of the fans. My mind continued its wandering momentarily. I ran down the field and slowly saw my feet rise from the snow and take to flight, like mercury gliding up the rocky slopes of Olympus, the icy wind whirling past my head, now whistling to me, now calling a name. . . . some name. "Leitrea," I heard a voice as soft as a snowflake's gentle fall. "Leitrea," the wind called. I laughed and shook the sound from my head. The hiss of the heater suddenly stopped, throwing my thoughts into quiet.The lights had come up and our offensive coordinator, Coach Chapman, had stepped into our circle. He slapped at the back of my head, and threw out mimeographs of the new pass patterns. This was game day, and Winning Was Everything. They took us in the Campus Shuttle to the stadium, whereupon we filed from the bus into the recess of our locker room. Football locker rooms are no place for the squeamish or the faint of heart. Immediately upon entering one is overwhelmed by a thick combination of stenches: heating goop, two-week sweat socks, urine, mildewed shower tiles, the remnants of grass and mud which coated the entranceway. Here, the fundamentals of nature cohabitated with the fundamentals of habitation. Football is not a gentlemen's game and The Lockeroom is the first and last refuge for the beasts who parade its banner. The heartiest of cheerleaders would resign their charter at once if they had witness to the putridity their heroes called home.

Dress out before games had all the attributes I could imagine must have existed in Roman times before the battles of gladiators. The injured and maimed were attended to first -- in the taping room -- with heating goop, gauze, support pads, wraps, taping and basically any miscellaneous protection an inflicted player might feel necessary to ward off the pain. In the first few moments of contact every stitch of our uniforms would be thrown into disarray, yet on game day special care was taken to get every seam in perfect line, every strap tightened and crossed with precision, so that the bulky, flapping of the pads fit over each muscle, bone and vein like the shell of some radioactive future species of man. We cleaned the dried grass from the laces of our shoes and ran a rag over our now scarred and multi-colored helmets. As we slowly put together the components of our game day armor, we also began the process of putting together our mental armor. Fear had to be shut out, visions of victory brought in. Some players kept to themselves, staring solemnly at the smelly locker before them. Others began punching things: laundry bags, walls, other players. The end of one bank of lockers had received so much abuse the sheet screws hung loosely from the caved in frame. Hate and viciousness were the primary emotions being pulled into our consciousness, and we pulled them from whatever dark veins we could mine. We knew, just beyond the concrete walls, our opponents were going through the same gruesome forethoughts and if for some reason we slipped in our faith, forgot to raise our courage to its finest mettle, we could be slain in our tracks and the battle, the war, and all, would be lost. The danger was real. It was not enough to win. You must also survive. We had the numbers on this Navy team. We'd beat 'em three years going and all indications were we spank 'em even worse this, my last, go round. As I pulled my jersey down over my shoulder pads and tucked the tail into my pants tightly I was struck suddenly by memories from last year's game with The Institute. They had a cornerback -- I think his name was Mabry, or Macally, something -- who (as I recalled the game more carefully now, re-playing the pass patterns, pulling back some vague fog of events) dogged me like a stray cat for four quarters. Macabe was his name (it came to me now) and he had eyes like a mole. He'd watch you from the corner of his vision, splitting the distance between you and the ball to the last inch, cutting off the angle at the last possible second, catching a single finger on the pass just before it reached your grasp. Few teams had the audacity to leave me in single coverage. They knew a single mistake would cost them six. Not so with this kid Macabe. Like me, he was All-League twice running. He considered the territory on his side of the scrimmage line his own. He made a receiver feel like he was stepping into a shadow, running through a loose and perfect web, unforgiving of the carelessness and the intruding.

We ran through the pre-game drills then returned to the locker room. Before our march onto the field we gathered near the door and went to one knee. Coach Rivers stood by at the doorway of his office, almost whispering to Coach Chapman, looking over us like we were infectious. He stepped out and began his address. As I listened I almost grinned when the thought hit me that my Dad would be president now if he could just speak half as well as our crazy coach. The Coach adjusted his cap and waited for silence. Hot air whistled into the room from the ducts over our heads. But otherwise there was not a sound as we knelt on the cool concrete and gave him our undivided attention.

The Coach cleared his throat, looked briefly at Coach Cooley, then addressed the team."Well, we got a battle here, gentlemen. It's gonna be cold. Cold as a bear's ass in an artic fish pond. But I think we've seen this before and we know what it takes. Only way to get warm and stay warm is to keep hitting. Contact will keep your toes from freezing up. We're gonna go right at 'em with the game plan we've been looking at all week. We've gotta move em' up front. Crane, Vellick, Cole:We're gonna pound that side till they get soft, then open up with the counters and the pass. Now this kid, number 17, the cornerback." "Macabe," I added."Yeah," The Coach looked at me and almost smiled, "if you throw that way make it quick and hard. He's a sneaky little bastard." The Coach raised up his chin and peered down at us through the slits that were his eyes like he was looking over a crop of bad peanuts, or a prison work farm, but at the same time with a spark of pride in the fruits of his labor, then he nodded at us. "Light up the fire, men!" and he threw the door open. A wisp of snow drifted into the room on the swirling breeze and wrapped around us in invitation. The school song blared from the bleachers, echoing across the stands and the schoolrooms and the haunts and hollows of the surrounding land, mixing chaotically with the roaring of the fans. We rose and stamped our cleats and took the field in a blaze of glory.

We were ready for the match, but no amount of fervor could put out the chill of this day. As I stood on the sideline watching the coin toss at midfield I turned to Jimmy. "It's days like these I get homesick. Probably about 65 degrees back in the swamps. Little humid." My words came out in thick vapors. "Good day for laying down by the viaduct with a case of beer, a tin of crickets and some cheap tackle."

Jimmy blew on his hands, then put them between his legs and looked back at me, grinning the best smile he could push through the cold. "You're a lost romantic, Colton. It's just a little snow."

"No," I countered, "a little snow just barely covers the field and melts down 'soon as the sun breaks through. It's a goddamn blizzard."

"Relax. We lost the toss. You got time to enjoy the winter wonderland. Maybe sing a few carols." Fred came up behind us and knocked Jimmy forward with a forearm. Fred never wore long sleeves under his jersey, regardless of the conditions. I thought this act of machismo ridiculous, but he had so few idiosyncrasies you had to let him pass. He stood looking over us, breathing through his nose quietly. "You see that," he said."Lost the toss.Should never let McClary call the toss. He probably doesn't know the sides of the coin. Colton." I looked up at him, my teeth almost rattling from the chill air. "You gonna put the tightrope on this little fucker?"

"You mean Macabe?"

"Yeah, Macabe, or whoever the little devil is. I remember his tricks. He slides right by you like a little snake. Or a worm. Never seems to make a solid hit, but he's always there somehow. I may have to plow him today. Look for me on your way to the end zone." He stuck out his palm for a hand slap and I whacked my slender fingers across his thick palm.

Our stadium was not large, perhaps holding 2 or 3 thousand folks, but in the past there was never much of a need for a lot of seats. Lately, we'd begun drawing a little better, what, with a chance at the Cup, and all.The field had been cleared early in the morning and only a light dusting still stuck to the frozen grass and dirt. The sky was clear, but I remembered Willie Patterson's forecast for snow and I looked to the west nervously at the few patches of white in the otherwise blue sky as we took the field and kicked off. It would be a game of breaks. In football, perhaps more than in any sport, the element of chance can play a critical role. You've got 22 men colliding in all directions, some of them moving with no real destination in mind; you've got a field with patches of dirt, mud and sometimes frost or snow, which makes each step an adventure; you've got the wind, rain, snow and bright sun or glaring stadium lights filtering into every player's eyesight, to intervene subtly in every play; and the ball you're charged with snapping, handing, tossing, passing, kicking, catching and holding on to is shaped like an elongated ostrich egg, with seams and laces and the tendency to bounce like a Mexican jumping bean. It's a wonder people see any order to it all.

Throughout the first half both defenses played well. We held Navy scoreless and all we could manage was a field goal. Jimmy kicked the ball superbly, dropping the ball in like a deflated balloon on the five, the 12 and the 13. When Jimmy was at his best it was a thing of beauty to watch. Only the more studied of the fans appreciated his talents. Jimmy couldn't kick the ball out of the stadium like some of the punters we played against. What he accomplished was a more structured feat: kicking the damn thing in the one place where you couldn't hardly bring it back.With a defense that roared onto the field and relished the idea of contact with any ball carrier trying to pull the ball out from inside his own twenty, Jimmy Piehler, probably as much as any other one man, gave us a decided advantage. He kept us in the Navy game this year, the last year for both of us.

You could hardly fault Coach Rivers' game plan. We figured we could move the ball behind Fred and Tommy on the right side. This was 1981. This was not the Navy team that beat every major college in the country back during the war. The whole idea brought home to me how far we had come as a society. The young men who now signed up for the sternest of tasks and stepped forward for the ultimate challenge -- WAR -- (young men not unlike my own father, full of pride, patriotism, and the will to endure); these fellows had somehow become the whipping boys for a bunch of rich and pampered future yuppies who'd never shot a rifle, except maybe one in a video game.

One of these beleaguered enlistees came into the program with a full and structured grip on the game now before us; and his name was Macabe. When the running game bogged down early in the first quarter Coach Rivers reached quickly for some of his old cards and called my number. Though my toes were numb from the cold, as were my lips, I stood ready for the challenge. We tried a slant. Shoals overthrew me.

We ran a stop and out. Macabe dove forward at the last moment and almost intercepted the damn thing. I tried a stop and long -- the sonafabitch mirrored me step for step like a goddamn bad dream; I had to knock the ball free from his sticky, greedy paws. Macabe was easily was one of the shortest guys out here, and certainly one of the smallest; yet he played with a vision and a reach that transcended his limited stature.

No one shut me down. No one.

The Coach paced the locker room at half time nervously. The players cleaned off the sludge and tried to warm up, giving each other encouragement and consolation timidly, apprehensive of what admonishments were forthcoming. The score was Three to Nothing. It was anybody's ballgame. The Coach started by throwing a cigarette out the door. His voice sounded like rivets shaking.

"Listen up! Somebody's gonna win this ballgame, gentlemen. We're gonna get out there and knock heads for two more quarters and get our fingers frozen and smashed and our noses stuck in the ice and then the damn thing'll be over. From what I've seen so far, Navy's not gonna just give it to us. I know we keep waitin', but it ain't happening. That means were gonna hafta' take it from 'em. At some point we're gonna hafta' convince 'em that this ballgame is ours. We haven't lost a game all year and this is not gonna be the one today. I'm gonna forget about the first half. It's a whole new game. We're gonna hafta' knock 'em off the ball with every snap, pound their asses backwards till they stink up their own end zone like a shitpot, and then we're gonna flush 'em out of our backyard. Now light it up!" And with that he kicked the door open and watched us pour back to the field, renewed with purpose and full of fire.

There are some visions only wise grandmothers ever fully realize. As the afternoon grew towards dusk the cold air crept in with the shade and the clouds became thicker. No amount of inspiration could keep the players from the realization that things had become more uncomfortable and when the snow started up again we all felt damned. We had made it midway through the third quarter, the score still at three to nothing, when the first flurries drifted into the stadium from the west. Our fans had practically deserted us and the snow quickly coated the bleachers and the field with a shimmery whiteness. They say Eskimos have 22 words for snow; you'd think some folks would get used to it, but I doubt it. Something about it when it comes floating down in big, feathered flakes on a calm, gray afternoon and starts piling up smooth and soft as a thick, down quilt; well, it warms up a part of a person's soul and awakens some hidden sense of wonderment. While the snow reduced visibility and made each step slippery, at the same time it cushioned each fall and added an element of grace to each sliding tackle or missed block.

As I watched the field turn white I hoped the snow would change my luck against my tireless antagonist, number 17, in blue, who was still shadowing me like he'd been in on the play calls. But not even God's own northern winds could stir his hold. I had caught two passes. Both were short stops over the middle, hitches we called them, hardly five yards deep and smack in the linebacker's lap. I had tested Macabe's speed and he seemed undaunted. I had tried out every fake in the book and nothing could break me free. I thirsted for the ball like an addict looking for a hit of dope in a Sunday School class.

"Reverse it!" I finally coughed out. We had just huddled up, after trying another sweep for a minimal gain. "Forty-seven pull, reverse. And get this fucker off my back!"

Shoals looked up nervously. His eyes were blinking from the moisture. "Coach wants a slant."

"Fuck the slant! You can't shake this motherfucker. I'm telling you. Give it to me back across and somebody pick up 17. I know I can break it."

Fred grunted, "I've got him, Tightrope.Give him the ball, Shoals." And the rest of the team voiced support for the plan. You could never tell what went on in Shoal's jittery mind. He always seemed on the brink of a nervous breakdown. Some people are not born for gambling. We lined up over the ball and came to our set position. Bucky looked out through the snowfall at the defense, then to his right where he met my eyes. I gave him a wink.

"Blue," he shrieked, our code word for an audible.

"Forty-seven pull, R-50, R-501" He looked my way again for a sign of encouragement but my mind had moved to greater tasks. Somehow Macabe sensed we were up to something and I saw him move a step in, as if to get a clearer reading on my thoughts. I took a step forward with the snap of the ball, then spun and moved at a calculated pace from right to left, four yards deep in the backfield. Bucky spun and handed the ball to Vellick, who tucked it away surreptitiously as we passed each other. It was a brilliant idea and Vellick pulled it off with style. I could see the entire defense sliding towards Vellick and the right sideline, towards a ball carrier with no ball. I saw the corner and made the turn up the left sideline, picking up speed with each step.

This was what I played for. This is where all the hours of practice, pain, blood and boredom paid their finest dividends: the open field. And only when you're there, will you know. Everybody has A Game and this was mine. I picked up a linebacker reversing across the field to cut me off, but he didn't know I was two moves beyond him. I cut back and he went by me, grasping for air. Another cornerback made the same mistake and I turned back toward the middle of the field. I couldn't see the yard markers, but I could feel the goal line, hazy and obscure, waiting like a veiled virgin somewhere in front of me. It was too easy. Another player made the same mistake and overran me; I graciously allowed him passage. Suddenly the world opened up and only the goalposts and a slaty thirty yards lay before me from here to the end of the universe, and I owned it all.

I guess I should've known better. Fred told me he caught Macabe with his eyes glued on my path through the backfield. He threw a 240 pound roll block at him which left them both buried in snow. But one of them rose from the grave. I felt the hand hit my ankle like a vine. I tripped and fell forward, and as I did the ball spilt out and skidded through the end zone. I looked back at the uniform attached to the thin, red hand which still had a firm hold on my leg. ….17 !

Of course. I should've known!

It just got colder that day and the snow thicker and the prospects for another score just got worse. When the gun finally sounded, marking the game's end, the score was still three to nothing. We got the victory, but neither team won this battle. Both teams congratulated their opponents on their grit, their guts and on their sheer survival. Arms draped over shoulders and linemen laughed and shrugged; this had been a battle of the brutes. I didn't know what to make of my own efforts. After all, what does another six points mean? I removed my helmet as we filed off and as I trotted across the field I saw a small figure walking my way through the drifting snow. This was it for us. A few more games, that's all. That's all we had left. Some people are not born for the Big Leagues. What passion and what magic we could bring to this game would be left here, on this field, and on every field we'd ever played on, and though someone might remember a game here or a play there, our day would wind down, just as the clock always limits a game, and the gun would soon report the end of it all. That's all we had left. Number 17 pulled his helmet off, revealing a sharp nose and chin and large ears which stuck out cleanly from his short military haircut. I reached out my hand and he shook it.

"Macabe," I said. "Colton?"

"Yep." I grabbed his hand tighter and gave his arm a tug with my other hand. We smiled at each other and I saw that his eyes were not so dark in this eerie snow-filtered light and in his grin I could see suddenly the depth of his love for this silly, stupid game. Neither team had accomplished much today: three to nothing the final score. This was a battle between small schools with unheralded teams. This was it for us. Macabe and I had battled out here for four years. He was the best I'd seen and I think he felt the same about me, though neither of us spoke a word. I ran a hand over his prickly scalp, now wet and icy with snow, and the kid threw an arm around my neck and pushed me toward the locker room with a laugh.

"Thought you had me," he said.

"Yep," I said, "Should've known better."

We were the last players on the field and as we started to drift apart toward our separate locker rooms I-stopped and watched him dip his head and start a jog toward the door. I couldn't help but yell at him.

Macabe!" He stopped and looked back.

"You're the best I saw!"

He smiled again, and pointed at me."You too Colton. You too," and with that we both turned and disappeared from each other lives forever.

I think about that little kid from Navy from time to time and about that game in the snow. We were just a couple of dumb kids pushing our passion for a dumb game to its logical limits, putting out there whatever magic we could whip up in our crazy, gifted hands and slippery feet.

There was a pureness to number 17's approach to the game, a virginal clarity. It is easier to appreciate the long pass or the clever open-field move than it is to truly delight in the more subtle tricks of the deflected pass by a wily cornerback. Even a stupid game, full of accidents and fortuity, can add a sense of wonder and joy to the hearts of simpler men. But what is life but a stupid game?I remember this game because it held a sense of wonder about it, a sense of the possible and the true, in the midst of chaos. My life would never be so simple again.

Chapter 9
This is no one night stand. It's a real occasion

That frigid Saturday night in Lassiter, Connecticut, Scoop Thompson threw a party at the house he was renting just north of town, up highway 20. Scoop's folks had money and he managed to afford a nice old three-bedroom house for an apartment, along with a brand new Datsun. Some guy named Phil rented a room from him and it was rare that a party didn't erupt out there at least once a week. The roads didn't appear to me to be in great shape for a country drive in the middle of the night, but Jimmy and Fred were committed to a night of joviality and I was never one to spoil the party. Even Karen agreed to drive me up and stay for a couple of hours. I guess the snow had touched everybody's romantic feather.

Because Karen was such a lousy driver -- even under normal circumstances -- riding with her over ice-covered asphalt tested every inch of my bravery and patience. I gripped the dashboard with both hands and tried to appear calm as we flew up the dark roads, sliding around every curve. We argued on the way, principally because I wouldn't ride with out to her parent's home in Simsbury and spend the night in the guest bedroom. Eventually, I gave in, partly due to the terror of her driving. Fred and Jimmy were there when we arrived, as were a good many of the other players and cheerleaders, along with a few faces I couldn't quite place. Jimmy had perched on the kitchen counter, hugging a Molson between his legs and he burped as we removed our coats and searched for a beer. You could hear the Mick Jagger chanting from the monstrous speakers that framed the den:

You make a grown man cry
Spread out the oil, the gasoline
I walk smooth, ride in a mean, mean machine
Start it up

"'Scuse me," he apologized.

Karen shook her head. "Jimmy. Where's Diane?"

Jimmy smirked. He and Diane had been split up for two weeks now. I nudged Karen with my hip and gave her a look in an attempt to quiet her down.

"Where's Fred?" I asked him.

"Don't know. Last I saw him he was trying to corner Kathy."

"Kathy Humphry?"

"Yeah."

"You're kidding?"

"No. I'm afraid not. And he's not even finished his first beer."

I shook my head and opened Karen's beer. I'd have to keep an eye on Fred tonight. I heard a howl from the living room and we looked out. Kyle McClary had just fallen back in his chair. Didn't take him long. I put my arm around Karen and guided her to the corner of the kitchen and tried to steal a kiss, but she turned her cheek and pouted.

"What?" I pleaded.

"You know what." She looked off with petulance.

"You still mad 'cause I wouldn't ride with you out to Simsbury? Jeez, Karen, I mean I'm already exhausted. All I'd do is sleep on the way out and be bored all day tomorrow." I knew the moment I said it that it was a bad choice of words.

"Oh, so that's it!"

"No. I mean, look, you know its hard for me to sleep knowing you're just two doors down and I can't get my sweaty hands on your petite and perfectly proportioned body."

It was the best I could do. She bought very little of it. "Yeah, right."

We faced each other as I leaned back against the pantry door. I locked my hands around the small of her back and snuck in a kiss. There was more truth to my excuse than she knew. As I looked over her shoulder I saw Scoop Thompson strut into the kitchen leading Michelle Puckett by the hand. He reached into the fridge and pulled out a beer and handed it behind him to Michelle. She noticed me and smiled cutely. She wore a red Lassiter sweater and looked as pure and sparkling as the fresh snow. I held Karen tighter and for a moment let my imagination run loose. As soon as Michelle got her beer she slipped away from Scoop and left him standing there awkwardly. Scoop and I never had hit it off much. He was a second rate ballplayer at best, who cared more about spearing unsuspecting ball carriers than he did about keeping his man from the pass. Scoop had white-blonde hair and tiny, brown eyes. He was a nervous lad, who seemed to be always blinking when he talked. Most of all, I was repelled by his best friend, Kyle McClary, who was having real problems adjusting to life within the boundaries of civilization. McClary had all the qualities you looked for in a middle linebacker, but none of the qualities you'd want in a friend. He lived life at a fast and furious pace, relying heavily on his penchant for violence to overcome any difficulty. He was a tough son-of-a-bitch, but almost no one on the team, or for that matter in the whole Lassiter student body, cared for him personally. McClary had taken Scoop Thompson under his wing and they made a ridiculous and idiotic twosome. Scoop regained his bearings following Michelle's brush off and called out to Kyle.

I heard Fred's voice in the dining room and I led Karen out of the kitchen and walked toward the big window which gave a full view of a sloping backyard. The snowfall had diminished to a few isolated flakes and they floated through the spot lit trees like bugs, dancing in the cold, swirling wind. Steely Dan thumped out a subterranean chant under the crackle of talk and laughter:

Drive west on Sunset
To the sea
Turn that jungle music down
Just until we're out of town
This is no one night stand
It's a real occasion
Close your eyes and you'll be there
It's everything they say
The end of a perfect day
Distant lights from across the bay

Fred indeed, was talking to Kathy Humphrey. I broke up their conversation.

"Hey man, what's going on?"

Kathy turned brightly. "Hey John!" she said.

"Hey Kathy. You know Karen?"

"Oh yeah. We had finance together, didn't we? Or Trig? Something like that." Karen seemed to be lost. Perhaps she didn't remember Kathy at all. Kathy was actually quite attractive, long, brown hair and a well endowed, if slightly chubby, figure. She just wouldn't ever shut up.

"Yeah," Karen finally said, "I think we were in Trig together." I looked up at Fred glowingly. He seemed to be embarrassed.

"Can you believe that kid?" I asked him.

"What kid?"

"What do you mean, what kid? Number 17, my nemesis." Bobby Dregorian, the trainer, walked by sprightly and I knocked him off his stride. He nearly dropped his beer.

"Oh yeah," Fred remembered. "I got that son-of-a-bitch. You know that? I laid him out flat. Fucker got up like he knew just where you were heading. Made a bee-line straight for the tackle."

"The kid's a trip. No doubt about it. Thank God I won't be lined up across from him again."

Kathy put her hand on Fred's arm."Boy, it was cold out there! I'm surprised you guys don't freeze to death. I mean, I was wearing two sweaters and this big, old parka and still just got colder and colder."

I looked at Fred again. He took a long swig from his Molson and smiled, struck by some silly thought. "You're right," he said. "We are a bunch of imbeciles."

"Now I didn't mean that," Kathy countered.

Fred consoled her and put his arm around her neck. She seemed to find the gesture comforting. Karen, meanwhile, excused herself to the bathroom. I sat on the edge of the dining room table, looking over the crowd. Jerry Lupestein and Bucky Shoals were leaning against the far wall, trading quips with their freshmen dates. Both girls seemed too young to be in college. Several teammates were taunting Bobby Dregorian to down a shot of vodka. He winced and coughed as he forced it down. I saw Jimmy breaking up a small circle with some absurd comment, gesturing wildly, eating up the spotlight. 'From around the corner Janie Sauer brushed back her hair and behind her Michelle Puckett worked her way through the chairs up beside me. I made a quick reconnaissance of the hallway that led to the bathroom. All was clear.

"Well good evening," she said, her voice hoarse and deep. I nodded and looked her over. She put her beer on the table and straightened the tuck of her sweater, thrusting out every centimeter of her long, full curves. Her light blue eyes caught the overhead light with specks of silver.

"Where's your escort?" I asked her.

"Oh Scoop? He's a twerp, isn't he? He's just trying to be a gracious host." She smiled at Kathy and Fred. "Hi Fred." Fred nodded back and introduced Kathy. Michelle shook her hand politely. I remembered, suddenly, the night we had the encounter at Mrs. Johnson's.

"Listen," I warned her, leaning closer, "don't let Kyle see me talking to you. He may get the wrong idea." Michelle shook her head and threw a long curl of her crisp blonde hair over her cheek. She touched my hand. "He's a little overprotective of the cheerleaders. He thinks were a bunch of helpless bimbos." I drew back my smile as Karen appeared from the hallway, walking solemnly towards us.I put on my most innocent expression and looked past Michelle as Karen stepped up stood beside me.

"Some game," Michelle said.

"Yeah," Karen countered, looking at Michelle like she was standing in quicksand, holding her own ground mutely. Karen began fidgeting with her diamond earrings, a nervous habit she fell to when the moment seemed uneasy.

Suddenly Michelle turned and spotted Scoop Thompson. "Oh Scooper!" she yelled at him, then turned and slipped away, saying, "See ya," to all of us. Karen looked me in the eyes, then said, "Doesn't look like she's feeling any pain." I smiled slightly. It was true, the smell of alcohol on her breath was overpowering. I tried to deflect Karen's speculations. "Hey, you know how it is. You were a cheerleader once." Karen was a cheerleader at Simsbury High, her sophomore and junior years, until her parents pulled her out in an effort to bring up her grade point average. "They're all drunks," I added. Once more, I had said exactly the wrong thing. I winced and looked out the window. I could see my own reflection like a ghost.Karen let loose of my arm and looked across the room. Fortunately, Jimmy Piehler was heading our way, toasting us with his cocktail.

The party moved on that night awkwardly, sluggishly. Every attempt I made to win Karen back to my graces was met with stubborn resistance. While most of the team seemed stimulated by our unlikely and fortuitous victory, and the capturing climate, and seemed anxious to quaff down any and all beverages, not even the numbing magic of the icy beer could steer my moods. It was often this way at parties with Karen. She refused to wander far, fearful, (perhaps rightfully) that devilry lurked in me just out of her reach. And few of the players were her type. Hell, I wasn't much her type either; I guess she tolerated me best she could. Karen believed in structure -- an orderly morning routine, never being late to class, planning every date to the nearest half hour, being sure our clothes didn't clash -- and a house full of drunken football players hardly met her requirements for a structured evening. Everywhere I turned, it seemed, my eyes kept falling on Michelle: bending to pick up a record, sucking at the straw in her cocktail diligently, running a hand down her neck. She stumbled and almost fell right at my feet once when I was reaching over Karen to catch a wildly thrown football. The whole night seemed out of joint. Karen left shortly after midnight with a brusque and short goodbye and as the party wound down I paired up with Jimmy as he made the rounds and kept the conversation lively.He tried to drag me into a back bedroom for a hit off someone's pipe, but I was in no mood for greater awareness.

"Jesus, Michelle is looking good tonight!" he said. I smiled, but did not respond. We stood in the narrow, paneled hallway, just outside the bathroom. I could see the drink and dope in Jimmy's eyes. He had been hurt when Diane had called it quits, but he was doing his best not to show it. "I can't believe she's hanging out with Scoop."

"Who? Michelle? I don't think she's serious."

"Jeez, I hope not. Did you see where Fred and Kathy went?"

"Yeah, they left thirty minutes ago."

"Oh God, what a pair. I had her in Anatomy. She asked more questions than Socrates. You know Dr. Levier? By about the third week he'd look right at her, with her hand waving wildly with some ridiculous question, and then go on to the next subject as if he'd never seen her. Look at that!" Jimmy nodded across the den, where Bobby Dregorian lay back in the easy chair, nodding in and out of consciousness. "That reminds me," Jimmy said, "You're driving."

"No problem."

When we left, Michelle was still there, as was Bobby, a couple of the players and their dates, along with a few guys I didn't know, who apparently were more preoccupied with getting stoned than enjoying any of the more subtle delights of parlor talk. The Mustang handled poorly on the slick highway, so I drove at a measured pace back towards Lassiter, thinking to myself as Jimmy caught some sleep. I couldn't put a finger on the cause of my discomfort. Surely, it was a combination of things. Had I been selfish with Karen? After all, one must always make some sacrifices for love. Perhaps I felt the sacrifices too great. Perhaps the change in our relationship I'd hoped for -- a change in Karen, really (to be more spontaneous, more relaxed) -- was too slow in coming. I had felt, that day, as the game ended, a strong sense of the impending end of my days on the field; and perhaps this had given me pause. Perhaps pure exhaustion, mixed with the chilling cold and tranquilizing alcohol, had set me into this puzzling fog. I bought Jimmy a cup of coffee at the Minite Mart, tested his wits, then sent him on his way home. It was a short trip from my dorm to his apartment. Then I pulled myself down the pale, green hallway of the dormitory, the floor dirty with dried mud, to my dorm room where I fell into the bed. I threw off my clothes and picked up the copy of Poe's short stories that lay on the floor, turned on the bedside lamp and turned to the story named Eleonora. I could see how it would take but a small leap for some to consider Poe as mad as his antagonists. I gave him the benefit of the doubt. As I read, the room turned opaque, the light as hazy as the light beyond a surgeon's eyes, when it is you on the table.

They who dream by day are cognizant of many things which escape those who dream only by night. In their visions they obtain glimpses of eternity, and thrill, in awaking, to find that they have been upon the verge of the great secret. In snatches, they learn something of the wisdom which is of good, and more of the mere knowledge which is of evil.

Silently and surely sleep overtook me. A football player can sleep only so soundly after a tough battle; the body is bruised on too many angles. I remember a dream. I sat at a desk in a classroom with just a few other students and the room was remarkable only because ice coated every surface in the room. My textbook would not sit on the slick desktop. Yet I felt warm, in fact uncomfortably warm. I wanted to mention this to the others in the room but they appeared removed from any sort of reality. "They don't care," I heard myself say and I continued squirming uneasily. No teacher stood before us and I looked around anxiously, waiting for the buzzer to grant me escape.

I awoke from the dream suddenly. Someone was knocking at my door. Who in the hell could it be? I got the lamp on clumsily, made my way to the door and cautiously pulled it open. In the hallway, his hair tussled and his eyes bloodshot, stood our demure trainer, Bobby Dregorian. He looked down the hallway nervously.

"What the h. . ." I started to say. "John," he whispered, "let me in."

I stepped aside and looked at him with amusement. No one who hoped to be a doctor should ever look this bad. He smelled horribly, as if perhaps he'd just thrown up on himself.

He continued talking, closing and locking my door, then moving over to sit on my bed. I leaned back against a chair, still in my underwear.

"Listen," he said, "You gotta do something. I just left from Scoop's. Michelle's getting raped."

The words hit me like a bucket of hot water. The wind suddenly whistled outside and we both turned, startled. I looked hard at Bobby, getting my focus together, trying to size up his sincerity and sobriety. His face was soiled.

"What's wrong with you man? You sick? You look terrible."

"I'm alright. I drank too much. Listen, John, I'm serious. I just left there. Scoop and Kyle have her in Scoop's bedroom. I think she passed out or something. We gotta go back out there."

"Jesus!" I said, rubbing my face, shaking my head to clear out the weird and wild tale that our dwarfish trainer had brought me in the middle of the night. "How do you know? What. . .what were you doing there? Were you there when this happen?"

"I left my cap. I had gone to the car and gotten sick. I think they thought I'd left.When I came back to the door I could see them through the front window. She was on the couch and she was nude.They took her into the bedroom before they opened the front door. I got my cap and acted like I didn't see anything. Come on, John. You can stop them."

I reached down and put on my socks, then began pulling on my jeans. I had no idea what I was fixing to do, I just knew I needed to prepare for something. Perhaps, in some noble pail of my sleepy dream-consciousness, I knew exactly what I was preparing to do. But I could not bring it into thoughts. "I don't know," I said, and continued dressing, pulling on a sweatshirt, lacing up my worn and weathered boots. "We just . . . . Are you okay to drive?"

Bobby looked up at me like his head was still spinning. "Yeah," he grunted.

"No. Look. I'll drive. We'll drive out there and see what's going on. But I swear, Bobby, if you're bullshitting me, or hallucinating or something, I'm gonna kick your ass!"

I put on my blue parka. "Give me your keys," I said.As he handed them to me I could see tears in his eyes. "Jesus Bobby, you're a fuckin' mess."

Bobby's folks had money too. He drove a crisp BMW 325i, metallic silver. The car was immaculate and it handled with a fine-tuned combination of ease and power, marred only by the smell of Bobby's vomit. I turned the heater on and found the button to glide my window down partway. Bobby sat next to me with his hands between his legs, gritting his teeth and licking his lips in a silent vow never to partake of the golden elixir again in his borne days. We both knew it was a hollow and transient vow. The night was darker and less forgiving at this hour, the patches of ice I'd maneuvered through deftly on the way home now shinning like small ponds in the yellow fog lamps. We pulled to the top of Scoop's street and coasted down quietly. I put the car in neutral and turned off the motor for the last half a block. I looked at Bobby as we came to a halt under a tree. His head was bowed and he looked up at me like he was on the verge of regurgitation.

"Come on," I urged him, "Let's go. Let's see what the fuck's going on."

Bobby shook his head no and ran his hands over his scalp. "I can't do it," he said. "John," he whispered, "You know I've never been any good at sports. I love it, John, but I'm just one of those guys. But you know I'm not the only one. We watch you, John. You're really something. You know how we all want to be like somebody. Somebody that kind of brings together all those things you'd like to be. I watch you, John, and I wish..."

I cut him off before he made a complete fool of himself. "You're drunk as shit, Bobby. Are you telling me you're not going up there with me, after getting me up in the middle of the night and making me drive out to the middle of nowhere in a bunch of ice n' snow? Fuck it!" I said, and handed him the keys. "You see me coming out, start the car and be ready to go."

I buttoned up my jacket and walked quietly up the steps to the front porch. I looked in the window off to the left of the porch. The light was on but no one was in sight. I turned back and looked at Bobby huddled in his car, looking up at me like a mouse in a glass cage. "Shit!" I said, under my breath, then I pulled open the screen door and rapped loudly on the front door. It was silent for several moments, then I could hear the vibration of footsteps. There was the muffled sound of voices. After a few more moments I saw Scoop step out of his bedroom, looking nervously my way, wearing only a pair of gym shorts. He turned the bolt lock and pulled the door open.

"Tightrope!" he said, his eyes lit up like he was glad to see me. "What the hell you doing out here?"

"Scoop!" I replied, and pushed my way past him. "Shwew! Damn cold out there."

"What you doing out here?" he asked again. I looked at his bedroom door. It was closed tight. Scoop turned momentarily to check it himself. Scoop's eyes were bloodshot and his best attempts could not keep them fully open. You could smell the Marijuana in the room and from his hair. Scoop somewhere had run into a bad crowd or something. He really believed that he was tough. I'd seen his kind. I looked him over as he stood holding the front door. The door was still open, and the bitter wind must have raised chill bumps on his legs. He pushed it almost shut and stepped back.

"Is Michelle still here?"

He laughed. "What? Are you kidding?"

"No. I'm not kidding.Bobby was just here. He saw you guys take her into your bedroom." Scoop drew back, then looked down at the floor, a weird expression on his face. He bit his lip.

"What?" he got out, finally. I thought I could hear, barely, voices behind his bedroom door.

"Listen," I said, "I don't care. Bobby dragged me out here and he thinks she's in trouble. I don't know what's going on. But I'm here now and I'm gonna look in your bedroom and then I'm going."I started toward the door and as I did Scoop moved up ahead of me and blocked my passage. "Alright," he said, "She's here. But listen, nothing's going on. She's fine." Just as he tried to reassure me I heard someone call my name; it was Michelle Puckett's voice, hoarse and weak. "John," she called.

"Let me in," I told Scoop. "Just let me talk to her and I'll go." I reached for the knob and he held his ground. He smelled of body odor about as bad as Bobby smelled of vomit. "What's the problem?"

"No problem. It's just, you're not going in."

I called out: "Michelle. Michelle." I could barely hear some jumbled response. "Scoop," I said, quietly, looking him dead in the eye from about six inches away, "I'm going to go in and check on her. If you want to stop me, then I suggest that you do it." My nose was about two inches from his own. I knew his kind. As I reached for the knob he slid to the side and allowed me by him. The room was dark, lit only by slivers of moonlight filtering in through Venetian blinds. I hesitated for a moment to regain my vision, when suddenly Michelle sprung up at me from the bed. Another figure, apparently Kyle, moved slowly from in the bed. Michelle ran to hug me, still totally nude. She had been crying and she put her head on my chest. Scoop tried to excuse the scene.

"Aw come on, John, she just got a little drunk. We were just having some fun. She went along with all of it."

"Oh God!" she said, crying and holding me harder now. I looked into the shaded room.

"Is that you Kyle?" The form shuffled, turning away, but did not answer. I walked her into the living room and sat her down on the sofa. "Give me her clothes," I told Scoop. He walked hurriedly into the bedroom and appeared momentarily with her jeans, underwear and her sweater. He handed it to her and stepped back arrogantly.

"Why don't you put your clothes on," I told her, then I stood and approached Scoop. He backed away nervously. He was unsure what I might do, whether I would attack him, lecture him, or call the police. His eyes blinked and he turned his face and drew back as I came closer.

"Listen, John. It's just, you know, nothing happened." His voice sounded like a rusted saw. "You know she wanted to stay." I didn't know what to make of it. The whole scene had the feel of unreality. It was like the time Sarge struck Lisa Rae. The whole room was spinning with confusion. I shook my head with anger and disbelief at Scoop's explanation, but I couldn't work out a sensible response, only an expression of rage. Michelle pulled her sweater on and I led her to the door. I turned back as I ushered her out, thinking Scoop might make one last incriminating statement, but he held his tongue and watched us silently, his face gone colorless.

Bobby started the car as we came down the icy steps. I helped Michelle into the back seat and moved Bobby over. He was still too drunk to be driving anything. Michelle was still crying and her head was down. There was an awkward moment of silence. Bobby finally looked over his shoulder. "You okay, Michelle?"

She sniffled. "Yeah, Bobby. Just great. You got a Kleenex?"

"No. Let me see. "He proceeded to look through his glove box, but found nothing of use. I could see in the rear view mirror that her nose was running something awful. I looked at Bobby's shirt.

"Here," I said and pulled at the top button of his flannel shirt. "Give her your T-shirt." Bobby looked at me like I'd lost my wits. I had long ago lost patience with him and the whole situation.

"What?" he said, just as I grabbed his t-shirt by the collar as if I might just rip it right off his chest from beneath his shirt. In another moment I would have. "Alright. OK," he said, and finally removed his shirt so he could pull off his undershirt and hand it to Michelle. She blew her nose voraciously. I looked at Bobby, scurrying to get his shirt back on, like he carried a pestilence.

When we got on the highway and the car began to heat up, I realized that whatever happened next in this muddled and strained night would be the moment of no return. It would be the moment when the whole fuzzy picture would develop into a clear and lasting image and be hung on the darkroom wall as a testament. Once it came clear, it could not be changed; all our lives would be hung on that wall, in that picture. In a moment the course of our futures would be turned unalterably down some dark passage where only one's conscience can rule the heart and only the spark within one's soul can provide guidance for the righteous. In my own dreams and hopes I'd never cast myself into the role of the hero, the rescuer, the martyr. I took enough of my mother's religion and her own gentle compassion along with me to provide a sense of fairness and sympathy, but my approach had long been to avoid the Real dangers, the Real challenges, to move the ball up field though cunning and cleverness, wisely knowing when the play was over and the tackle was made.

I drove as fast as the road would allow, the car pushing quietly through the air. We would be in Lassiter soon and the region we approached made us all look out at the dark farms and closed up gas stations with distraction. I tried to get a feel for Michelle's state of mind.

"Where's your car?" I asked her. She had stopped crying, but her eyes were swollen red and mascara stained her cheeks. She looked out the window momentarily. We were slowing down through an intersection. A lady in an old Cadillac waited to cross at the light.

"I left it at the field," she said, her voice a whisper. "Jeez, it's probably snowed in."

I grimaced with misgivings. She was right. Bobby's BMW would be her only transportation this night.

Michelle leaned forward, resting her hand on my shoulder and her chin on the seat back. I could smell the alcohol on her breath, mixed with the sweet perfume of her hair. "John," she said to me, "Do me a favor. Let me stay with you tonight. I don't know what to do. I can't go back to my apartment. I can't see Julie tonight. I can't see anyone. I need time to think. I just . . . I don't know, John. Just tonight."

I grimaced again and turned to look at Bobby. He remained crouched over, his eyes black beads. I looked at Michelle in the rear view mirror and she caught my glance with pleading, swollen eyes. My stomach was churning so that I almost felt nauseous. I slowed down and made a U-turn at Juniper and 2nd Street, then guided us back the way we came till I reached Holcomb Street. The dorm was half a mile down on the right. I made the turn quickly. It was too late to turn back, the compass had been set and the flags raised. Yet I could feel the surf tossing our ship unsteadily, and while I couldn't make them out in the purple darkness, I knew that somewhere in the windy channel dark rocks lay waiting. I held the wheel with both hands, looking out at the snow-covered lawn outside The Asylum as I rolled to a stop. Our headlights reflected in the snow like Christmas lights. As I helped Michelle from the car, I kept thinking how peaceful I would've been sleeping right now, if not for Bobby's inability to hold his liquor, and his lousy choice of accomplices. Bobby got the car going and onto the street clumsily. At this hour, his odds of making it home were much improved. Only the old lady in the Cadillac poised a threat.

I made a point not to speak as I escorted Michelle down the hallway. It would serve no one's interest to have another unlucky soul cast into this tragic and surreal scene. As we came to the bathroom we stopped and both of us leaned up against the concrete wall, staring into each other's eyes. I could feel my head beginning to ache and I held the fingers of my right hand up to my temple. I pressed her on the issue at hand.

"Michelle. I don't know what happened there. But I think if you're gonna do something about it, if you're gonna contact the police, you can't clean yourself up." What did I know about such things? I spoke with the authority of an attorney, though my widest experience with the law came from second-rate TV dramas. Michelle put her hands to her mouth and suddenly she began crying again, this time bursting into a torrent of tears. She fell into my arms, sobbing, and I pulled her inside the door of the men's bathroom. A draft chilled our feet on the damp, tile floor. The bathroom smelled of ammonia. I held her loosely by the first sink, our reflections like a dream in the row of mirrors beside us.

Whatever happened out there tonight, it had affected her deeply. She sobbed like a baby. I could offer no comfort but my presence. She began speaking through her sobs. I pulled out some paper towels to dry her face.

"I can't do it," she began. "I can't do it John." She had the look of a five year old that'd lost her only doll. "You don't know my parents. My mom....." Once again the tears broke out. "It just.....it would kill them. John, you can't. Please don't."

"I don't.....Don't what?"

"We can't let anyone know. We can't let anyone know." She spoke as if she were speaking to the walls, her voice echoing quietly. I shook my head, which was now banging with pain, and leaned back on the sink next to us. Her face was splotched, and her eyes were still mapped with red, yet I found myself drawn to the gentle curves of her cheeks and chin, her almost plump nose and the light brushes of blonde above her eyes and around her ears. Her lips were as full and red as apples. I wondered how such a beauty could ever find her in the middle of a single night without a sophisticated and established escort. I realized suddenly that there was more than one puzzle at work here.

"Listen," I said (she turned on the water and tried to wash her face). "You gotta make this decision. I don't know what happened. I just want to be sure you're okay. I want to be sure that everything's OK. I'm afraid we can't go back."

After she washed, she dried her face on my shirt and looked up at me. She gave me a crazy grin, like somehow she'd finished the sorrow and was ready to go on with her life. I admired her courage and grinned back, but behind our thin smiles we both knew nothing had ended, and perhaps the craziness had just begun.

"I think I need a hot shower," she said. "S'pose I can borrow a towel?"

I laughed, wondering if in fact I had a single clean towel to offer her. As I shook my head with agreement the bathroom door suddenly opened and Frank Zimmerman stepped in, wearing a pair of flowered boxer shorts. He stopped and looked at us for a moment, baffled and half-asleep.

"Hi Frank," I said. He was speechless.

"C'mon," I said to Michelle, and led her out of the bathroom and back to my room.

I guarded the bathroom long enough for her to clean up, then found some old sweats that she could get into. I gave up the bottom bunk and threw together a blanket and a half for myself on the top mattress. It was after five thirty when I turned the lights out. In my room you could always see shadows at night from the twisted branches of an elm tree just outside.The thin shadows would dance through the blinds when the wind was up. There was a quiet breeze that early October morning and the dance of the shadows moved slowly on the walls, the arms and fingers of a grandfather and grandmother in a sleepy waltz. The heater hissed quietly under the window. Michelle rolled over and seemed to cocoon herself in the covers below me. She asked me a stupid question.

"How come you don't have all your sport's stuff on the walls in here?"

"What sport's stuff?"

"You know, all your trophies and stuff. I mean, Jeez, you're in the paper every week just about."

"In the Lassiter Beacon? They don't have much to report on. Besides, I send all the clippings back home."

"Back home?"

"Yea. Lumberton, Mississippi." I heard her giggle. "What's so funny?"

"Oh, nothing. I just never thought you were from Mississippi."

"Well, keep it to yourself."

I heard her roll over again and sigh. "Our little secret," she said, softly.

Suddenly, I felt a tear come to my eye. I looked at the shadows, moving up the wall like the smoke of Indians, and I echoed her promise. "Yeah. Our little secret."

Chapter 10
I might still be out there, chasing squirrels.

Sometimes a person moves ahead with an idea or a job, not a thought about the worth of the work, or the value of the task. We can't always judge such things.

My Grandfather, Justin Colton, owned six acres of pecan trees when I was a just a little peanut myself. I remember how my dad used to put me out there with the help, gathering up the pecans in early September. They had a machine that would hook around the tree - I think they called it a shaker -- and it would rattle the ripe nuts off the branches. Only way they could figure out to get 'em up, though, was with a bunch of folks and some burlap sacks. The crews Grandpa hired in were always black folks, and Mr. Cooper was always the most familiar among the bunch. I'd try my best to keep up with Mr. Cooper's crew and contribute a sack or two, but the work couldn't keep my mind occupied and the sacks, for a third grader, would start to get awful heavy after a while. I remember how they used to tell stories about hunting possum and deer, and chasing down wild boars. Mr. Cooper had a rope across his backyard with a bell on it that would start clanging whenever some wild animal stumbled across it. Sometimes you'd hear a shotgun go off in the middle of the night and I'd imagine Mr. Cooper bagging a wild hog or some stray bear. He had two sons who usually worked with us who seemed to be always cutting up and firing the nuts at the crazy squirrels that cowered under every tree, their bushy gray tails darting with what could be either excitement or nervousness, depending how you saw it. Sometimes I'd even sneak in a shot, but you couldn't hit the damn things; they were quick as lightning and could dart up the side of a tree before you could set up for your next shot. I saw a big old gray squirrel once, when we were out collecting, dive off a branch way above me and he fell right into another web of branches like he was stuck in a net. He caught his balance and scurried to a larger limb, then to a main branch. As I looked up at him I could've sworn he winked at me and grinned, but by the time I called out for the rest of them to see the crafty devil, the old gray had pounced to another tree and disappeared, probably into a hollow spot. I guess they paid the help by the bushel, but it couldn't have been much money, 'cause most people, even those who needed money and wanted to work, refused to do it. Whatever nuts I managed to gather in I turned over to one of Mr. Cooper's sons, who'd turn it in for credit. I guess I'm lucky most of those trees died off. I might still be out there, chasing squirrels.

One thing about being at Lassiter: you never ran out of projects. I awoke that Sunday morning and got Michelle to her car and dug her out, then trudged back to the dormitory cafeteria for an early lunch before holing up in my room and working on a paper I had coming due in Russian History. The Czars, Cossacks and Bolsheviks provided more excitement to the exercise than I'd imagined going in. But my mind was too weary and confused to make much headway. Every time I paused, my gaze would fall on my Poe collection and the smallish print would appear as a vision. Finally, I gave in and turned to the middle of the book and started in on The Purloined Letter. I'd read it more than once, but it still stood up to another reading. Many have called this one story the first of the detective genre. I'd never tag Poe as a detective writer, however. I think he shoots for a cleverer and less apparent theme. In the story Poe pulled me away from the riddles that had come to rest in me that Sunday. I found, for a short time, solace and peace, my mind subtly carried through the winding tale of emotions and intrigue. My eyes began to drag after just a few pages, but I knew the story could not be delayed for my rest. Poe lugged me to the end and at the end I smiled and closed the paperback book, then fell back on my bed and with the faint perfume of Michelle's hair still on the pillow I fell into a sweet and forgiving sleep.

There was a mood which used to cover me up back when I was attending Jackson High School, brought on by the fermented redolence of the hallways, a mood which followed me around from classroom to classroom like a cloud. On the first Monday of classes following the encounter at Scoop's my mood seemed unfocused by a similar type of thick fog. I could've been stoned on Columbian Red and more aware of my surroundings. The air began to warm up a little, but my atmosphere was charged with its own dim light. I ran through ideas, dilemmas, and hypotheses with every new corner I turned. Was it out of my hands now?

Just as I was walking into the Tillman Building toward Professor Strache's class a big icicle broke off a tree above me and exploded on the steps beside me. The ice shattered like glass and skidded down the incline of the steps through the slippery feet of the approaching students. We were all lucky the shard didn't catch us in the head, but we all got a lift from the bizarre moment. I turned and looked back down the easy, snow-covered slope and the students lit up with surprise and delight, and I grinned and winked, then turned inside.

The classrooms at Lassiter were almost always too warm during the winter and too cold in the late spring. Big, thick coats lay draped over every chair back. Some of the more casual students even threw them on the floor in a back corner. The Professor wore a yellow short sleeve shirt with a dark plaid bow tie, brown slacks and hushpuppies. By the looks of his hair you'd think he just got up. His eyes seemed tired also, but with a special light nevertheless.

He had a habit of starting the class even while everyone was still shuffling to get comfortable. His voice seemed full of smoke. He wrote on the board: Process (then, under it) Reality (and under that) Dreams. He stood looking at what he'd just written for a few moments. I thought he was going to erase it, but instead he walked over to look out the window and then began talking, as if to the wintry landscape outside.

"Art, you know, is as original and important as it is, precisely because it does not start out with clear knowledge of what it means to say. Out of the artist's imagination, as out of natures inexhaustible well, pours one thing after another." He threw out his hand, as if he were throwing out candy. For a moment, he looked directly at me. "The artist composes, writes, or paints just as he dreams, seizing whatever swims close to his net. This, not the world seen directly, is his raw material." The Professor made his way slowly toward the back of the room, still pausing to look out the windows between every sentence. I kept following his gaze to see what he found so captivating. "This shimmering mess of loves and hates -- fishing trips taken long ago with Uncle Ralph, a 1940 green Chevrolet, a war, a vague sense of what makes a story, a symphony, a photograph -- this is the clay the artist must shape into an object worthy of our attention; that is, our tears, our laughter, our thought." Several of the students took down notes wildly, but I knew this lecture could not be captured so I closed up my notebook and let The Professor wail. When he reached the far back corner of the room, precisely where the coats lay piled up, he looked back at us and smiled warmly, crossed his arms and leaned back on the window sill.

"Students of aesthetics used to say that art combines fancy and judgment. Schiller once put it in a letter to a friend, what happens in the case of the creative mind is that the intellect has withdrawn its watchers from the gates, and the ideas rush in pell-mell, and only then does the creative mind review and inspect the multitude.'"

Once again he threw out his arm. He moved across the back of the room and carefully up the inside wall, back toward the front of the room. "Think of how you solve a puzzle, any puzzle, say a crossword. You look for an immediate solution first; what jumps out at you, is there something obvious? If nothing comes right away, then you start a free association. What word starts with a J and has four letters? When this doesn't do it, you work backwards, look again at the clue, in this case let's say: Used in swimming. You picture a typical swimmer at the beach, or perhaps someone swimming in competition. You try to work by a process, but you'll take any idea which comes to mind, that is, as long as it fits. Finally, you throw up your hands and go on to the next block, hoping more letters will lead you down the right path, or if you're stuck at that block you secretly solicit help from someone who may have a broader knowledge of aquatics, or you put the puzzle down until you can refresh your mind, but always on the look out for some subtle comment or picture which will lead you to success. It's your senile grandfather, of course, who reminds you that swim trunks, in his day, were called jams." Every face in the class looked toward the Professor with a smile. We could see the whole scene as he drew it out. He searched for the piece of chalk he'd used just a few minutes earlier. It was not in the chalk tray. Finally he gave up and pulled a new piece out of his desk drawer, then wrote on the board and circled it: Technique.

It was easy and natural to get lost when The Professor led you down some winding dirt road toward the day's thesis. You didn't have time to be concerned about whatever assignment he might throw at you, or whatever other problems you'd brought with you into class. I stopped at Professor's Strache's desk on my way out to congratulate him on the day's lesson.

"Clever work, Professor," I told him. He had pulled his chair out to sit down, but stopped when I approached him.

"I hope I didn't ramble too much today, John."

"Well. Just enough." Phil Burrels pushed me on his way by. I'm sure the whole class thought I was a brown-noser with Professor Strache, but I hardly cared. I wasn't sure exactly what I wanted to say to The Professor that morning, or if I wanted to say anything at all. In some way I needed a connection with something real, something I knew to be honest, something unpolluted by the oily currents of the times. The Professor pulled the chair out and sat himself down as the last student exited and I rested myself on the corner of his desk, putting my notebook between us. He fumbled at my notes as he talked.

"This whole idea of process. It gets us into more trouble than we'd like. Did you ever finish *The Real Thing* by James?" I shook my head disparagingly. It was another in a long list of stories and books which The Professor had recommended to me and which I'd never had the time or the energy to take on. I always felt as if I'd let him down somehow, even though during football season my free time was quite limited, yet he never let my omissions keep him from suggesting more and more works for my fertile but untilled mind. Someday, I kept telling myself, I'd read 'em all, and I'd call up the old man and give 'em a shock in the middle of some long, sleepless night.

"James wonders about experience, reality and the growth of the artistic mind. James was probably too smart for his own good. Don't you think?"

"Yeah. He reads a little haughty."

"I agree, Mr. Colton.We seem to agree a lot on these simple matters. You should keep with your idea of being an English teacher. If you ever make it, you'll have half a chance of putting some kids on the right track." He laughed at his remark, his teeth small and yellow. "Where're you gonna settle down, Colton?"

I looked at the desk, musing on the idea. If everything here in New England were as warm and stimulating as Professor Strache I would be easily transplanted.

"I don't know about that. Allot of snow up here." The Professor nodded slyly. He was as at home in the frozen drifts as a silver mink. "Besides, if I'm gonna get kids on the right track, they probably need me worse down where I came from than they do up here. But who knows? I might get drafted by the Jets." I had to laugh myself at that idea.

"Oh well," I sighed, gathering myself to leave, "I guess I better get on. I just wanted to tell you that I enjoyed today's class. I might stop by to talk about some things later this week. You'll be on campus?"

The Professor looked up from the book he was flipping through, his brow furrowed. "Mostly," he said. He handed me a scrap of paper with some titles on it. "Here," he said, try this out when you get a chance. On the paper he had written:

Life and Song, Sidney Lanier Tennessee's Partner, Bret Harte
4 Preludes on playthings of the wind, Sandburg

I took the paper, folded it into my top pocket and bid him adieu. It was 11:40. On Mondays I always met Karen at the Student Union for lunch, but I knew I had other tasks to complete before I could fulfill my appointment.

The Smythe Library had been constructed in 1901. When you entered the door you could see the stacks on the first two floors from the central atrium. Elevators and new lighting had been added, but the place still had the feel of antiquity and the sturdy scholarship which existed at the turn of the century. The library had individual cubicles around the perimeter of the second and third floors. Whenever I was stuck on campus and needed to put in some serious study time, or wanted to get into whatever I might be reading, or simply needed a few moments to remove myself from the day's rush, I would sneak off to a cubicle on the third floor along the east wall where they kept most of the older, classic works. Not only did the heavily varnished and warped wooden floor fill the quiet air with a thick, encompassing smell, but the old, decaying books cast off their own peculiar odor: the smell of knowledge.

It was in one of these narrow cubicles that I found myself thumbing through a collection of Sandburg's poems until I located "Four Preludes on Playthings of The Wind," written in 1921. People in libraries tend to be serious about whatever task is before them; there is always a quiet and intense shuffling of pages and footsteps. A person might be standing three feet away from you, searching through titles for five minutes, and never make enough noise for you to turn and notice them. I dropped into my own little world as I finally found the poem and began reading, my mind searching each metaphor with The Professor over my shoulder.

> *II*
> *The doors were cedar*
> *And the panels strips of gold;*
> *And the girls were golden girls,*
> *And the panels read and the girls chanted:*
> *"We are the greatest city,*
> *the greatest nation; nothing like us ever was."*
> *The doors are twisted on broken hinges.*
> *Sheets of rain swish through on the wind where the golden girls ran and the panels read:*
> *"We are the greatest city, the greatest nation;*
> *nothing like us ever was."*

Well, it might just be true. We were a nation of superlatives. Certainly no country could match the richness of this land, both in physical and intellectual terms. We were at first simple and God-fearing folks. Folks who would risk everything for the freedom to worship. From the beginning we were gamblers. It's always been in the American Spirit to put it all on the line with a single throw of the dice. But what began as a simple dream, grew beyond all proportions. Perhaps it was our faith which seeded the clouds of fortune, transforming the simple refuges of free worship into conglomerate, media empires so corrupt even many politicians wouldn't be seen on the grounds. Though it's not as if the shadow of greed grew up new and re-formed from the

American Dream; greed has always been the main fuel of the engines of progress in "this greatest city." With freedom come certain compromises. In "this greatest city" we are all Icarus ascending, in danger from the fires which burn everywhere above and below us. With freedom comes confusion, the conundrum of too many voices un-silenced. Suddenly, as I stared at the faded page before me, I felt a cold breath on my ears and I pulled my shoulders in protectively. I turned to look behind me. A gray-haired lady stood just down the stack, with her back to me, fumbling with her selections. She was mumbling quietly to herself.I could swear she was saying, "You have sinned." I shook my head to throw off the chimera and I pulled my collar up to smooth down the hair on my neck. I remembered at once that Karen was waiting for me at the lunchroom. When I looked back again the old lady had disappeared.

"Well," she said, her eyes almost crossing, "I was just about to give up on you." I laid my books down on the table next to hers and sat down meekly.

"I had to talk to Professor Strache about something. I'm sorry. I . . ."

"What is it with you and Professor Strache?"

"What do you mean, what is it? He's my teacher for Chrissake! You know, we're in school here. It's like a college, you know. You see all these kids walking around with books and stuff, studying over their shitty ham sandwiches. It's like being in college. Jesus!" I folded my arms and looked away. I was making no sense at all. Karen straightened her books and followed my gaze toward the cafeteria line.

"Alright," she said, "Jesus, you don't have to go on about it. It's just I'm starving and I thought you'd be here at twelve."

I didn't know what to tell her."Look, I can't.....I just.....You want to eat?" She sighed and stood up and we made our way to the line. As we picked up some sandwiches and sodas we seemed, the two of us, as disconnected as ever. But I was disconnected to everything. Or at least to everything but my own disordered cerebration. Nothing of what was bothering me had anything to do with Karen. She had not changed at all -- in fact she appeared changeless -- it was me. We sat across from each other and ate quietly; the food here was actually not too bad.

"What is it?" she asked me. Her light blue eyes seemed gray in the bright overhead light."What's bothering you?"

I tried to smile away her concern, but I had always been a lousy liar. "What do you mean?" I came back.

"Are you upset because of the other night?"

My face went flush suddenly."What . . . other night?"

"You know. Saturday night. Are you still upset about all that?"

"Oh, no. No, that's nothing. I was acting stupid. I guess I was just tired, that's all."

"You sure were acting kind of weird."She shook her head at me like a mother counseling her son.

"I know I've had a lot on my mind lately. You know, I've been screwing around with this stupid game for twenty years. Twenty years! Can you believe it? I'm not sure it hasn't all been a big waste of time. I'm not sure whether I'm gonna miss this shit or not. Does that make any sense?"

She took her napkin and wiped my chin. I didn't even realize I had drooled some milk. "I know, John," she tried to soothe me, "I guess its kind've like parting with an old friend."

She giggled cutely."I think you're gonna miss being The Star!" She took my hand and kissed it and I smiled at her, once more drawn into the warmth of her heart.

"The Star!" I laughed. "No, I won't miss that!"

But I lied.

"Listen," she said, "You need to come out next Sunday and have brunch with us. My brother is going to be back for a few days. You've got to meet him."

"Is this the one who's in the Navy?"Her younger brother had enlisted after flunking out at Lassiter. Karen had suspected he had gotten into drugs.

"Well, he's not gonna be too happy to meet me. I mean, we just got through beating his team."

"Barely."

"Yeah. I guess that's true."I thought suddenly of Number 17, smirking at me with his prickly scalp. "Yeah, sure," I said, confirming the date with feigned excitement.

Her folks were just too formal to make for a relaxing Sunday afternoon. I would have much preferred to drive out and see The Professor. Or maybe just take a drive with Jimmy and Fred out toward Blue Hills, pass the pipe and talk philosophy. I smiled as my mind ran through the images. I would sure miss these guys.

Chapter 11
Gone to Carolina in my mind

I dressed for practice Monday nervously. My locker was next to Jimmy's, but he was always late. Down from Jimmy there would be Lupestein, who delighted in insulting both Jimmy and I at every opportunity. I would have welcomed his barbs that day, but he too was running late. As my scrimmage uniform came together I could hear behind me McClary and Thompson shuffling into the locker room. They were laughing over some joke, their snickers like the grunts of pigs. I knew they could see me from their lockers and I could feel their eyes on the back of my head. I pulled my helmet on and pushed by them toward the door. Scoop stepped aside courteously, but Kyle held his ground and looked down on me with contempt. I looked down and slid out the doorway.

The field had dried up a good bit since Saturday and the sun shone clearly in the cloudless and cool afternoon sky. As I jogged up the sideline Willie Patterson ran by me, made a cut, then reached out to pull in a spiral thrown from way downfield. He stopped, put on a move as if evading an invisible cornerback, then shot toward the goalpost.

"Willie, Hit me!" I yelled. I took off across the field. He fired the ball in a high, wobbly arc and I raced under it, but could not control the spin. It bounced wildly off my outstretched hands and landed at Coach River's feet. He looked at me sternly, making no effort to pick up the ball. I jogged up to him and scooped it up.

"Afternoon, Coach," I said.

"Afternoon, Colton. You warmed up yet?"

"Oh yeah," I yelled back, tossing the ball towards Willie and taking off in another sprint. "I forgot."

Some people can take the fun out of anything.

We were scheduled to play the University of Massachusetts on the next Saturday, away. They had played decently early in the year, even beating Navy by 30, but had faded in the past few games. They had a spirited passing attack, bolstered by a quarterback named Burnworth, who they said had a chance of going pro. We all doubted it seriously, but he definitely had an arm and would be welcome in my backfield on any fall afternoon. U Mass would be game 7 of our 12 game season.Only Thanksgiving, two weeks away, would give us any release. Only five more to go. Five more victories and we'd be undefeated. Five more wins and we'd make history for Lassiter. Five more wins and we'd own the Cup. Five more wins to finish out my final year. But now it was hard to focus on these familiar dreams. I moved through practice with the sluggish grace of a matador's bull, my horns always inches from digging my target, my eyes dark and woeful.

Late in the practice we broke into teams and had a short scrimmage on half the field: first team offense against second team defense and vice versa. I came violently to life during the scrimmage. It happened during a pass to the weak side. I had been loping lazily across the middle, with no intention of blocking anybody. Out of nowhere Scoop Thompson caught me from the blind side and knocked me off my feet with a stick right under my chin. I spun to the ground dizzily. Even Coach Rivers was shocked by the hit. He even walked out to see how I was and at the same time dress down Thompson for his poor sportsmanship. I looked up at The Coach groggily and slowly pulled myself to my feet. There was the color of pink in all shades of light and the motion of the players walking back to our respective huddles seemed totally chaotic; every helmet on the field, it seemed, had turned to watch me as I shook out the cobwebs and finally made a focus on the offensive huddle.

Regaining my bearings, I re-joined the huddle. Fred grabbed my jersey and looked me in the eye, gauging my condition. It weren't the first time I'd been stuck! I knew the feeling. A few specks of color might stay in my vision for a while -- an eerie, unwelcome hallucination -- but my .grasp on reality would quickly reappear. I looked back toward the defense and saw Scoop Thompson standing boldly at the scrimmage line, split out to the right.

"Split right, 72 hitch," I said.

"John!" Fred said.

I turned to Bucky and stuck my facemask up against his own. "Call it, fucker!" I told him, moving him back with the force of the strain in my neck. Bucky looked at Fred and Fred nodded his concordance.

"Alright," Bucky spouted, "72 hitch. Break!"

I don't think Scoop knew I was out to get him on this play. He lined up right across from me as if he owned me. It was true my eyes were still half full of stars, but like I said, it wasn't the first time I'd been stuck.

On the snap I made a quick fake to the right, then pushed by him up field about seven yards, pumping my arms as if breaking into full stride. Scoop didn't possess the greatest speed and I knew he'd take off vigorously to catch me. That's when I stopped and moved back to the ball. Bucky laid it out for me perfectly and I grabbed it and spun. Scoop was a good four yards up field and struggling to regain his balance. The cobwebs had left me. Everyone knew what was happening. I juked him four ways from next Sunday, till he stood so far back on his heels I thought sure he would stumble and fall. Then I tucked the ball under my left arm and caught him with a right forearm and shoulder that threw him flat on his back. I stepped forcefully over his helmet and started up field. But the passion had now boiled up in me. I felt the anger of the bull upstaged, the hostage turned victor -- so I stopped dead.

Scoop had barely made it to his knees, but I knew he was no quitter, and I knew he'd charge after me with the deranged fury so prevalent in his species. One must know one's game, which fields lay before you, dusty and foot worn, properly ripe for a parapet, where, at the last reach of the engagement, to draw one's sword.

I rested on my toes, awaiting his attack. It was like a dog jumping after old socks. I offered a leg and jumped aside, then came back at him as he tumbled by me, jumping side to side until every direction must have seem to him the wrong one. He cursed and swore as I jogged backwards toward the goal line.

"Colton!" he yelled at me, still in hot pursuit, "You fucker!"

I stopped at the five and made one more clever move, so that his fingertips just brushed the edges of my cleats, then I spun wildly, stepped into the end zone and fired the leathered spheroid into the turf, right at his face.

"Motherfucker," I said to him, so only he could hear it, then I turned and walked toward the showers.

Coach Rivers blew his whistle. "Colton!" he yelled, his voice raspy. "Where're you going, son?"

I didn't even turn to answer but walked on to the locker room and began undressing. Our offensive coordinator, Virgil Chapman, stepped inside as I removed my shoulder pads.

He looked at me for a moment from the doorway then walked over and sat beside me. Coach Chapman was a slender man who kept himself in better shape than half my teammates. His large nose held mantle over a thick, gray mustache, giving him a distinctive visage more at home in an earlier American century. He slapped at my head and looked down over his nose as he questioned me.

"What da fuck is wrong with you boy? Dat was some show."

I smirked in response and looked at my feet.

"What's bothering you? You know, I noticed you weren't looking too good all day."

I ran through my recent actions in my mind; I must've looked like I'd lost my mind. Coach C was the kind of coach you could trust with a problem. He had a knack for keeping the offense focused when Coach Rivers dressed us down. He had a simple approach to the sport and a simple approach to people. You always felt like he was with you, like he was one of the boys. Me and Jimmy had even had a beer with him one night in an old saloon near the river. Somehow we had ended up there on a warm Friday night in last year's spring semester. I guess we'd seen the place on the way home from some party, or a wild excursion towards the river to blow a joint. Our appearance in the smoky bar drew attention from every well-wrinkled face hunched over their drink. It looked slot like the Majesty Bar back in Lumberton. These places I guess are the same everywhere. We'd ordered a draft at the bar and were checking out a waitress when we noticed that Coach C was hunched over his own drink right beside us.

"Now I thought these football boys didn't do no drinking during the off-season."

For a second we were startled, but when we saw his gray eyes light up and his warm smile welcome us we both broke into laughter.

"Coach C!" I said, throwing an arm around his shoulder. "What the hell you doing here?"

"Well, Colton. What does it look like? I'm partaking of a whiskey. The more proper question is: what are you boys doing here?"

"Partaking of a whiskey, of course," I answered. The waitress we had been ogling glided up beside Coach C, put her arm around his shoulders and looked us over.

"So this is how you boys train in the off season, driving through the countryside, pounding brews and chasing women?"

Jimmy defended us. "Shit Coach, we got a tip said you been hanging out here and we knew wherever you were the pretty women would soon follow."

"Fuck you, Piehler!" Coach said.

His blonde, curvaceous friend piped up. You boys on the team?"

"They were on the team," Coach answered for us."We're looking to weed out the troublemakers and ne'er-do-wells and these two will be the first ones to go."

The waitress looked me in the eye dreamily, like she'd had a beer or two herself recently, then she reached across Coach Chapman and offered me her hand.

"Hi, I'm Sarah," she said.

"John," I said. "And this is Jimmy."

"Charmed," she said.

"Jesus," Coach C said, swirling his bourbon. I caught .his eye in the mirror behind the bar. Coach C had had four kids, but his wife had left him some time back. None of the coaches made much money at Lassiter, so they all kept second jobs. Coach Millen and Bursey were teachers. Coach Chapman sold real estate. He drove a black corvette and was often seen escorting attractive women through the parking lot after a ball game. All the players admired him for that (and for the fact he could still throw a perfect spiral forty yards). He didn't bring a lot of new ideas to our offensive attack, but he had enough sense to let us use our own judgment when the mood struck.

Jimmy offered a toast. "To ne'er-do-wells and troublemakers!"

The bartender poured Sarah a shot of whiskey and the four of us raised our glasses and threw 'em back. Jimmy and I stood to leave and Sarah gave me a wink. I smiled, slapped the back of Coach C's head and ran for the door.

Coach Chapman had no clue as to why I'd suddenly lost my wits in practice that Monday. I was as puzzled by my behavior as he was.

"I don't know," I told him. "I guess that hit just made me a little dizzy, raised up my gander."

"Your gander?"

"Forget it. It's a term my old high school coach used to use.He was an idiot. Well, not really. He was OK. Anyway, let me get on out of here. My head is killing me."

"Alright son. You go ahead and take off. You let me know if something's eating you, OK. You let me know, we'll take care of it."

I nodded my thanks. I wish it were that simple.

When I got back to my room at the dormitory a note lay at my feet just inside the door.

Dear John,

I'm sorry I've caused you so much trouble. I just wish things had been different. I'm so mixed up. I feel so bad, so...

John, I want to see you. I need to talk to you.

I'll be in the library tomorrow at noon. Please stop by.

Your secret friend, Michelle

My only class on Tuesdays was Russian History, which took place at 10:30. I walked up the hill toward the center of the campus toward the library when the professor finally let us out. The snow had melted a good bit so that it left only piles here and there where it had been shoveled off the sidewalks and streets. A deformed snowman stood an eerie watch over the yard, enjoying its last few moments in the sun. Someone had jabbed a curved stick into the sculpture so that it protruded perversely from the groin. No one had enough energy or interest to pull the stick out.

Michelle sat just inside the library door, looking over a copy of Cosmopolitan. Her hair was pulled back behind her in a pony tail and she smiled at me over her magazine as I entered and moved her way. The only seat left was right beside her so I remained standing.

"Good afternoon, Michelle."

"Hey John. You found me."

"Yeah. Some trick. What's going on? You wanted to see me?"

She put her magazine on the coffee table and stood up. Her silky blouse, leather jacket and designer jeans accentuated her already accentuated curves. Her perfume washed over me when she stood.

"Well, yes," she said."Would you like to have lunch?"

"Well, I'm not so sure it would be good idea. Karen might not understand. She has a suspicious mind and she's always hanging out in the lunchroom."

"Oh my! I didn't mean in the cafeteria. Let's get off campus. You don't have a class do you?"

"No. I don't have any more. You know I don't have a car?"

"Yeah, well, I'll drive. C'mon, let's go." As she spoke she pulled at my arm as if to drag me out the door. We walked into the crisp sunlight and moved briskly toward the parking lot. I tried to look off as we walked, to give the appearance that we simply happen to be going in the same direction, and also to keep a lookout for Karen. No explanation would ever assuage her worst fears. I could feel the moisture from the sweat under my arms. I remembered something suddenly as we neared her car.

"Wait. Listen. I don't have but about five dollars. I hadn't planned on spending much today." What I didn't tell her was that that five dollars was supposed to last me till Friday. Sarge had me on a strict allowance, controlled vigilantly by limiting the deposits he made into my checking account. Michelle looked at me and smiled. Her teeth were perfect and full. It was a mouth any orthodontist would gladly put on the wall of his waiting room.

"Oh c'mon," she said."I've got money. Besides, it's the least I can do."

We piled into her black Grand Am and she took off toward Hartford, driving confidently. It seemed a prerequisite for the women at Lassiter to have a nice set of wheels -- they all drove in Daddy's Hot Rod Lincoln -- filling up the parking lots like The Shearson Lehman garage, or an exclusive country club. They'd be members some day, but they didn't have to wait to get their ride. It was a different world.

Michelle Puckett came to Lassiter from Pennsylvania. They said she had almost a full ride for academics and whatever expenses were left were covered by cheerleading. She made straight A's but no one would ever mistake her for an intellectual. While every member of the team lusted after her, in the same breath they made light of her grasp on reality; but none of us could say we knew her more than casually. She had been dating some guy from Scranton the whole time I knew her -- even had an engagement ring. He was out of school and apparently, whatever he did for a living, was doing well. When you were around her, you almost got the feeling that she was saving herself for marriage. That's part of what made the whole scene at Scoop's so misplaced.

She took us to a restaurant in the corner of a north Hartford mall called Shack's. I'd never eaten there, but it was high on the A list for the country club lunch set. She was paying, and she did "owe me," so the smell of grilled seafood which hit us as we entered brought my already ravenous appetite to full blossom.

We were led to a table overlooking the mall and Michelle ordered us a beer and some chips while we looked over the menu. Once thing I'll always say about New England: they know their fish! Jimmy, Fred, Karen, The Professor - everyone - took delight in introducing me to more varieties of seafood than I ever knew inhabited the ocean. They laughed at my squeamishness upon first inspecting mussels (though after a couple bites I overcame my diffidence and ordered more); they showed me how to take on a Bar-B-Que'd cut of shark, or swordfish, or tuna; and they instructed me in the fine art of dissecting a three pound lobster (tender flesh so juicy, sweet and succulent that it made my eyes water); they even took me to an honest-to-God New England clam bake. Where I grew up there were few things that could top a fish-fry down by the Crowder's Lake. But this was New England. And seafood was supreme.

I ordered a grilled tuna sandwich and some fries and looked off at the shoppers scurrying busily. As we sipped on our beers Michelle looked at me intensely. Her expression became more subdued.

"How have you been?" she said.

"Oh, okay, I guess. You know, I stay pretty busy."

"You do?" she mused on the thought. "Well, I guess you do. I know I wouldn't want to play football and go to school here."

"No. You don't want to play football."

"But I do cheerlead."

"Yeah, I suppose that's true. Tell me, how did you get into that, anyway?"

"What are you saying?"

"Nothing. Just an innocent question. Just wonderin', that's all. You did it in high school?"

"Yeah. I did it in high school." She sipped at her beer devilishly. "Listen. It pays for my books."

I could tell I'd struck a sour vein, so I moved on. "How is school going?"

She looked down at the table, pursed her lips. "Hmmmm. Fine. I'm doing OK. This year's not too tough."

"You're taking finance?"

"Marketing."

"Oh. A salesman."

"Salesperson. But I want to get into advertising."

I thought: she'd have no problem making a living as a model. But I held my tongue.

"What about you?" she asked.

"Oh, I'm majoring in English. Can you imagine that?"

"English?"

"Yeah, I know. Shocks the sensibilities."

"That it does," she said, smiling and leaning forward so that her breasts almost sat on the table top. She pressed me for more of my history. "Is your Dad a teacher, or something?"

"My sister."

"Really. Where does she live?"

"Biloxi. On the coast. She's married, has a kid." She seemed genuinely interested in my past, but like most women I knew, I could get only a shaky read on her expressions. Though I felt at ease with her, other nagging memories made the whole conversation seem unnatural.

"My mother used to teach," she said.

"S'that right. Now, where was this?"

"Oh, she taught Elementary school in Philadelphia. That was before she met her second husband."

"Your father?"

"Of course, do-do brain."

"What's he do?"

"Brian's a dentist."

I couldn't help but laugh. That explained a lot. "You call your father Brian?"

"Yeah, why not? That's his name."

"Hey, fine by me," I said, just as our sandwiches arrived. The tuna was tender and delicious and as I attacked the poor fish Michelle ordered us another beer. I kept noticing how every male who walked through the mall took a second look at our table. As she held her sandwich I noticed the close cut of her nails on her long fingers. She had the hands of a wide receiver, strong and controlled. She smiled at me as we ate, yet her eyes seemed tired.

"You know, you haven't called me," she said. "How come?"

The question took me by surprise. "I... Uh.... I didn't think you wanted me to. I got the impression you wanted to forget about everything, including me."

"I don't think it's that easy."

"Yeah, I know."

"You do?"

"I mean, you know, a lot about this whole thing has been bothering me too."

"Like what?"

"Nothing. Forget it."

"No, I tried that. It doesn't work. What's the problem?"

"Nothing. I just . . . you know, I've got to play with these fuckers every day. They don't know what I know, what I'm gonna do, who I'm gonna tell. And I guess Bobby's in the same boat. It's not your fault. I mean, there's nothing you can do about it, I'm just telling you what's going on." Somehow, letting her in on my travails didn't lessen my anxieties. She reached for her purse and pulled out a Kleenex. She had begun to cry suddenly. "Michelle, I'm sorry. Don't..."

She looked at me angrily as she dried her eyes, then slowly unbuttoned her right shirt sleeve and rolled it up, revealing a brown and purple bruise covering half of her bicep. The imprint of someone's thumb was as clear as if someone had drawn it in with a marker. Then she rolled her sleeve down.

"My god," I said.

"They raped me, John," she told me.She was still angry, but I no longer felt the anger directed at me. "They drugged me or something. I only had two or three beers. I swear. You gotta believe me."

"I believe you," I said.

"I think Scoop put something in my beer. I felt really weird. My whole body was tingling. And I passed out." Her tears came back in a flood. I wanted her to stop. I reached out to hold her hand, console her best I could. She put her fingers to her forehead, half covering her face, and went on. "When I woke up, Kyle was on top of me. It was disgusting. He's a fucking animal!" She lurched forward suddenly and nearly vomited. I stood and reached to her arm.

"Let's... let's go," I said. "Why don't you go to the bathroom? I'll take care of the check." As she stood and grabbed her purse I remembered I had no cash. "Wait, I'm sorry," I stopped her. My helplessness almost made her smile and she found her billfold and handed it to me. I paid the check and waited for her at the door. Every housewife in the mall seemed to be looking at me like Judas.

Michelle looked a little bit better when she came out, but not much. As we exited into the plaza she grabbed my arm and swung me to her, then gave me a kiss on the cheek.

"I'm so scared, John," she said, grabbing my hand and pulling me across the street. "I don't know what to do. Don't leave me," she whispered in my ear. As we sat in her car and she got it running, I turned to her and asked her to wait for a moment. I still had some questions eating at me. She looked terrible.

"Michelle, have you gone to a doctor?"

She nodded her head no and sniffled back her tears. "How could I explain this?" she said, holding out her arms.

"But are you okay? I mean, if they hurt you in some way…"

"Oh, they hurt me, John. They hurt me plenty. I just thank God you came back."

"Well, thank Bobby too."

"Poor Bobby. Oh poor Bobby. How's he doing?"

"I suppose he's a nervous wreck. To be honest I haven't talked to him. But I'm not worried about him. I'm worried about you. You see, what you do about this affects all of us. You seem to be unsure. Perhaps you need to tell someone."

"John, you don't know. What could I say? Who could I tell? Who would believe me? It's my word against theirs."

"Jesus, Michelle, your arms look like you've been beat up by a fuckin' heavyweight boxer. I don't think your credibility is a problem."

"No . . . No. You don't know. I know something about this. I had a friend in Wilkes-Barre: Christy Kernan. He left her at a motel. She was such a fool! He raped her alright. But she couldn't prove it. Everyone in the whole fucking town read about it. And he got off. She ended up moving to Albany. She hasn't been the same. She's bitter at everyone. Do you see John? I don't want to live the rest of my life like Christy Kernan. It's not worth it. For what? For justice? For what, John? I just got fucked and that's the end of it!" Her anger had come back. Her hands, where a few minutes earlier they had been so virile and restrained, were now shaking. I reached out to hold them. Though it was 40 degrees outside and dropping, the sun had warmed up the car so much that both our palms were sweating. We sat there in the parking lot with the engine running. I could barely hear on the radio an old song by James Taylor:

A silver tear appearing now
I'm dying, ain't I
Gone to Carolina in my mind

"Look at me," I told her. "You're right about this: there's a lot I don't know about a lot of things. All I can say is: I'm here, and I'll help if I can."

"Hold me, John," she asked. And I held her to me as she wept on my shoulder.

Chapter 12
We are the stuffed men

My old man didn't believe in tears. He believed that only old ladies and little girls should be allowed to cry. I guess I never heard him say it to me quite like that, but he made his philosophy clear nonetheless.

"Crying don't solve nothin'!" he used to say, when either myself or someone else in the family broke down. Half the time it was because of something he'd said to us. He believed in utility. If you asked him if you could spend the night with Red he'd tell you didn't need to that night. It had no purpose. He had totally missed the point. In war there are real tears; there is real pain; there is real death. This domestic life brings only shallow challenges, which at their worst should be met with a gritted jaw, determination, and a renewed commitment. Like much of his philosophy, he found it easier to espouse than to live by. Some are born to be fighters. Some are raised.

Every now and then, when I find myself pressed to draw up my last pail of courage, determination, and commitment, I see my father's face. I can see him standing boldly in some mystic yard or doorway, eyes as untainted with sentience as the eyes of a worn, brass sculpture, his lips so peacefully poised you knew at once that the matter -- whatever it might be -- would be ended here and now. I would occasionally take on such a countenance, looking at the world through my father's eyes (best I could bring them to light), filling up with a strength of purpose that might just boost me to overcome whatever fears eddied nearby.

It always took too much gristle to maintain such a stern posture over any long run. It would drain your soul and, before long, run off your friends. But as children we believed Sarge could shelter our family from all harm, turn back a spring storm with his unyielding gaze, his thick forearms crossed in front of him, his eyes clear and calm, focused on the thunderhead. Sarge had the nose of an Indian and like an Indian he seemed unafraid of death. I was the Indian/Sargent's son, but somewhere along the way I'd left the tribe.

Later that night I tried to call Lisa Rae collect from the pay phone in the dormitory lobby.

"Hello John," Roger answered.

"Roger," I said. "What's going on?"

"Nothing. Just got through giving Jamie a bath. He's watching Sesame Street. He keeps calling Big Bird, Beebee." I pictured the little blonde hair kid sitting a foot and a half from the TV screen, squinting to make out the silly characters and ridiculous dialogue. He was a cute little kid. Thank God he didn't have the Colton nose. Must've gotten it from Roger.

"Well, at least he's got the right letter of the alphabet."

"Yeah. He's a regular genius. Lisa Rae is trying to teach him to sing." Roger had a quiet, gentle voice. Nothing ever seemed to change its timbre.

"Oh God, no!"

"You looking for Lisa Rae?"

"Yeah. She around?"

"No, she's at her oil painting class."

"You're kidding?"

"Naw, she goes every Tuesday. They meet at some gay guy's house downtown."

"Oil painting? When did this start?"

"She's been doing it about three weeks now. She's not much good yet, but don't tell her I told you that."

"Trust me. I know how she takes constructive criticism. Well, anyway. I guess I'll call back. Hey, good to talk to you. Tell her I called and tell Jamie I said hi."

"You got it, tiger."

I hung up and soon found myself watching the Tuesday night movie in the lobby with the guys. Willie Patterson and another black dude— I think his name was Jerald — were laying across the floor in front of the three ragged sofas. Nothing about our dormitory was designed to be warm and homey, but after four years it had grown on me. Someone popped some popcorn and we sat around drinking sodas and making jokes about the girls in the movie. I had planned on calling Lisa Rae back, but the hour slipped by me, so I gathered myself back to my room, read a couple of poems from T.S. Eliot and fell to sleep. Eliot sang gently.

We are the hollow men
We are the stuffed men
Leaning together
Headpiece filled with straw.
Alas! Our dried voices, when
We whisper together
Are quiet and meaningless
As wind in dry grass
Or rats' feet over broken glass
In our dry cellar
Shape without form, shade without colour,
Paralysed force, gesture without motion;
Those who have crossed
With direct eyes, to death's other Kingdom
Remember us -- if at all -- not as lost
Violent souls, but only
As the hollow men
The stuffed men.

When I arrived for practice the next day Coach Rivers called me into his office. He sat on the edge of the desk with his arms crossed and he asked me to sit down. He seemed to look at me through the corner of his small, dark eyes.

"What's the problem, Colton?" he asked.

"I don't know, Coach. I guess I just got a little dizzy yesterday."

He showed me his yellowed teeth, the best smile he could produce. "Dizzy? It seems to me like you were pissed about something. Now, I know Thompson gets a little carried away out there sometimes, but we got a team here. We can't just take off in the middle of practice every time we get pissed off. We'd never make it through a practice. You see what I mean?"

I looked out the big glass windows which paneled two sides of the office. I saw Kyle McClary and Scoop Thompson walking by slowly, looking at me and The Coach anxiously. As I watched them my mind didn't even register their presence.

I was chewing on what The Coach was telling me.I shook my head in agreement and looked down at my feet. His office floor was just as dirty as the rest of the locker room, though it didn't smell quite as bad.

"Yeah, I know Coach. I just... you know sometimes, you just get sick of it. You just . . . you just can't deal with all the crap anymore. I don't know. Listen, it's over. I'm OK. No more problems out of me."

"Well, good enough then. Let's get on out there." As I stood and opened the door The Coach spoke again.

"Colton," he said. "You're my man." And he winked and tugged at the bill of his cap.

I pushed myself through that week hurriedly and distanced, not the Indian/Sergeant, not the man of resolution and action, but a man of dreams and voices.I tried twice again to reach Lisa Rae, but each time she was out on other errands. I began to talk to Karen like I barely knew her, while Michelle kept leaving me notes and sneaking up on me in between classes. We played against Princeton, at home, and beat them 33 to 3. I ran through the plays clumsily, stepping from one zone coverage into the next, avoiding any chance I might be mistaken for a clean target. Their offense couldn't get a first down the whole first half. The fire had been smothered quickly. The same small steps which could get you open could keep you away from the ball and I was in no mind to leave my mark on this game. Why, the school record for catches was 356. I'd need 120 to match it in the last four ball games; I didn't see it happening. We were 8 and 0 after beating Princeton, on the verge of history, but my vision of The Team had become slowly and irretrievably shaded. What had The Game become when it no longer had conviction? What kind of Team could be called true winners without probity and courage? Alas! Were we all stuffed men?

There are dreams and nightmares, illusions and dark visions, and there are quiet, deep-flowing hopes, and there is the occasional quick sense of danger one gets in a dark room, or when one suddenly sees one's own reflection from a suddenly revealed mirror, and each of these have their own meaning and their own purpose, and each are different and yet part of the same thing.A once remembered dream tells us: we cannot even know our own mind.

I was awakened from a peaceful sleep on the Saturday night after the Princeton game by a quiet, but incessant knocking at my door. No dreams were in my head; the room was dark and warm. These were the days of voices in the night, so I pulled on my shorts, unlocked the door and opened it, expecting nothing, awaiting no one.

There were two of them, and they wore ski masks, and the larger one held a pistol, pointed at my face. When he spoke I recognized the voice as Kyle McClary's, and I knew the smaller fellow was Scoop Thompson.

"This way Colton," he said. His accomplice reached out and pulled me into the hallway. Their leather gloves grabbed me at the arms and pushed me forward down the hallway. A tube sock was put in my mouth and another wrapped over my eyes. I moved with them toward the lobby wearing nothing but a small pair of blue shorts, the barrel of the gun up against the back of my head. My entire body had tensed up – I moved like I was made of wood – but no avenue of escape came into mind. There is fear and resignation at the other end of a gun barrel. I could not believe they would go this far. As they moved me outside through the sliding glass door in the back of the lobby into the frigid cold, my thoughts raced around this idea: they would not EVER go this far. They would not go this far.

I was shivering noticeably when they pushed me into the backseat of the car. I could barely make out the seat cover under the blindfold. I knew it couldn't have been Scoop's Honda and Kyle was driving, so I figured it must be his old Chevy. Scoop pushed my head onto the seat and rode beside me. I could still feel the cold steel of the gun on my neck and leather gloves twisting my head into the seat as the car pulled out onto the street and sped off into the night. I tried to speak but all I could do was grunt unintelligibly.

"Shut up!" Kyle yelled back from the front seat. "Tell it to the Judge!"

Once again, they pushed my head into the soiled car seat and jammed the pistol barrel into my neck.

"Jesus," I tried to say and then I stopped trying to talk and began listening, listening for every rev of the engine, every stop, trying to calculate every turn and hear the sound of any car which might pass us, or any train which might blow its whistle in the lonely night. We drove on a highway for some time, perhaps 15 minutes, with only one stop. They must have made it to some road leading out of town in a hurry. They weren't heading for Scoop's place; there'd be a bunch more turns and stops. Eventually the car slowed and turned to the right onto to what appeared to be an unpaved road, or a road in bad repair. Twigs and leaves cracked under the car wheels. I could hear the wind blow in the trees to either side. Then we came to a stop and Kyle turned the engine off to an eerie quiet.

"Take him out," Kyle said and then Scoop pushed me out into the cold night air. There were rocks on the ground beneath my feet and the air brought up chill bumps immediately. I was lead into the woods about twenty yards and pushed up against a large tree. The gun was moved under my chin and I could feel them pulling a rope around my wrists. In moments my hands were tied behind me around the tree. Every time I moved the frosted bark bit into my back and arms. They moved away from me and I heard them whispering.

'My God!' I thought,'Would they leave me here? Jesus! What had I done?'The air was so cold on my skin now that I shivered uncontrollably. I imagined suddenly, without warning, what it might be like to freeze to death. I'd read about such things. They say the cold brings intense pain, a throbbing in every joint and bone, then numbness comes on, then nothingness. The pain had begun. I yanked on my cords and tried to scream out, a hollow lament which raced through the bare trees and fell into silence without respect.

"Colton," McClary said, an empty, ragged voice, a sound that would be at home in the deep forest. "What did you tell the coach?"

I shook my head from side to side, then I felt the sock come loose over my mouth. I gasped for breath desperately and worked out the muscles in my jaw.

"Nothing," I said. "I didn't tell him. Michelle is not gonna tell anybody. It's done. She's through with it. She can't deal with it."

"Deal with what?" McClary asked. Each time he spoke his voice made me shudder.

"Whatever happened. Jesus Christ! I'm freezing to death here! My feet . . . My feet . . ."

"How can we trust you?" It was Scoop's voice.

"What about Bobby?" Kyle added.

My mind was spinning, trying to juggle the words I'd need to be set free and fight back the sharp pain from my feet and hands. I could feel my lips getting numb. Speaking was becoming difficult. There was a noise in the woods somewhere, like a tree limb had fallen, then suddenly I heard an explosion, a bang like a cannon. An image of Mr. Cooper appeared suddenly, standing broadly in the pecan grove, then I heard the voice. It was like an Angel on Judgment Day, deep and sweet as molasses. It was Willie Patterson.

"Motherfuckers," he said, "Drop your gun."

I heard a gun re-cock. It must've been a shotgun, from the size of the report. A moment of quiet ensued, then Willie spoke again.

"Go on, motherfucker. Test it out. You bad, huh? You ain't bad. You're just a big, fucking baby. Good. Now just wait there."

I heard footsteps coming towards me. Willie cut loose the rope at my wrists and I fell forward onto the ground. I could barely work my fingers to pull off the sock around my head. I grabbed myself and rolled up into a ball, unable to stand.

"Your coats," Willie said. "Give him your coats."

"Fuck you," McClary said.

"Colton," Willie turned to me, "What should we do with these motherfuckers? We'll leave him here and call the police."

I looked at the two hooded thugs. Warmth was my only objective. "Give me your coat, Kyle," I barely got out. "We'll talk about this later." He threw me his coat and Willie helped me put it around me. Then Willie demanded his boots and Kyle slowly obliged. It hurt to pull them on. The frost had crept into my bones.

"Take a walk," Willie advised them.He stood over me, with the gun pointed at them. They spoke something to each other, then turned and walked into the woods. The boys had made two mistakes: they thought I'd squealed on 'em, and they hadn't planned for some crazy kid like

Willie. When they were out of sight, Willie lead me back toward the road. As we passed Kyle's car he reached down and stabbed his switchblade into the front tire. The tire exploded with another bang.He helped me into the front seat of his Thunderbird and he took off down the highway. Never had heat felt so warm.

As Willie drove he told me how he had heard the noise in the hallway earlier. He had been up studying, he said. When he saw me being escorted out he grabbed his keys and somehow managed to tail us to the highway. They didn't go for firearms in the dorm, so he kept his 20 gauge in his trunk. He'd been hunting at his Grandpas just last Sunday. He told the story like he was talking about someone else, as if he were describing a late night movie. It was not till we were almost back in town and my body had temperature had returned to normal, that it occurred to me that I might be frostbitten. My feet and hands still ached terribly and a vicious headache had taken residence just behind my eyes. Willie drove silently. Perhaps he realized that when I had some answers for him I would speak.

"My feet," I said, finally. "I think they may be frostbitten. Do you know anything about it?"

"No John, not me. We should see a doctor."

"They seem to be working," I told him. "They just ache like crazy. I guess I'll wait and see, huh?"

"I guess," he said, then: "What the hell's going on, anyway, Colton? You owe these guys some money or something?" I laughed, best I could get out, and looked over at my rescuer. I realized suddenly there were tears in my eyes.

"Money," I said. "Do you think I would borrow money from those fuckers?"

"I wouldn't do it, but they seem to be pissed about something."

"It's a fucked-up story," I told him. What could I tell him? He deserved some version of the truth. I remembered Michelle's words: "Our little secret." It wasn't our little secret. It was bigger than both of us, and it seemed to be growing. I had to tell someone about this. I could never keep it all to myself. It would eat me up from the inside. But Willie, the crazy little motherfucker. Pulled a goddamn shotgun out on the motherfuckers! His voice still rang through the crisp wind: "Motherfuckers." The song of Judgment. The voice of salvation.

"Willie, it's a fucked-up story," I began, then I proceeded to tell him the story of another wild and vicious Saturday night. It never was "our little secret." From the moment Bobby rapped his little knuckles at my door, the secret was out. Willie displayed the same astonishment that I had displayed when these facts first came to my attention. Michelle Puckett? She was the one piece that didn't fit in the puzzle.There were a dozen girls you could imagine in a compromised situation late into a Saturday night party, but Michelle was not one of them. Willie tossed around the conundrum as we walked through the dorm and he saw me safely to my room. I took half a bottle of aspirin, turned up the thermostat, hid under the covers and fell asleep. There was another mistake The Boys had made: they'd help me to make a decision which had been stuck in the mud of my brain for a week. I tossed in and out of sleep all morning with the dreams and voices from the trails before me, until I was awakened by another soft knocking at my door. I had forgotten that Karen was coming out. We were due to join her folks for Sunday brunch at two. She was surprised by my appearance, but I shook off her barbs and washed up for the trip. My body still ached and with the first sneeze I felt a head cold take root in my sinuses. There are secrets, and there are Secrets.

Karen's mood was ebullient, though perhaps it was all show -- you never could tell; she could change her personality 180 degrees in a minute. It was a nice change for me, however, from the past few days. The sun came out brightly and lit up the soft, rolling hills which made up the ride from Lassiter to South Windsor with a warm, golden quiescence. We talked about her week and I tried to forget all about mine. Her soft and gentle face fell naturally into the sunny Connecticut day.

"Dad's cooking steaks," she piped up. "T-bones."

"I can deal with it."

"And mom's making Egg's Benedict."

"I thought in Connecticut it was called Egg's Benedict Arnold."

She laughed. "Do me a favor, don't tell my Dad that joke."

"Why? He's got a good sense of humor."

"Not when it comes to politics . . . or me."

"Naw, your Dad's all right. He's less conservative than you think. There are secrets only men tell each other."

"S'that right? Secrets about me?"

"Maybe. Maybe about your mother."

"Oh no. I don't even want to hear."

"Good.'Cause you're not."

I could see suddenly, as the light flashed through her hair and lit up her eyes, her mother's sharply-structured cheeks and chin, and neckline. I reached out to her and pulled her face towards me.

"Slow down," I said.

"What now?" she asked, slowing the car to near stopping.

"It just hit me. I can't go another mile without a kiss." She smiled and I bent over to kiss her. She stopped the car in the midst of a long, unadorned stretch of Connecticut countryside, filled up with shadows and light, and we embraced for several minutes. I looked for an empty barn on the horizon, but I spotted nothing we could work with, so I bade her drive on, her small warm hand in mine.

The McIntyres had such a beautiful house we'd have called it a mansion if it sat somewhere down Cooper's Trail, a few miles outside Lumberton. Their front lawn was always perfectly manicured and it stretched wide and full down the slope to the street. Only the presence of the other homes in the neighborhood, all of which were large and beautifully built and kept, diminished somewhat the sense of awe that hit me whenever we pulled up the drive. They had a polished and closely trimmed wood floor in the foyer made from richly colored oak and cherry and a staircase with the same fine woods winding in alternate steps up to the second floor. Only once had we sat in the living room; it was taboo, and too neat and clever for anyone to feel comfortable in anyway. I suppose it was partly the purity and opulence of the McIntyres' home which lent me the odd sense of ill-ease I would experience on most occasions there. Even Karen insisted we clean up any soiled dishes at once and put the magazines back on the coffee table in the same order we found them. I was always afraid Mrs. McIntyre would flag me for a social faux pas and send me back fifteen yards from Karen's petite and perky breasts.

I took in a great sense of excitement and joy one afternoon when her folks had left us in the house alone. We'd snuck up to her bedroom and made love till our shrieks and clatter filled up the whole house. We were laying half across one another, sweaty and exhausted, when we heard the front door slam. I made it to the bathroom and somehow Karen got on her shorts and T-shirt before her mother stepped in. Karen smiled and stepped to her window and engaged her mother in a conversation about dinner. When I re-appeared I noticed the bed had been perfectly made and Karen looked fresh and unblemished. She had it down to a science, but I doubt Mrs. McIntyre was fooled for single second. The lady kept herself slim and well-put together and when she had a glass or two of wine she might even lean over and flash me a quick view of her breasts or walk just an inch or two too close to my hand with her backside. She knew how to get inside a man's head, a craft Karen had only dabbled in. We ate brunch in their solarium/dining room on a glass table and wicker, cushioned chairs. I was plenty hungry after my anguishing night in the woods and so I ate everything Rudolph McIntyre put before me. We talked about the football team and schoolwork and how Karen might have an opportunity to work at a PR firm in New Haven, if the connections come through and her grades stay solid. Mrs. McIntyre didn't say much, but we could excuse her one morning. They were good folk I always thought. A little too polished, just like the floor of their home (for me anyway) but basically good folk.

When we moved into the den towards the TV and some Sunday football, that is, some Real Entertainment, I was surprised when Mrs. McIntyre took me aside and told the rest of them to go ahead on in, that she wanted to talk to me for just a minute. The living room was clear at the other end of the house from the den, so when she led me onto the plush green carpet and offered me the sofa for a seat we could barely hear the sounds of the TV whispering down the hall.

I thought at first that she might ask me what my intentions were concerning her daughter. I supposed that soon, indeed, we'd all want to know. Only one and a half semesters were left for foot-dragging. But she looked at me with a strange, unfocused expression which quickly made me reconsider her motives.

"I've got a question for you, John," she started off. She sat in her chair with her feet flat on the floor, her knees together and her hands clasped in her lap. "What are you doing to my daughter?"

"What?" I offered in response. The whole scene was baffling.

"Do you think she's just some little plaything? Something to be picked up, played around with, then sent home whenever you need another toy?"

I still had no clue where she was coming from and I looked at her and pleaded for some rung of sense to grab on to.

"I saw you last Tuesday at Town Center with that girl. She's a cheerleader, isn't she?"

My face went flush. I looked at the ceiling and exhaled loudly. How could I get out of this one? It was unbelievable. Just then Karen walked in, a puzzled look on her face.

"What's going on you guys?"

Mrs. McIntyre smiled at her. "Oh, nothing dear, it's a secret and that's why we don't want you to hear."

"A secret about what? What's all this about secrets today, John?"

I put my face in my hands. It was unbelievable. "It's nothing. Listen, Karen, give us a minute. I'll tell you the whole story. You'll love it."

"Alright, but hurry up. You've got five minutes. I can't take anymore of watching football with Dad and he can't take much more of me either. Okay?"

"Deal," I said.

When she left we looked at each other and renewed the battle.

"Mrs. McIntyre," I said, "You are right about this: I was there with that girl. Her name is Michelle, by the way, but it's not . . ."

"What? You're gonna say it's not what I think? Do I look like a fool to you? I saw you, you were holding hands! You kissed her."

I fell back. More disbelief. She'd actually tailed us into the parking lot. I tried to get my words together but she cut me off.

"John, I want you to know, Karen may not be the kind of girl you're used to. You know, we tried to raise her with a little bit of culture and a little bit of a sense of obligation to people. We've tried to teach her to look for friends who had just as much loyalty and honesty as herself. Perhaps we weren't such good teachers."

"Please. Can I just . . . . you know, you're not making any sense to me. You don't know what's going on. Not with me. Not with Karen. I don't see why you're bringing all this to me. Why not just tell Karen? Didn't you teach her how to look out for herself? Ask her own questions?"

"You're a mean little man, Mr. Colton, and my daughter doesn't know how mean. I'm trying to keep her from being hurt anymore than she has to. You just don't get it. Karen's not right for you." As she laid it on me tears began to fill up her eyes, and her hands began to shake. "She's a McIntyre, goddammit! We have a little sense of decency about us, a little sense of honor. I won't have you ruin my daughter or this family!"

"A McIntyre," I said, "She's a McIntyre. Jesus, what a shock! All this time I thought her name was Karen." I stood up and walked to the window. There was no one in sight, no little blonde haired kid rode his bike down the perfectly trimmed sidewalk, nobody played catch in the yard or chased their dog, or just walked up the street lazily taking in the sun and telling some delightful and forgotten tale. Someone had clipped the grass close and clean on every lawn and every expensive car shone with fresh wax, but for a moment, from this one window, the life had gone out of everything.

"Naw, we don't know about those kinds of things where I come from. We're just simple folks. Soldiers, some of us, school teachers, simple folk who sit in church and pray for forgiveness on Sunday. Hell,I used to think waffles were uptown till I made it north! But I guess if I hang around long enough I might learn something about honor and about respecting other people's rights and about putting it all out there on the line when you're the last person who can help! You keep teaching Karen all you know. I'm sure one day she'll be a fine McIntyre. Don't worry. This Colton will leave her be. I don't want it on my conscience."

How the rest of the day ended I can't hardly remember. I never told Karen the little secret that day, not on the ride home, and not after she pressed me for it repeatedly in my room. She wanted to make love, but I turned away her advances stodgily. None of this was her fault. I hated what was happening to us, hated all of this crazy story, because in a part of my backward, uncultured heart, I loved her, and always would.

Chapter 13
And I've kept track of the parts

I finally reached Lisa Rae on Sunday night, the 19th of November. Her voice, when she finally picked up, came through sweetly, the voice of angels, the voice of salvation.

"Why Johnnie Junior," she said. "You finally caught up with me. Have you gotten too lazy for letters, or you just felt the need to run up my phone bill?"

"Both. And neither. Besides, you know I'll reimburse you for everything, one day. All the pain and heartache. How have you been?"

"Oh, busy! I lead such a wild and exciting life, you know! Just a thrill a minute."

"Yeah, I heard you were getting into oil painting."

"Hah, what did Roger tell you?"

"Nothing. Just said you were beginning to talk in French and you were always asking him to pose in the nude."

"Oh, is that right? Yeah, well none of that had anything to do with painting. We're just a kinky couple. You know life doesn't end after marriage, it just gets weird."

"That's what I heard."

"Well, how about you? You and Karen still going out?"

I shook my head and looked across the dormitory lobby. A couple of freshman football players were tossing a football back and forth over everyone who sat trying to watch the TV. Soon, they'd knock over a lamp and the resident manager would come out and raise hell.

"Yeah, I suppose. I ate over there for lunch today. Or, excuse me, that is, brunch.Me and her mom don't get along too well. She has the strange notion that all us rednecks from the Deep South lack manners."

"Well, tell her you're from Lumberton. The deep south is another 80 miles east."

"No, the deep south, to her thinking, is everywhere south of New Jersey."

"Well, don't let her get to you. Jeez, Roger puts up with a father-in-law who won't even speak to him. Which reminds me, have you talked to mom lately?"

"No, I've been busy too."

"Well, there are more problems on the home front. Mom is in a terrible way. I'm worried about them. Mom has talked about moving out."

"You're kidding?"

"I wish I were. He's gotten worse. Mom says all he does is stay at the store or work in the yard and he's just acting downright mean lately."

"Maybe you should just go see him."

"What? There must a problem with the connection. I think we're picking up static from New Jersey. You think that's gonna help the situation. Listen, I've tried, Junior. He hears I'm coming by and he disappears. He's afraid I might cast a spell on him, turn him into a warthog or something. No, I mean, you know I'd do anything in the world for our mother. She is the dearest and loveliest person I've ever known. She deserves a better life than this."

"Well, I hate to add more leather to the whip, but I got some crazy news from up north."

"Don't tell me: she's pregnant."

"Jeez," I laughed, "I wish it were that simple. It's something you won't believe when you hear it. How I get caught up in these things I don't know. I must be paying for the sins of my youth. Anyway, let me give you the basics."

Lisa Rae held silent while I shelled out the agony and discord which I suddenly found orbiting my world. I could hear on the other end the sound of her sucking gently at her teeth and sighing with each revelation. She was a deep and powerful storm when her winds were at sea and you never knew what mix of breezes would push her off shore. I looked to her for guidance, another hand at the wheel. But at the same time I hoped her gale would not blow us too far off course. We were in this together. She would be the light, she'd once told me. It was up to me to do the legwork. When my tale was spun I could hear her crying softly.

"Johnnie," she said, "Oh Johnnie, what have they done? I tried to warn you about those jocks, didn't I? They're just missing some pieces, that's all. There's a reason why people smash each other in the face. It's not normal. Do you think the girl, what's her name?"

"Michelle. Michelle Puckett."

"Do you think she's gonna tell? You think she's gonna change her mind?"

"I don't know. My sense is that she's gonna keep it with her. She calls it our little secret, but she's wrong. You can't keep it hidden. It comes out. And now I'm the one who's got to watch my back. These guys are crazy, they're really scared and they know I could ruin their lives forever."

"John, you've got to do something. I know that you can't . . . That is, I know you're out there by yourself with this one, but my God, there must be something you can do. We are living in the worst of times."

She didn't really believe that, I knew. Her brooding and cynical language hid an eternal optimist. She truly felt, if nothing else worked, then her own persuasion would be enough to turn the world around, make it spin backwards on its axis if the cure called for it.

"I'm thinking it through, Lisa. It's been damn cold up here. You know we have a week off for Thanksgiving after Saturday. I wish I was down there with you. Hell, I'd settle for a quiet weekend in Lumberton. We're playing U Conn Saturday. We'll probably kill them, but I don't really give a shit. It's no longer my season, sis. I've lost all interest in it. I'm not even sure I can go through the motions anymore. That'd be a shock, huh?"

"No, John, you've gotten this far. You gotta get through another year. You know it has nothing to do with me. God knows your father doesn't value education. But you need to think about you, about the future you're gonna be living in. I'm gonna be alright, even without a birthright, cause I married a beautiful guy with beautiful teeth who makes beautiful children, but I want to see you get everything you deserve."

"Well, I've gotten my share of desserts. Some things are meant to be. I'll be alright, sis. Like you, I land on my feet. Hey, remember how Grandpa Justin used to talk about being an Injun? How he could hear voices in the wind? Gives you an edge, you know. Besides, I got the moves."

"We miss you, Johnnie. Perhaps you'll come home for Christmas? Maybe me and Roger can come up with a plane ticket for ya."

"Please, Lisa, don't worry. I gotta go.You know I love you, sis. If anything weird happens I promise I'll call — collect."

"I love you too, hun. Goodnight."

I hung up the phone after our conversation deeply troubled. My old man had always had a temper and been a little hard to live with, but I couldn't believe he'd let mom slip from his life. It went against everything I thought I knew about him. He was so committed to the values of flag and family that he crushed the breath out of both of them. I sat at my desk and wrote a letter home, reminding myself to pick up a late edition of Sunday's paper. I stared at my notebook under the white light from the desk lamp with my eyes only inches from the page. I was spent, both physically and emotionally. It was all I could do to finish the letter.

> *Dear Mom and Pop,*
>
> *It's Sunday night about 10 o'clock here in the luxurious Lassiter Hilton. I've just come from the sauna, whirlpool and massage room and I sit pondering the elaborate room service menu. Should I order the filet mignon and a Rothschild? Perhaps I'll just munch on some of these week-old potato chips and pick up a can of coke down the hall. It better fits my mood.*
>
> *You can see Pop that we put it on Princeton yesterday.*
>
> *If we keep playing this well there's rumors they'll have to move us out of the Ivy League and make us play college teams, though nobody from the SEC (thank the Lord!). I heard that Ole Miss almost beat Bama yesterday. The ghost of The Bear still haunts us. Will we ever be Free at Last?*
>
> *We get a break after next week for a few days. It'll be a good chance to catch up on some of this bookwork here, but I'd sure love to be home.*
>
> *I'm so lucky to have parents like y'all.*

Some of these kids; you wonder. Well, until next week's victory.

All my Love,

Junior

I didn't know where I stood any more in the mix of things, who I could turn to, which corner to keep an eye on. When you are a student you are consumed with study, with getting through the next assignment, passing the next test. Time is your enemy and every classmate on the curve an impediment. You might have a heart attack on the quadrangle and go undiscovered till mid-terms passed. It was easy to feel alone.

I ran through the drills at football practice Monday like a man in a dream. I laughed at Jimmy's jokes and fawned off Fred's concerns, but my mind kept running over the same words. I stayed on the field and showered slowly, so I could catch Coach Rivers after the squad was gone. He hadn't noticed I was still in the locker room until he was just starting to turn out the lights.

"Coach!" I yelled at him.

He looked back at me in the dim light, startled. "Colton," he said. "What the hell?"

"Coach, I've got to talk to you. You have a minute?"

"Yeah, I suppose." He pulled off his cap and ran a hand over his bald head, then put his cap back on nervously. He stepped over to a bench and put his foot up, resting his hands on his knee. In the empty, concrete room our voices echoed as if in a tomb. A leaky showerhead dripped methodically -- plop, plop, plop - behind me. I walked closer and leaned against a locker, looking at the floor and at my feet and everywhere except at The Coach as I talked. Some folks you just can't read.

"You were asking me what was bothering me the other day, Coach."

"Yeah, I guess."

"Well, you need to know what's going on. I don't know how to tell you. It's so unbelievable and tragic."

As I went on with my tale and told him about the crime committed by two of his players, and how they'd nearly killed me in the frozen forests north of highway 305, and how one girl had been maimed and damaged for life and even how the fragile, little Bobby Dregorian had put himself into harm's way because it was the right thing to do, The Coach almost didn't change his expression. It was like his face had turned to stone. What little light remained from the window had gone out and only the blue ceiling lights set off the shadows in his taught face. When I'd finished he looked away from me, towards his office, putting a finger to his tightly pursed lips. He spoke quietly, his voice raspy.

"Colton, I can't believe it," he said. "This girl, you say, Michelle; she wouldn't do it. She's the straightest girl on the whole squad."

"I know that, Coach."

"And why wouldn't she go to the police? I mean, I would think, if you got raped. I mean, shit, what are you gonna do? These guys, what are they supposed to do? She should have gone to the police, John."

"No. She couldn't. Well, I guess she could. But you don't know her situation, Coach. She's got more to lose by going to the police than by keeping silent. It's just . . . I don't think we can let this just go . . ."

"I talked to Michelle Saturday. She seemed fine."

"Yeah, you're right, she looks fine. But listen to me, I've seen it. Her arms were nearly purple."

The Coach looked at me strangely. I knew at once what he was thinking.

"I don't know what I can say. You've gotta believe me."

"What about Bobby?"

"He . . . What about him?"

"I haven't . . . He hasn't said a word."

"Well Jesus, Coach, the guy's scared to death. I'm telling you, I thought I was gone the other night. You gotta do something."

"Are you going to the police?"

"No. Not for my sake. My name's in the papers enough."

"Well I don't know, John. I don't see what I can do."

"What do you mean?" I looked at him incredulously. I turned away toward the lockers and took a deep breath, then held one of the locks in my hand and squeezed it tightly. I felt like I could pull it off the door with a single yank, I was so incensed. His words seemed to echo back and forth throughout the room: "I don't see what I can do," the voice came back: "I don't see what I can do." Some folks you just can't read.

"Alright then," I said, and thought about saying more, but stopped. "Alright then," I repeated, gathering my books and exiting.

It was a dark, crisp evening.The snow had melted and the moon stood full in a cloudless sky as cool and clear as a painting. It took a moment for me to notice Willie Patterson standing off to the left ahead of me in the ragged parking lot. Some other folks were gathered around a car near him. When I came closer he spoke. "Hey John, come here," he said. His voice, even in the vacant lot, rang out like a bell. "I want you to meet someone," he said.

I looked anxiously at the three fellows near the car. "You can relax," he said. "McClary will leave us alone."

Three black dudes leaned back against a black Pontiac. One of them, the tallest one, wore dark glasses.His moon shadow fell out across the parking lot like a big old oak and he looked just as solid. I could see, barely, the glint of a gold tooth. In the bright moonlight his shades almost made sense.

"Tightrope," Willie said, "This is Reginald. This is Mitchell and Jess." I shook their hands, then looked at Willie and laughed.

"Don't worry," he said, "We just gave them the news."

"What news?"

Willie looked at his friends and laughed. "Hey, Tightrope, don't worry. These guys are all college grads. Reginald even pledged Delta."

My mind ran back to the stuffed panther which held dominion over the entranceway of the Delta Chi fraternity, and I couldn't hold back a chuckle.

"Class of '79," Reginald said, a voice as deep but not as resonant as Willie's. "Played defensive end. You guys got a damn good team."

"Well thanks. But we got our weaknesses, you know."

"Yeah, Willie told me. You got a couple of fuck-ups that think they're bad." Reginald smiled and his friends shuffled tensely. Even I was suddenly frightened.

"Well, I guess we'll see. It's a pleasure to meet you," I said, and I shook their hands once again and jogged off towards home in the sterling evening light, feeling at once full of spirit and at the same time cast over with doubts.

Perhaps the little wide receiver from North Hartford High with slippery moves and a lazy roll block had come through with the critical downfield pick when the game was on the line. Could be he'd even opened up a lane through which I could drag a leg and push the ball on towards the chalk. But even in the open field, even when there seems to be nothing but daylight, there is always someone there, your number 17. There are hazards to everything.

Certainly, for the next few days at least, Willie's reassurances seemed to be based on reality. McClary and Thompson gave me a rigid swath over the next few days of scrimmage. Something had made an impression on their minds, something which made them look at me distantly and removed, yet with eyes full of schemes. I was too young to realize how quickly a rumor can spread and how a small secret can grow and transmute with each whisper and every ear, and how what appears to be the truth may be only rumor, and how a secret, sometimes, can be a lie.

I always got the sense, sitting in Professor Strache's classroom, that his tutelage was tuneless, preserved from the fickle swerving of current events and whatever teaching method might be popular this semester on American campuses. There was The Professor, and The Class, and this vibrant (if sometimes murky) exchange, and then there was everything Out There. Even with all the worries that I carried with me like a knapsack over my shoulder I could still be washed away in his stream and cleansed with ideas. He was late to class on Wednesday and the students were restless.

"I'm so sorry," he said, closing the door hurriedly, then spreading out his books and papers on the desk, looking for whatever materials he might pick out for today's class. He found one wrinkled page, examined it, then replaced it for another. He walked around to the front of the desk and cleared his throat.

"Meetings. We have meetings, you see. This is how a college works. We meet and talk and then we meet some more and then, if we have time, we squeeze in a little teaching.

"Oh well, you will attend your share of these meetings in due course." He pulled on his glasses clumsily and read from the paper.

"Men and women are equal
When it comes to broken hearts
Because I have been a party to this
And I've kept track of the parts
Men and women are equal
When it comes to being kind
Equal in love and honesty
The finer qualities of the mind
Men and women are equal
Having no choice in the way
They look upon the world
See the gentle eyes of a new golden day
Having seen this
I Could not refuse
The two-way dreams and the two-way blues
Smoothing out the waves

"Well, I know it must be unsettling, but this is a poem written by me. Albeit, some years back, in an age and time when you could still get away with being a romantic, but nevertheless from my own pen. I'd be careful about such a poem today. Let's say this: It's okay to write one, just keep it locked up. I suspect one day they'll come back in style."

He looked at the wrinkled, worn paper once more, smirked, then set it back on the desk with the other papers. He looked through the mess for something else to present, but couldn't seem to find it, so he shook his head and walked to the board. He wrote in his distinctive, bent cursive:

Assignment - A Poem - Yours - Friday

"We used to do a lot of reading in class when I was in school, folks. Like romantic poems, it's kind of gone out of style. But I'm all for bringing it back. I think we'll start a trend here in English -- what is this?

533? 560? Hmmm?" Even the students had forgotten the course number... "Well... anyway." The Professor threw up his hand, as if throwing the dust of the muses into the air to seed the shallow furrows of the students' captive minds. "On Friday we'll read our poems, your poems, before the class."

He sat on the desk and looked at us devilishly, his fingers curled up, covering half his face. "I see you squirming uneasily already. Don't think for a moment I take delight in your anguish." He broke into a smile and chuckled to himself. He had definitely sent shock waves through most of us. Probably only Shelly Fogle, in this group, could take much delight in such an assignment.

I shook my head and smiled. Poetry. I could say a thing or two, alright, if I could get it into clever words. I could talk about broken hearts, alright. I could make 'em cry, given a chance. Hah! Who was I kidding? I was a lanky ballplayer from the sticks, a character perhaps, but not a poet. We'd have to wait and see about that.

When we left the class we were all a buzz with the prospects of reading our own works aloud before the class. Funny how these kinds of things make the biggest cowards of almost everybody. I will never forget the way Sarge sweated over the simplest of speeches. As I walked in no particular hurry toward the library with the intention of starting right away on the assignment a sudden scent drew my thoughts away into another world. It fell into my senses like a bank of honeysuckle. I felt her arm clasp around my own, and her breast push into me softly. She leaned to me and kissed me softly on the ear. When I turned and politely pushed her away Michelle smiled cutely.

"What are you doing, girl? Do you hide behind the statues and wait for a chance to ambush me?"

She hooked her arm back in mine. "Well, I've been found out. I'll have to come up with a new tactic."

It was too much trouble to keep her off my arm, or perhaps I'd begun to enjoy it. "How have you been?" I asked her.

"Okay, I suppose. I cry sometimes. I'm a little lonely. I think about you, sometimes."

"Me?"

"Yeah, I wonder about you. What you think about me." She stopped abruptly. We stood in the middle of the campus. The old Smythe Library, five stories of gray stone and ivy, cast a shadow over us. The cracked and broken sidewalks came up the hill towards us and met in the quadrangle like a web from all corners of the college. The huge bare sycamores and oaks waved above us in the light winter breeze. I looked at her sweet face framed by this courtyard which held so many memories for me, both sweet and sour, and I had to smile. There were questions in my mind about everything still. I didn't even know for sure if I'd get out of here with a degree. But when I stood there and looked at the dark, weighty buildings, the sun catching the specks of flint in the stones and throwing a prism's rainbow on the moisture in every golden leaf sprawled around every dusty window, and then looked quietly at the students walking purposefully up the hill, following the broken paths of the broken sidewalks, intent on panning out whatever gold might be left to peddle from this rich campus, and looking mutely at the lovely girl in front of me I couldn't help but fill up with a sense of pride and ownership in the old school, and the few specks of gold I'd mined here myself. I couldn't give Michelle an answer to her question.

"I don't know, Michelle. I don't know."

"What do you mean? You don't know."

"Let's walk," I said, and began walking down the hill, beyond the library, then beyond the student union toward the gymnasium, no destination in mind. I tried my best to put into words how mixed up I was, while she just added to my confusion. Some folks you just can't read. "I just don't know, Michelle. I mean, I think you're lovely. You know how football players are -- blondes, cheerleaders -- we have a natural weakness."

"Well, it's nice to hear you have some natural weaknesses."

I looked at the worn, stone path which led up to the steps of the student union, reminded suddenly of how many times I'd hurried to meet Karen McIntyre there for a quiet lunch. She'd stand waiting for me just inside the doorway and hand me her books to carry before planting me a kiss. "Yeah, well my weaknesses all begin with women, natural and otherwise."

"Why do you suppose that is?"

"Why do I suppose what is? That I can't figure women out? I'm sure it has to do with my crazy sister."

"What d'you say her name was?"

"Lisa Rae."

"And she still lives in Mississippi?"

"Biloxi. On the coast.It's really beautiful down there. Hadn't been all built up yet like a

lot of the Gulf coast. Great place to relax and enjoy the beach without a bunch of loony tourists everywhere."

"Me and some friends went to Lauderdale once."

"Spring break?"

"Yeah, my senior year. We thought we were cool."

"Well, I'm sure you didn't have any problems finding a date."

She laughed. I must've sparked a memory."Yeah. We were pretty wild back then."

"Well, Biloxi ain't quite like Fort Lauderdale. Not that I've been there. But I've seen the pictures. Girls like you and your friends, wet with sea-spray, running up and down the beaches as far as the eye can see. Our senior trip we went to New Orleans."

"Oh, I've been there too. It's so hot!"

"Yeah, I suppose so. I think we were too drunk to notice."

"You didn't get into trouble, did you?"

I tried to remember those crazy nights running up and down Bourbon Street with Pete Kaufman and Red Simpson. I tried to land some fat gal at two in the morning. Thank God her friends rescued her. "Naw. We just took in the scenery."

"Everyone is so nice in the south."

"You believe that?"

"Yeah. They are. I mean, we've been to Houston, and Atlanta."

"Well, that's not the south. I don't think either of those towns qualify for the real south. Atlanta is like, I don't know what, a southern Chicago or something. Nobody that lives there is from there. And Houston, well that's in Texas."

"Well, I don't know. Everyone seemed so nice to me."

"With that smile of yours. how could anyone not be nice to ya?"

"Are you making fun of me?"

"Actually not. I guess I'm just expressing a little more of my complete ignorance when it comes to the ways and means of the opposite sex."

She hooked my arm once again. We had reached the gymnasium and turned north on the sidewalk which climbed up along the side of Keaton Lane. The breeze came down the hill and chilled our faces.

"I'm not so hard to figure out. I'm just a little moody sometimes," she confessed.

"I heard you had a 4.0."

Her eyes lit up a little."No. Now who told you that?"

"Oh, you know how guys talk. There's nothing like a high G.P.A. to get us excited."

"I'm sure."

"Well, actually, it is amazing to me. Not just you, of course. 'Cause hell, I don't know anything about you. But the fact that anybody can make straight A's here. I don't see how it can be done."

"Well, when you have no life, it helps."

We stopped at the corner and let a car pass. A student in a wheelchair crossed with us at the corner. He too, couldn't resist a long glance at Michelle's backside. When we got to the opposite curb I helped him pull back up onto the sidewalk. He winked at Michelle and rolled quickly toward the Administration Building. We were heading back towards the library now, the afternoon chill was picking up and I needed to get back to do some studying, so I walked steadily. Michelle was doing well to match my step. As I cut between the Administration Building and the Faculty offices Michelle suddenly grabbed me again and held me still. We stood alone in shadows of the alley.

"John," she said, pulling me off the walkway, "You're still dating Karen, aren't you?"

"Well, actually, I don't know."

She leaned back against the wall of the Faculty Building and pulled me to her."Are you afraid of me?"

"I don't think so, Michelle. I'm not . . ."

"Then why do you keep pushing me away? What do you mean: Actually, I don't know?"

"It's a long story."

"Everything is a long story these days."

"Yep. I suppose that's true."

Michelle put her hands to my collar and studied my face, her light blue eyes turned navy blue in the late afternoon darkness.

"I need you to kiss me," she said, her voice quiet in my ear.

"Michelle, I just....." Then she put her lips to mine. Our coats were so thick we could hardly get our faces together, but after the first sweet touch of her lips I could not pull away. Her perfume flooded over me suddenly and I felt as if I were falling into the dark shadows of the earth. I kissed her soft and long with our feet in the cold grass and her back pushed against the cold stones. She began to cry and I kissed her again and tasted her teardrops.

"John," she whispered in my ear, "Don't leave me."

"Oh God, Michelle," I told her. "You don't even know me."

"Yes, I do, John. I feel like I've known you forever. Like you're the best friend I've ever had."

We stood holding each other in the cool shade of the alleyway like two kids who'd snuck out of the junior high sock hop.

"This is crazy," I said, but something about her gentle kisses made perfect sense. I was lying to both of us. This feeling felt as natural as the evening wind whistling around the corner, throwing her long, blonde hair around the back of my head and tickling my neck. We drove back to her apartment and dove into her bed. The same flowery smell rose from her covers, enveloping me like a warm towel. We both had our weaknesses. Some people you just can't read.

Chapter 14
Who is the gaucho, amigo?

How could anyone ever leave such a lovely face? Michelle possessed such extraordinary beauty that the image of her smile alone seemed to stay with me everywhere. Her sweet words, whispered in my ear from her warm bed, kept me entranced as I walked across the campus.

I could still smell her luxuriant perfume as I sat at my favorite cubicle on the third floor of the library and tried to work on a piece of poetry.Knowing I'd have to read my work before the class made each idea more painful to express, each line more studied and every completed verse full of troubling non sequiturs. Poetry was the essence of literary expression. I had trouble writing grammatically correct sentences. Thus I travailed, thesaurus in hand, hoping against hope to pull together some thread of allusion which might make sense to at least someone in the crowd -- Shelley Fogle even. The day grew dark and the building quiet (though I felt alone the entire time, isolated from all intrusions) and eventually they ran me out of my spot, inspired but with work still to do.

I lucked out in class Friday. We ran out of time before my turn came due. I'd have the weekend to work out the kinks. I thanked the Lord, folded my shoddy lyric into an old textbook and slipped out of class, a forgiven man.

One more ballgame I had to push the old body through before Thanksgiving break. We would travel to play the University of Connecticut, just down the road in Hartford. I walked to the Administration Building with Willie for an early team breakfast. The morning was quite cold, but clear. Willie always seemed to be full of energy. He gave me the day's forecast.

"Yeah. It's gonna stay clear today. Won't be too bad. Little bit of orange on the horizon. Look out for Catholics." He grinned widely and winked.

"Catholics, huh? Willie, I don't think you know the first thing about predicting the weather. That one game -- you said it would snow -- pure luck, nothing more."

"Bullshit, Tightrope! I can tell about these things. It's in my eyes. How else d'you think I saved your ass at four in the morning?"

"More pure luck I'd say, though mine on that occasion."

"You don't believe in magic, John?"

"Magic? Like bending spoons through a wall? Reading someone's mind? Neaw. Doesn't seem likely."

"You ever studied physics?"

"They made me take trigonometry once. That's the same thing, right?"

"Well, close. But anybody who's studied physics will tell you that everything we know, we know from guessing. Nothing is absolute."

"You sound like Professor Strache."

"Wait, bear with me." We were walking into the cafeteria line now, warming up our

hands, scooping up some scrambled eggs. Willie's voice came down, to keep everyone in

the room from listening in on his diatribe. "Everything is illusion, all life a dream."

I looked up at the gray haired lady serving out the bacon and sausage and smiled. Her eyes met mine and for a moment I thought she was blind.

Bobby had not made it in yet so we sat by ourselves to continue the morning's dialogue. I didn't buy in to much of what Willie was saying, but he impressed me with the expanse of his imagination. I welcomed his distraction, for The Game lacked a true sense of fascination for me now. It all seemed ridiculous, as remote as the humid Friday nights long ago when I played the stupid game on the ball fields of south Mississippi. After a while Jimmy and Fred arrived and joined us. Neither looked particularly excited to be up at eight in the morning.

"Morning, gentlemen," Jimmy addressed us. Fred sat down politely, his plate filled with two portions of everything. "How's the grub?"

"Adequate," I answered. "Ain't no biscuits and grits, but then what can you expect from a bunch of Yankees." Fred stuffed his mouth full and looked at me sternly.

Jimmy went on: "Well, someday we'll all catch up with you down there in the swamps and you can show us what southern cooking is all about."

I laughed, remembering the truth of what I knew about it, how Momma used to dish up white cream-corn, vine-ripe tomatoes, fried okra and snap beans, with a slab of pepper ham and biscuits, or a platter full of deep-fried catfish. And the indescribable taste of a steaming-hot peach pie topped with homemade ice cream. It was a long way from here, but they'd sure be welcome if they could read the map.

We rode the bus quietly to the U Conn campus, catching up on sleep and lost in our own thoughts. It wasn't till we began to unpack that I realized someone was missing. I caught Bucky's attention as we found our lockers and began undressing.

"Bucky, where the hell's Dregorian?"

"He left," Bucky said, surprised that I hadn't heard. "What?"

"Yeah. Hampshire."

"You're kidding?"

"Uh-uh. Nobody knows why. I don't know what happened. I heard it from Lupestein. Maybe they found out he was gay." I looked at him without expression, or rather, with the expression of someone who is suddenly without words or thoughts. Bobby had wanted to be a doctor.

He met the profile.

Coach Rivers talked to us about the upcoming contest before we took the field. I could barely hear him at the back of the crouching players. He described some aspects of their offense to look for. Asked if there were any quit. Quit school. Moved back to New questions. I looked over at Kyle McClary. His eyes blinked incessantly. I thought he looked stoned on something. The door flung open, the crowd roared and we pushed onto the field. I slowed as I went by The Coach.

"You asked if there was any questions, Coach," I said. "What is it Colton?"

I pulled off my helmet so I could better see the dim light from his eyes.

"Where's Bobby?" I asked him.

His stare met mine like he could push a rip-tide back to shore. The stands cheered and I turned and joined the team. I can't remember what happened when the guard hit me. I was running across the middle, looking for a linebacker to take out, when my left leg caught behind me and I spun to the ground in pain. Fred nearly carried me off the field. The new trainer didn't know what to make of it. All I knew was that I couldn't stand up for the pain in my left hamstring.

We were up by 10 points when I went out, but the margin shrank quickly. U Conn ran back a punt, then tied it up with a field goal at the start of the fourth quarter. They'd put a leash on Lupestein and every time Bucky looked up a U Conn tackle was in his face. Willie had gone in to replace me, but Bucky couldn't find a lane to throw through. Something was up down here in Mudville. Somewhere, someone didn't like a bunch of upstarts running all over the Ivy League and Southern New England. They'd come up with a plan.

Willie sat beside me, out of breath, shaking his head. "Fuckers," he called them. "I can't get a block." Fred stood over me.

"How you doing?" he asked me.

"Great. I just can't walk."

"What the fuck did you think you were doing out there?"

"What do you mean?"

"I mean diving into a pile of linemen?"

I looked at Willie and he looked back at me, anxious for a reply.

"Seemed like the right thing to do at the time."

"Yeah, right," Fred responded. "You gonna be alright?"

"Yeah, I told you, I'm like a cat. Besides, I'm part Indian."

They both looked at me strangely.

"Play to win," I said, grimacing.

I knew the kid would get it right one day. It was just a matter of time and a few chances. You could see it in his eyes. At our own 42 yard line, third and long, Bucky broke free of a blitz and spotted Willie streaking back towards him. He threw sharply and Willie brought it in, then turned to the sideline. He made a quick move, lost the cornerback, cut back across the path of the safety, then broke for the corner. When I saw him break free I hobbled to the sideline and joined my teammates screaming for a touchdown. The son of a bitch left 'em like they were walking home and crossed the goal line picking up speed. We raced onto the field in such a delirium the refs had to warn us to clear out. Willie fought his way through the crowd towards where I stood at the sideline. Grinning, he tossed me the ball.

"That's . . . how you do it!" he said.

I looked up at the blue, cloudless sky and had to agree. I gave him a high five, lost my balance and fell flat on my back.

On the bus ride back to the stadium the players were raucous and full of energy. We'd pulled another one out, by the luck of the draw and our own wiliness, and everyone knew the next week belonged to us. No practice, no films and only two days of school before break.The weak pain relievers they gave me were of little help. They just made me dizzy. Fred helped me down the steps into the parking lot across from the locker rooms. As he helped me hop across the asphalt Michelle appeared suddenly from nowhere and hugged my neck. Fred stopped for a moment, puzzled.

"Oh John," she said, "you poor thing." She gave me a kiss and hugged me again. It seemed everyone was watching us. I turned and in my hazy vision made out a slight figure standing in the middle of the lot, her hands clasped over her heart.

"Karen!" I yelled to her. But it was too late. She jumped in her car and sped off. I looked at Michelle and shook my head. She gave me another kiss and told me everything was okay. Everything was alright. I turned away without a word and Fred helped we move inside.

This night belonged to Willie Patterson. A missed tackle, a keen throw, a copied move and a ton of foot-speed had put his star on the sidewalk. Jimmy and Fred were going by Delta Chi for a while. I persuaded them to take me and Willie along.

The old fraternity had changed little over the past few years. The Deltas still took little pride in their standing amongst their brethren Greeks. They were more interested in style than in class. They had never led the school in academics, or athletics (or anything for that matter) but these were the guys who I always thought had the answers; these were the guys who I always thought would end up being In Charge. They were smart alright. Smarter than me certainly. But not too smart for their own good. Someone once said that when it's third and short you don't give the ball to a milk drinker. My boys almost carried me into the entranceway of the frat house.

"Tightrope!" I heard some drunk yell at me. I, too, was half lit and I smiled. Then I saw Lupestein making time with a loopy coed by the stairs. He raised his beer at Willie Patterson.

"Shotgun!" he saluted our new star.

Jimmy laughed, popped a fresh beer and swung Willie into the limelight. "Shotgun!" he echoed. Willie's grin lit up the rest of the room. Hah! Just what he needed. We were full of youth and moonlight, cold beer and optimism. We sang and laughed at our own nobility. I heard, from a distant room, a timeless Becker-Fagen lyric:

Who is the gaucho, amigo?
Why is he standing
In your spangled, leather poncho,
With the studs that match your eyes?
Bodacious cowboys
Such as your friend
Will never be welcome here;
High in the Custerdome.

They carried me up the stairs to someone's dark bedroom and we passed a pipe around. Willie looked at me and laughed with a bright, wide grin and a broad, full voice.

"I never suspected," he said. "Especially you, John."

"Shocks the sensibilities, huh?"

I sucked in the hot smoke and passed him the small, wooden pipe. The coalescence of pain killers, alcohol and THC had discolored my thought processes. The light from the corner of the desk made his face appear green. Jimmy Piehler played the drums on a couple of textbooks while Fred Cole walked to the window and looked out at the small crowd on the lawn. Two other students sat on the bed, looking at a magazine. The smoke drifted slowly in the filtered light. Another song took flight, an other-worldly rhythm, pulling away my senses:

Long distance runaround
Long time waiting to feel the sound
I still remember the dream there
I still remember the time you said goodbye

Touching the time and holding to the light of the room I talked to my friends and smiled and sang. We were an unlikely collection of confreres -- a teacher, a politician, a comic, a magician -- young men on the brink of adulthood with nothing but the limits of our own dreams to keep us to this earth. Willie smiled and winked at me.

"Our little secret," I said aloud, passing him the pipe and blowing out a smoke ring. The white smoke caught the light and drifted slowly up to the ceiling. He gave me five and once more let out his brilliant smile.

When I dragged my broken body home I found, taped to my door, a note. It was the handwriting of the resident grad student.

Your mom called Call home ASAP

Chapter 15

"Ever hear of a team from Connecticut winning the Sugar Bowl?"

My Momma's voice was broken and filled with weariness when at last she picked up the receiver. She approved the charges and reached to turn on the light.

"John," she said.

"Yes, it's me. I'm sorry it's so late. I just got word you called."

"John?"

"Yes, Momma, it's me."

"Oh goodness. It's . . . Oh . . . It's so . . late."

"I know Momma, I'm sorry."

"Oh, John, I'm so glad you called. Your father's sick. They put him in the hospital in Jackson. They think he may have cancer."

"Oh God."

"We don't know yet... what all it is. But they said he has lymphomas in his colon. They might operate, John."

"How are you, Momma?"

"Oh, I'm tired, you know. I haven't hardly slept the last few days. Where have you been? I've been trying to call you all day."

"We had a game today, and I went over to some friend's house."

"Well, your father's holding up alright. You know how he wudn't ever tell ya if he was hurtin'.I think he's been sick for a while. He's just a stubborn old man sometimes."

"Yeah, that's the truth, alright.So when do you think they'll find something out?"

"Well, they'll know in the morning. I need to ask you: Can you take off from up there?"

"Of course I can. Anytime."

"Well, your uncle Bill says he'll buy you a ticket, round trip, to Jackson. He's gonna air mail it up to you. You remember Uncle Bill."

Uncle Bill was the husband of my mom's sister Daisy. He was a real storyteller and had apparently made some money in real estate. I remember he had a silver handlebar moustache and he smoked a large, hand-carved pipe.

"Yeah, I remember Uncle Bill."

"Can you call him tomorrow?He said he could work it out."

"Sure, Momma, I'll call him.You get some sleep. Listen, now: I'll be down there in a little bit. Everything will be alright. And listen, Momma: I love you."

"I love you too, Johnnie."

"Call me when you talk to Bill."

"Alright. Now go to bed, Momma. Goodnight."

"Goodnight, Johnnie."

The best times I remembered of Uncle Bill was at some of the family picnics. He loved to cook so he always seemed to be hanging out around the kitchen or the bar-b-cue. He loved to wear suspenders over his plaid shirts and he'd wear any sort of hat which might fit the climate or occasion. Mom and Daisy were always cutting up when they got together. Daisy was much better on the piano and could play everything from John Wesley hymns to Stephen Foster, or even some old Gershwin tunes, and they both could carry a tune well enough to impress the neighbors. Uncle Bill would appear with a pot full of baked beans, or some jalapeño cornbread, waving his towel over it to cool it off and at the same time circulate the aromas. While the kids played and the parents gossiped, my father would always find some project to work on, cleaning up the garage say, or patching that little hole in the screen door that had been there for weeks. Uncle Bill would yell for him to come on and he'd appear suddenly from some hidden corner of the yard, dusting himself off. Uncle Bill would cajole Sarge for his industriousness while he rounded everybody up. He was one of the few characters I'd ever seen who could tell Sarge when to cease his toil.

Jimmy Piehler gave me a ride to the airport. As we drove he briefed me on the finer points of modern air transport. I was a senior in college and this would be my first jet flight. The sky seemed clear enough, the temperature hovering around 38. It seemed like a perfect day for flying, though perhaps I should have checked with Willie on the forecast before shoving off. "The main thing is, pick out the cutest stewardess in the cabin and keep asking her stupid questions. They think it's cute and before long they'll all be bending over you to see how you're doing. And if the seats aren't all filled they'll let you move around. Try to get a seat with a view of the stewardess's little work station. That's where all the action is!"

"You ever pick up a stewardess?"

"Of course not, I'm just a goofy college kid. They all date pilots and traveling salesmen with big bucks."

"Then what's the point of all this?"

"Hey, you're the one who asked for the advice."

"Well, I brought along a book, so I'll probably just read a little and sleep."

"Yeah, that'll impress 'em."

I laughed and slapped at the back of his head. As we sped down the highway I looked out the window at the skyline of Hartford. A light brown haze lay over the city, but the sky above was clear blue and calm.

Jimmy waited with me at the gate until they called for us to enter. I shook his hand and thanked him, then boarded the plane anxiously. Eventually I located my seat on the aisle. As we pulled away from the concourse and taxied across the runway, I surveyed the faces of my fellow passengers on this high tech air ship heading south. None of them seemed as unsure of what to expect as I did. I was seated next to a portly, graying businessman. He wore bifocals through which he read intently from his Wall Street Journal. A young boy sat just ahead of me and he kept peeking over the seat and making faces. I winked at him and tried to appear reassured, pulling my seat belt tighter. The engines began to whine, the plane rolled forward and began accelerating to an incredible speed. I watched the runway flash by in the window as the plane took to flight and quietly rose over the city and turned towards Atlanta.

The plane ride was smooth for the first hour and I tried to settle in and get into the novel I'd brought along, but my mind was full of other images. Every voice around me sparked a jumbled memory. I thought of Karen McIntyre standing in the blue light outside the stadium, clasping her hands to her heart, watching Michelle hug me as I hobbled toward the lockers. I could still see her turning away with disgust and driving into the night. Perhaps it was best this way. Perhaps it was easier for her to believe I'd found another. It might be painful, but at least it would be quick. She would never understand what really happened, even if I tried to explain it.

After all, Karen had Mrs. McIntyre to set her straight. They were both resourceful. It wouldn't take them long to find the Blue-Blood type they both really needed. We had had some times, though. I'll never forget how shy Karen was the first few times we made love and how excited she eventually became about every prospect. We learned a lot from each other, but I'm not sure we ever fell in love. Perhaps, I thought, when I return . . .

Suddenly I felt the plane lurch. We bounced slightly, then leveled off. I looked out the window and spotted the thunderheads on both sides of us.The Captain came on the speaker.

"This is Captain Fowler. We'll be going through a little turbulence for just a few miles, here. Please fasten your seatbelts. We should be by this storm in just a few minutes."

Suddenly the plane bounced again and I heard a lady behind me curse. I pulled my belt tighter and looked out the window, as if I might help the Captain spot the next culprit. The businessman next to me picked up on my nervousness.

"Aw, it's just some air pockets. We're coming down from the cruising altitude. We'll be through it in a second."

He looked out the window, fascinated for a second or two by the majesty of the clouds, then he turned the page of his newspaper and continued reading. I tried to take some comfort from his experienced nonchalance, but with each sway of the wings and mild rumble in the atmosphere my grip on the arms of my chair became more diligent. My book fell between my feet and I couldn't even bring myself to reach down and pick it up. I closed my eyes for a moment and said a prayer. It wouldn't be right, with my father in such a state, for his only son to die on a trip home. God works in mysterious ways, Momma used to say, whenever we had a question she couldn't quite answer. I figured my prayer would come through easier up this close to heaven.

Like the Captain had told us, the turbulence subsided after a short time. The plane continued its descent and came down through the clouds over North Georgia. We circled by Stone Mountain and came roaring in to Hartsfield. The modern Atlanta skyline reflected the afternoon sun, shining like a modern version of Oz. After we touched down and my nerves settled somewhat the man next to me introduced himself.

"My name's Rick Patterson."

I chuckled. "Hi. John Colton."

"You live here in Atlanta?"

"Oh no. I'm catching a flight to Jackson."

"Mississippi?"

"Oh, yeah."

"You don't fly much, do you?"

"No. Not that much? Could you tell?"

He looked at me slyly, folding up his newspapers and tucking away his eyeglasses. He cleared his throat as if clearing out his response. Then he looked out the window.

He spotted someone he knew and he waved.

"Well, only when you almost tore the cufflink off my shirtsleeve."

"Oh, sorry. I didn't know."

"I'm just kidding, John. You know it's a hell of a lot safer up there than it is down here on these crazy highways."

"Yeah, that's what I've heard."

"Sit by the window and enjoy the scenery," he advised. "Thanks."

"Sure. Enjoy your trip."

We stood and squeezed our way out. I met the gaze of the blonde stewardess at the exit and she smiled politely, as she did at every customer who looked her way. I remembered Jimmy's advice, but two hours too late. I stopped at the door and gave her my best puzzling look. "Is this the way out?" She laughed politely and pointed the way to safety.

The flight to Jackson was less eventful. I was even ready to try out some of Jimmy's stupid questions, but none of the attendants struck my fancy. We when we touched down at Hawkins Field it was nearly four o'clock, but we'd lost an hour going west. After flying over Hartford,

Philadelphia and Atlanta, the diminutive buildings of Jackson made the town appear from the air like a western crossroads from another era. In many ways these impressions from above told a real story.

We disembarked and I met my mother at the gate. We gave each other a deep, long hug.

"Oh John," she said, tears in her eyes, "I'm so glad you're here." She held me back to look at me. I looked at my mother's face, her high soft cheekbones, lightly blushed with rouge, her fine, brown hair, pulled back around her ears, her full, rounded chin: her entire face had tender slopes on every curve.Her eyes were a delicate and rich blue. She must've been quite a beauty in her day, though to me she was still the loveliest of all creatures.

"You still look beautiful, Momma."

She brushed back a tear. "Oh, John," she said, holding my hand and turning me around."Come on. Let's get your bags. Visiting hours are over at six."

She led me down the concourse to where my luggage came out and across the lot to her maroon Delta 88 Oldsmobile, which still had a dent in the left side from where I'd once backed into a fencepost when I and Susie were out parking. Dad refused to get it fixed just to remind me of my carelessness. If I ever got a job I vowed I'd get that dent repaired with my first paycheck. When we walked outside and I felt the warm afternoon sun hit me I stopped for a moment and looked around me. Heat rose in waves from the cars. It was late in November and everyone was in short sleeves. You couldn't mistake the warmth of Mississippi for anyplace else on earth. I gathered myself and threw my bags into the trunk.

Momma was trying her best to be strong, but she was new at this. I looked over at her as she drove to the hospital, wondering how she'd hold up in a world without Sarge.

He took care of everything. He had always held her back from making any decisions around the household when it involved anyone other than herself. About the only thing Sarge let her decide for herself was where she would shop for groceries and what friends she might invite over for a game of bridge on Wednesdays. I could remember many times when she'd make a suggestion for a place to stop for lunch on some dreadful vacation. He'd shoot her proposal down then become incensed when she didn't understand his logic. But she was a bright lady. She knew the King James' Bible inside and out and she used to love to read any novel which took place in distant lands. She'd read to me and Lisa Rae some nights, when we were kids, up in the room we once shared, just fresh from a warm bath (we'd be cuddled up in our matching pajamas, tucked into the covers like twins) and we'd sit on every word as Momma sat beside the bed in an old, broken rocking chair, reading under a weak yellow lamp, our bedroom window wide open, letting in the warm breezes and the sounds of frogs and crickets from the woods all around the house. She could make the simplest of stories come to life, her voice full of song, then suddenly at a whisper, raising goose bumps on my legs when she described a dragon, or a ghost floating through an old, stone mansion. She broke through my dreams.

"Your father's sick," she said. "They're gonna hafta operate, John." She bit her lip.

"He's got cancer in his colon."

"When are they gonna operate?"

"He goes in tomorrow morning."

"How's he doing?"

She looked at me, thinking over the question. "You know your father. He just... well, you know how he is." She put her hand over to mine.

"Well . . . so what do the doctors say?"

"They don't know. I think they think he'll be alright. You know, a lot of people have problems with this. They do this operation all the time. And this doctor, Doctor Lewis, I think he's the best."

I thought suddenly about Bobby Dregorian, wondered where he was. Perhaps when I return . . .

We came down the long hallway toward my father's room quietly. My mother still held my hand, her fingers slender yet firm. The light overhead was pale. A window at the far end cast a reflection of silver sunlight off the waxy floor.

An old man with a walker was being helped by a nurse in a light blue dress. She looked tired and withdrawn. Momma raised up her chin, collected herself and led me into Sarge's room.

He didn't look at us at first. His eyes were closed, though he didn't seem to be asleep. My mother stepped up beside the bed. As I stood beside her she reached her hand to his. The old lady in the adjacent bed looked over.

"John," she said, stirring him to life.

He shook out the dreams and brought us into focus. I saw the old man grin.

"Johnnie," he said, thrusting out his hand, his voice hoarse and gritty.

I shook his hand and looked him the eye. It was all I could do to keep from crying, but I knew he wouldn't go for that. Suddenly he pulled me forward with a powerful grip. "You're getting bigger, boy."

"You think so?"

"Well, of course. Must be that Yankee cookin'."

"I doubt it. They can't even do grits!"

He tried to laugh. "Well, you know we keep that secret to ourselves. Hey now, I got your clipping last week. Looks like you boys are gonna win 'em all."

"Well, we got a good shot."

"Good shot, hell!' Scuse me Momma. All you got left is Yale and Boston College. For Chris sake, a good high school team could whip them boys!"

"Only from Mississippi, Daddy."

He coughed and readjusted his eyesight. "Well, maybe that's true. Say, they don't play football up there like we do down here."

I remembered the Navy game, trudging through the snow with ice frozen on my facemask, slipping into the clutches of a stunted cornerback.

"You kidding? Neaw. Ever hear of a team from Connecticut winning the Sugar Bowl?"

Once again he tried to laugh, but I could tell he was fighting back the pain. The disease had worked on him. His face was pale, his body thin. His once powerful forearms were now wrinkled and purple from the IV's. He was not the same man. There was no place in Sarge's psyche for mortality. Growing up he'd always made us believe he could turn back the Mississippi River if he wanted to. He seemed capable of withstanding the surges of a gulf hurricane. And perhaps he still could. He coughed again and cleared his throat. He looked for a moment at Momma, trying to collect him from the pain that had just hit him. The sun was beginning to set and it left long shadows from the blinds in the window. His face seemed ghostly. I looked at him solemnly and my mother put her hand to the back of my head. I could tell she was running through the same remote reflections.

I heard footsteps from the hallway. I turned slowly and looked behind me just as her voice called out.

"Hi Daddy," Lisa Rae said.She stood in the doorway with Jamie in her arms.The little boy's face was pink from the sun, his white hair stuck straight up in the air and his blue eyes were wide open and full of life. She walked around to the other side of the bed. My father looked over in awe.

"Say hi to your Granddaddy," Lisa Rae said, and she held Jaimie down to my father's arms. "Hi Granddaddy," he said, in his small, beautiful voice. My father took Jaimie into his arms, held him and gave him a kiss on the forehead.

"Well, you little son of a bitch," he said. "'Scuse me Momma." I looked at Lisa Rae and we both laughed.

Daddy kissed him again and held Jaimie up. "The kid does look like me!"

"I told you," I said.

Daddy bounced him around. Any pain that he'd felt a moment earlier had left his face. "Got big legs. Might be a roundballer."

"They all have big legs at this age," Lisa Rae said, My father held Jaimie closer and looked at Lisa Rae. She reached her hands out and clasped his face.

"I love you, Daddy," she told him.

He handed Jaimie to my Momma and pulled his daughter to him. As the light fell out of the room they hugged one another and cried. The old man in the other bed looked over at us and smiled.

"I love you too, honey," he said. He held her closer and spoke into her ear."I'm sorry little girl. I'm so sorry."

"It's OK, Daddy. It's OK."

"He's beautiful, Lisa.I love you, honey. You know that . . ."

"I know Daddy."

They hugged and kissed and the tears flowed out of both of them. I turned to my mother and gave her a kiss on the cheek.

"He'll be alright," I said. "He's Sarge." I led her out of the room and left my father and sister alone to make their peace.

"Besides," I reassured her, "He's got you on his side."

Mom had a room for me at the Holiday Inn just down the street from the hospital. We ate dinner there and shared some pecan pie and ice cream with our coffee. The place was almost deserted even by 9 o'clock. I guess Thanksgiving week's not a popular time for eating out anywhere. We all spooned the cream in our cups -- because we all took our coffee the same way -- then we dug into our sticky desserts.

"Daddy looked so thin," Lisa Rae said.

"I know, honey," Momma said. "He can't eat anything, you know. He's been fed intravenously for two days."

"Jeez, you never think."

"Well, the doctor says it comes from not eating right. He says he sees this kind of thing all the time. I don't know. He does look awful. I think he'll get better though."

She looked at her pie and laid down her fork, disturbed suddenly by some thought. Lisa Rae spoke to her.

"What is it, Momma?"

Momma shook her head. "I don't know. You know he's been sick for a while now. I knew something was wrong. He just wasn't acting the same. Always staying up late, eating half his food. He's just so damn stubborn, that man."

I agreed with her. "I know, Momma. Maybe it's something he was born with. Who knows? When you been to war maybe it changes the way you look at things. He never would let anybody help him with anything."

"And you all," Momma said,"I feel so bad about all this."

"What do you mean?" I said.

She looked at Lisa Rae. "I mean the way he's been acting. He knows he was wrong.You can forgive him for that, can't you, honey?"

Lisa Rae took her napkin and dried Momma's cheek. "Momma he was always forgiven."

Chapter 16
Where was Roget when you most needed him?

The waiting room at the hospital had orange chairs and two beat-up rust colored sofas and no window. The ceiling lights were bright, not at all soothing. Just down the hall stood a pop machine and beyond the receiving area were the bathrooms. In the hallway, nurses and doctors walked by us talking and reading charts constantly, too busy about their day's work to even know we were there. The only magazines I found worth reading were some old Sports Illustrateds, about two months old. They were addressed to a Dr. Hafeez. He must've donated them after he'd caught up on the inside stories of the sporting world. I was glad that Dr. Hafeez subscribed to Sports Illustrated and that he was kind enough to leave his back copies here.

Momma brought around some crochet work, but couldn't keep her mind on it. Every few minutes she had to get up and pace the floor, wash her face, or step outside for some air. Lisa Rae tried to calm her down, but all three of us were anxious and could offer each other little solace. I knew Sarge would make it through this operation. That was not my concern. But I worried about the longer term, about whether they could get to all the cancer, about how Sarge could adapt to a life where he had to depend on others. That might be a harder task than facing his disease. I spotted Dr. Lewis walking down the hallway, untying his mask and scratching at his ear. He was a tall, light-haired man whose chin stood straight out as we moved.

He had an air of calm and in-control about him which permeated the whole floor. I dropped my magazine to the table and stood up. Momma and Lisa Rae remained seated and held each other's hands.

"He's fine," the doctor announced. You could see the pride of accomplishment in his eyes. "He's gonna be sore for a while. He's gonna need some TLC, but he's a strong fellow. Just watch his diet and don't overdo it and he'll be fine."

My mother hugged Lisa Rae and began crying. She stood up, wiping away her tears as fast as they fell, and she walked over to shake the doctor's hand. Dr. Lewis shook her hand politely and smiled with confidence like he performed miracles all day long, every day. Perhaps he did.

"Thanks, Doc," I told him.

"Sure," he said, his voice low and relaxed. We couldn't offer the doctor much more than our thanks. We didn't have any season tickets at Ole Miss or a vacation home along the Gulf for him to stay at.We hoped our thanks would be enough.

My father was well enough to receive visitors by late afternoon. He was full of pain killers and hooked up to a bunch of tubes, but the fire in his eyes still shone through. He was giving his nurse the business when we walked in.

"Well, it said that the game started at 8:30. Now if you're puttin' out the lights at 8 then I can't watch my ballgame! You see what I mean? And fix that there. I don't want that hanging out there for everybody."

The nurse straightened his pillow and looked over at us, exasperated by his demands. Apparently, he was recovering quickly.

"Evening," he greeted us. He pushed his head up slightly to see us better, but couldn't seem to move much else. "They got a TV guide here says the Braves come on at 8:30, but they shut everything off at 8. Now what kinda sense does that make? Hell, I'm paying for the damn cable TV in here anyway."

Momma began crying again as she went to him and gave him a kiss.

"Oh honey," she said, "You're gonna be fine."

He gave her a peck back. "If I could just get my ballgame on." He looked at me, like I alone would understand the importance of his request.

"We'll see what we can do, Dad. How you doing?"

"How do I look?" he asked sourly.

"You've looked better. But then you looked a lot worse a few hours ago."

"That's something's for sure. You seen Dr. Lewis?"

"Yeah," Lisa Rae answered.Jaimie had gone fast asleep on her shoulder. She handed him over to me and I tried awkwardly to make him comfortable as he napped.

"Well he's a fine man, isn't he?"

"He's wonderful," Momma said.

"You tell him now, when you see again, that he's a fine man. And I mean that!" He looked down at all the contraptions covering him up. "Shew! Look at me. They got me tied up for sure now, don't they?"

I was worried they might have given the old man more pain reliever than he needed. I carried Jaimie around to the other side of the bed. The old man next to us smiled at me.

"Hi," I said, "I hope he hasn't been too difficult a roommate."

"Oh no, he keeps me entertained. What a lovely child."

"He is, isn't he?"

"Do you suppose I could hold him for you?"

I looked at my sister and she shrugged her shoulders.

"Sure," she said and I handed the sleeping boy over to the old man.

"His name is Jaimie," I told him.

"Hi," he said, speaking to all of us, "I'm Bill Holland." He cradled the boy carefully and wiped the drool from his chin

My father looked over at Bill. "Bill's an old Navy pilot, John. I told him how they almost clipped off your perfect season up there, in the ice bowl."

"They've got a tough squad this year," I said. "Well, they used to have some teams."

The phone suddenly buzzed by my father's bed. Lisa Rae picked it up.

"Yes. Oh, great! Yes, come on in."

"What is it?" Dad asked her.

"It's my husband. He just flew in. He had to be at the bank this morning."

Roger opened the door slowly and stood just inside.

"Well, come on in!" my father announced, "Everybody else is here. Might as well make it a party."

Roger walked to my father's bed and held his hand. They looked at one another quietly for a moment.

"How are you, Mr. Colton?"

"Well, as you can see, I'm not ready to enter the Olympics just yet. But I guess I got a few friends here tonight."

"You surely do. Lisa tells me you should be out in a couple of weeks."

"Week and a half, I figure."

"That's great. You let us know if you need anything. Come on down to the beach sometime and we'll go fishing. They'll still let you do some fishing, won't they?"

"Far as I know. You mean out in the gulf?"

"Yeah, out in the gulf. My father has a boat that we use sometimes."

Sarge winked at Lisa Rae and looked back at Roger. "I'd like that, son. I can't remember the last time I went deep sea fishing. Can we take Junior along?"

"Why sure. We'll need somebody to cut bait."

Sarge laughed and gripped Roger's hand tighter. "Well, we'll just have to do that then. It's good to see you, son. That's a whale of a little boy you got there."

"Yeah, they say he takes after you."

"Well, let's hope he can just meet somebody as nice as your Momma, and maybe have some kids this special."

"We'd all be lucky at that, Grandpa."

Suddenly Jaimie yawned loudly and we all looked over. Bill Holland had gone to sleep with the child in his arms. Jaimie stretched out till he got comfortable, then he rested his head under Bill's chin and went back to sleep. Lisa Rae was crying when she at last took him back into her arms.

We all ate dinner back at the motel that night and afterwards Momma took Jaimie with her back to her room. We wandered into the lounge, had a few cocktails and chatted about old times, current news and our futures together. As one of my worlds was falling apart, another world was coming back together. Lisa Rae was excited about finally breaking through with Dad. It was a shame that it took something like this to get them back together, but his ill health might have been a big part of the reason he stayed so ornery, not just about Lisa Rae, but about everything. My big sister had won Teacher of the Year in her school district and already sold one of her wacky oil paintings. I warned Roger about the possible consequences of his invitation to Sarge. Dad would have every nick and scratch on the boat fixed up before they made it out of the docks. Lisa Rae was tired, but after two quick glasses of wine she was ready to dig at me. She put her hand on Roger's arm to draw his attention away from our waitress' backside.

"Junior here is dating a real life, true-to-God, Connecticut debutante."

I cautioned her about jumping to conclusions without all the facts. "Wait a minute now. Karen's fixing to graduate. She's closer to a dilettante. Besides, we're not on the best terms right now."

"What?"

"Yeah. Me and her mother had kind of a falling out."

"Well, screw her mother!"

"I don't think it would help. She... wants her daughter to marry someone with a little more class. Someone like Roger, maybe." Roger let out a burp and returned his gaze to its previous target.

"Well jeez, Johnnie. Here I was I thought you had found yourself the perfect little bride: sophisticated, intelligent, beautiful, rich."

"Let's not forget spoiled rotten, and a snob. Oh, and pretentious."

"Hey they can't all be perfect, like me."

"Thank God for small favors."

Lisa Rae smiled then took on a sudden change in her expression.

"Tell me John. Whatever happened to Michelle?"

I swirled the ice in my drink, musing on all the loose ends in my life. What about Michelle? I honestly didn't know. She was beautiful, but strange. She had a unique ability to captivate, but the closer I got to her more mysterious I found her.

"I don't know about her. She's doing okay. She's a little mixed up I'd say. We talk from time to time. I don't know."

"So she's not going to do anything about it?"

"I don't think so. It's a little late now. I think the time for her to act has passed. She's kinda put me in the middle of things. Roger, I suppose Lisa's briefed you on all my calamities?"

"Yeah, we've talked about it. Sounds like you've got a few nuts up there."

"And I forgot to tell you: Bobby -- you know, our trainer -- he left school. They got to him somehow."

Lisa Rae set down her glass and looked at me somberly. "This is terrible," she said. "How can these things happen?"

"You remember, Lisa, how our little connection enabled me to get by the academic requirements at Lassiter? Well, we probably broke some rules, stretched the truth. All for what purpose: to win some football games.Now this is a lot different, of course, but it works the same way. The whole school is caught up in our success. I don't know. I've got a few tricks left. We'll see."

"What do you mean by that? Don't you do anything stupid now!"

"No, I wouldn't do that. I'll be alright." I turned to Roger."Did Lisa Rae ever tell you she was part Injun?"

He smiled and took a sip from his drink.

"At least we think so, we're not sure. That's why she's so sneaky. And that's why she can't hold her liquor."

My sister leaned over and gave me a big smooch on the cheek. "Sometimes I just love you," she said. "But not often, Junior."

We closed down the Delta Drive Holiday Inn Lounge that night. Our reflections became fuzzier as the hour grew late, our language more liberated, our voices louder and our love for one another cemented in our common hopes and histories. I looked at Lisa Rae, laughing sweetly, and I knew for a fact that she'd already made it out of the swamps. She'd been on dry land for a long time now. I should've known what she was up to. I'd do the legwork alright. But she would always be the light and the stars in this family.

My flight left Hawkins field for Atlanta at 4:26 PM. We stopped by and visited with Dad for a while early in the day. As he regained his strength and wits, his knack for taking charge came back to the surface. He had the hospital staff watering Bill's plants and delivering sodas to his visitors. Sarge would be alright. It was the hospital I worried about. My family walked with me to my gate and saw me climb aboard Delta flight 201 to Atlanta. I gave my sister and Momma a hug and started down the walk when Roger called out. He walked over and stuffed a twenty in my shirt pocket.

"Enjoy the ride, Junior. And stay away from the flight attendants."

I looked down at his gift, nodded a thanks and stepped on board.

The flight back was smooth and restful. I'd taken Rick Patterson's advice and requested a window seat. Perhaps I was getting used to air travel. The flight to Atlanta was over in minutes. After a quick stopover I boarded my flight, and as the sun fell over the Atlanta skyline the plane took off for Hartford.

No one took the seat to my right so I stretched out and enjoyed the view and the privacy.There was nothing but mountains, it seemed, between here and Connecticut. I looked down and spotted my usual transport tooling along in the slow lane thousands of feet below us, being passed by every motorist on the highway. Once you got used to it, this was the only way to travel. I'd have to remember to send Uncle Bill a thank you note.I thought about Sarge, recovering his strength and verve, keeping the nurses on their toes. He had bribed an orderly to flip the game on for him, he'd whispered to me with delight. He wasn't afraid of anything but his own emotions. He'd be on his feet I'm sure before too long. Maybe not pushing the mower, but working on some important project, re-working the shelves in the hardware store or something. He taught us never to quit on anything and he made sure we knew the value of hard work. He wouldn't let you beat him at his own game, but he helped us in ways he never understood. I looked down at the book I'd brought along; I'd hardly finished a page. I thought suddenly about the poem that I'd composed for Friday's class and had the good fortune to miss out on reciting. I took out a pencil and tried to remember it, get it back in front of me for some more editing. The words came back but they no longer seem to fit right. What would Professor Strache think about this? He was a generous man, particularly when it came to the creations of his own students, but he knew real art when he saw it. I looked over the not so subtle allusions, pulled out a rhyme or two, fought with the right word to end every line, re-worked the commas. I knew Lisa Rae must teach in a way totally different from The Professor, but I knew they had the same magic. Both could enthrall and excite, and in both their eyes you could see the sincerity and sympathy and care. A student will pick up on those sorts of things. Where was Roget when you most needed him?

The stewardess came by and took cocktail orders. I asked her if they had Stoli. She leaned down and took my order, placing the light scent of her perfume in my nose. She turned to take the next order and I looked out the window at the dark landscape. Football practice would start back Monday. We traveled to New Haven to play Yale on Saturday, then for our last game we played Boston College, at home. We weren't really worried about Yale. It was BC that had us shaking. Why couldn't they have scheduled one more patsy for our last game? Poor scheduling can cost many a team a perfect season. Coach Rivers could smell this perfect season like his proverbial bad fart in a locker room; you couldn't get away from it. Everyone had jumped on the train and someone had thrown the brake out the window.I leaned my head against the window and gazed down toward the deep valleys and rolling hills. The lights were mere specks now, no movement on the land, no flashing caution lights. What is it in this land that creates such heroes and heartbreak? I looked for my quiet crossroads hidden in the tall pines along the Appalachian Trail. Some young man down there was probably out in his front yard right now, calling for his dog, taking in a deep breath of the crisp and luxuriant mountain air. He probably took notice of some light way up in the sky and for a moment he'd look at it, wondering what kind of people would ride so fast across the Virginia sky on such a beautiful night. And then he'd hear his dog running from out of the woods and he'd not give that soaring light another thought. He'd turn and walk towards the house, his dog jumping up at his legs, excited to be loved and wanted, and I imagine the old boy would stop at the door before he went in and he'd take another look around at his small expanse of the land and, for a moment anyway, feel like he owned the whole world. I felt a hand on my shoulder and I turned suddenly.

"Stoli," she said.

"Thank you," I said, taking my drink. "Listen, can I ask you: are we gonna be going over any big cities?"

"Hold on," she answered. "I'll come back in a minute and show you the route."

Chapter 17
There seems room enough here for all the uncultivated

There were two games left in this season. That was the end of it. The end of the sweat, the thirst, the crashing of heads, the nagging bruises, the long days, the glory. A person decides to keep playing college football for a number of reasons. It might be a financial decision, brought on by the ever-increasing costs of the American University System. For some folks the game helps them center their lives, gives a focus to all their pent up energy. For others it gets to be a habit, just something to keep you busy. No doubt many a man put up with the anguish of practice for the few chances to grab some of the spotlights on game day. I played the game for a little bit of every reason you could name, but no single reason I'd stand up and brag about. I was taught to finish a job once you got started. I was taught to play to win. But I was also taught to stand up for your principles.

Jimmy Piehler met me at the airport. Everyone else had split town for the holidays. As I pushed my way out of the crowd he grabbed my bags from me.

"Welcome back," he greeted me."How's your pop?"

"He's doing fine. He's a tough son of a bitch, you know. I'm more worried about the hospital staff than Sarge."

"Well, that's great. So he'll be going home soon."

"Yeah, it looks that way. Saw my sister. She came by to see him."

"Lisa Rae?"

"Yeah."

"They hadn't seen each other in a while, huh?"

"No. It's been a while. It's a shame what it takes for some people to admit they made a mistake."

We picked up my luggage at the baggage claim and stepped outside towards Jimmy's Mustang. The cool air sent a chill up my back. Jimmy spoke in broken English as we moved haphazardly through the cars in the long lot.

"Well, listen, John. I was thinking, uh, my sister and brother-in-law are in town and we're just having a little get together for Thanksgiving at my Mom's house and, uh, if you want to you, you ought to join us."

Jimmy's older sister was a gorgeous brunette, just like my own big sis, and though his mother was certifiably unbalanced, she was quite attractive also. I'd hardly ever been over there when her and Jimmy didn't get in to it about something or other. But she always stocked a full bar; the hour was late: it was the best offer I would get this turkey day.

"Well thanks. I'd like that. Otherwise I suppose I'd be eating at the Coffee Klatch."

"My mother probably won't top the food, but at least the company will be better. We can go by Mrs. Johnson's for a beer if you want. Maybe crash at my place and head over there after noon."

We stopped by the dorm so I could drop off my bags and get a change of clothes. On our way out through the lobby the resident grad student called out at me and handed me a letter. It was postmarked from New Hampshire. We hopped back in Jimmy's 67 Mustang and headed for Mrs. Johnson's as I tore open the envelope and read the letter nervously. It was typewritten and somber in tone. When I finished it I folded it back into the envelope and looked quietly out the window at the streaking lights flashing in the dark streets around us.

"What is it?" Jimmy asked.

"It's nothing. It's a letter. I . . . I don't know."

"What?" he asked again. "What's wrong with you?"

Jimmy Piehler was a smart and intuitive cat. He'd selected History for his major, with the Middle American period as his concentration. When you spoke to Jimmy you had to be sure - like my sister - you had your words in the proper order. I don't know why he took such stock in the course of human destiny.His parents had been divorced twice.He'd moved five times, before settling in West Hartford. He'd never had a stick of good luck. I guess he knew better, had a sense of the odds. I guess he knew his number would some day come up.

"It's a letter from Bobby," I said, unsure what story I should tell him, how much of the truth I should share.

I looked over at Jimmy. He drove casually, waiting patiently at each light, his mind disengaged from everything around him. Jimmy possessed an active and imaginative mind. No one could hold him down. He loved to laugh and joke, tell outrageous stories which only the trusting could believe in. While some of the players would shake their heads at his crazy comments in the locker room and walk away, I always felt he was someone I could read.

We pulled into Mrs. Johnson's Bar and Grill and quickly found a table. Only a few other students sat in the booths to either side of us, students like us who either lived in town, or too far away to make the journey home a good investment. On the night before Thanksgiving we could look at each other over a cold draft beer and feel at home, comfortable in the shallow depth of our puerile philosophy.

They had gotten to Bobby. In his letter he told me some things I'd never repeat to anyone. He was having trouble sleeping. He wouldn't be coming back. His dad was going to get him into Maine University. They had a good pre-med school. It was a letter of thanks. But what had I done? All I could think about was my failure.

I spilled my story to Jimmy. The shaded lamps which hung between us modulated the darkness to a soft amber. A few girls sat in my vision a couple of booths down the wall, but I couldn't find the energy to meet their gazes. What could you make of all this? What of law and order? What about principles? Were we all stuffed men? Jimmy sat and watched me talk, tossed between disbelief and understanding.

He had no trouble believing that Kyle and Scoop could cross such dangerous lines. They fit the profile. Jimmy had never liked either of them. But he was surprised about what I told him about The Coach. He asked me what he could do for me. There was nothing for him to do. Keep his silence. Offer his friendship. That would be plenty. These were puzzles I'd have to work out on my own.

I ate Thanksgiving dinner with Jimmy and his mom, and his sister Patty and her husband Jacob. Miss Piehler had picked up a whole collection of hors d'oevres and New England Pilgrim-type goodies from some caterer she knew. About her biggest contribution to the whole meal was heating up the biscuits and finishing off the sweet potato pie. Everything had some sort of liquor in it; every dish put a tingle in my mouth on the first bite, but I soon got used to it and eventually found myself pressing her for second and third helpings. I was a growing boy after all. Jimmy's mom worked in advertising and still got cash flow from her second divorce. Jimmy's real father, his mother's first husband, lived in Albany, New York. He had re-married and then had another son. Jimmy said he was a likeable person. He just couldn't deal with his mother's chameleonic coquetry. What was it about these dames in Connecticut? It was true I'll tell ya: his old lady reminded me of Mrs. McIntyre, and even Karen -- when she made certain gestures -- always dabbing at the corners of her mouth with her napkin, reaching her small hands out and touching whoever she talked to just so lightly, excusing herself every time she stood up from the table: I'd've laughed if it wasn't so damn charming. And she had the same habit of making eyes at young college jocks like me, pushing out her best angles and bumping into you when you were looking the other way. Perhaps it was the top-shelf spirits.

I thought about how we used to sit around the Thanksgiving table back home, atour small, but solid cherry-wood dinner table, passing around my mother's vittles quietly, because even at Thanksgiving -- particularly at Thanksgiving -- my dad didn't go for much conversation. There'd be a small but juicy turkey (maybe 16 pounds at best) stuffed with carrots and onions and cracked pepper and fresh garlic and some of Momma's cornbread dressing which is to this day the best I've ever tasted anywhere (even countin' that fancy Hilton in New Orleans); and usually she'd dish out some white creamed corn (which was another of her specialties); and over the turkey and dressing we'd lop on a full ladle of Momma's secret-recipe gravy -- thick with boiled eggs and all the plump juices of the bird; and of course we'd have some of that fresh cranberry sauce that the Pinckney's sold in their produce market near the river; and always a taste of sweet potato pie, mashed up with cinnamon and pecans and topped with marshmallows; and for dessert she'd bake a tender pumpkin pie and carry it out to the table in a thick towel, her face all lit up like she was carrying a newborn, and even Sarge would lick his lips and clear his plate to make room for a slice. My mother would pray a beautiful prayer before we took part in this meal, all of us holding hands, thanking the Lord for everything he'd given to this little country, and to our little family.

Well, after the meal me and Jimmy retired to his mother's spacious den and laid out in front of her spacious TV to enjoy the plethora of football games which always came on Turkey Day and before long I was near napping. And sure enough Jimmy and his mom were into it about something stupid.I had to come to from my slumber and make a few jokes to keep them from swooping at each other's throats. We'd all had too much wine and too much heartbreak.

Fred came back into town Sunday night and we all got together for a few drinks (of course my two best friends splitting the tab for me). I got drunk and when Fred asked about Michelle I told him most of the story. None of us might ever amount to anything, but we always felt like we'd have each other to depend on. Fred was brilliant in a different way from Jimmy. He had a feel for the mathematical, the scientific. Where he might not have a quick grip on a fresh acquaintance, he understood the natural world in a deeper, more philosophical way; he knew everything in this world revolved around science, and all science revolved around mathematics. Fred was as big as a truck and just as solid in his emotions. I let the ole' boy in on "our little secret," I was drunk. And besides, I had a plan.

The next morning I awoke with a mild hangover and gave a few long thoughts to staying right where I was, rolled up and covered in the morning darkness. But The Professor's class met today; I had an obligation to meet and I missed his abstruse and delicate guidance. The pavement and grass of Connecticut was still cold and dried-up with winter. I'd never have enough clothes to keep out these winter breezes. Trudging insistently towards class every student looked intently toward their destination, too weary and uncomfortable to look up for a friendly face across the walkways. I settled in to Professor Strache's class and slowly pulled off my coat and scarf, pretending to look over some old notes in my notebook while actually re-appraising the bony, sentimental lines of a country, pastoral poem.

The Professor arrived a moment before the bell, or a moment after -- I don't remember exactly -- and proceeded his usual ritual of throwing his coat, hat and scarf in three different locations and situating his books, folders and papers all over his desk so he'd never be able to find anything on the first couple try's. He looked at me for a moment and gave me a warm half-smile. He walked over to my desk and asked me: "I heard your father was sick, John. How is he?"

"He's fine," I told him, "He had a little surgery. But he came through with flying colors. Probably be home in a week or so."

"Well, that's great. I wanted to invite you and Karen over for Thanksgiving, but they told me you left town. Carolyn was so disappointed."

"Well, tell Carolyn that I'm disappointed too. I would've loved to join y'all."

"I'll do that, John. We'd planned on finishing up some of those readings today. I know you've had a lot going on; a lot on your mind. If you'd like . . ."

"Oh no, it's fine. Let's get it over with it," I reassured him, smiling nervously.

Any room you have to stand up and speak in is always too hot. You could be inside an igloo, looking over an ice-covered podium and sweat would drain beneath your armpits. The Professor called my name from the furthest seat. I slowly made my way up front, unfolded my poem and began reading, a sound not unlike rivets shaking.

Because I have been hurt and bruised by love
I am a cautious wanderer on love's properties
Picking carefully at fallen limbs with a stick
Unable to defend myself from a sudden many-footed brute.
Childish, and like a child, excitable,
Quick to flight when alerted by a jay-call or the snapping of a crisp twig on an otherwise silent floor.
Please! Thou who art landholder of these folds,
I am wounded and without guard.
Be not unduly alarmed at my clumsy trespass into your curious garden.
The grasslands are ungathered.
The pine straw unexplored by my shoes.
There seems room enough here for all the uncultivated,
And in these streams play crayfish and newts.

When the dawn fog makes the closest aspect indistinct,
Turning all thoughts hazy,
We listen carefully for the Dance of the Elves,
Trying to pick out some repeating rhythm,
The hum-hum of a rondo,
The slight raising-up of the willows wind-whisper
In the undefined bog.
Listen,
listen
But now it is gone
And over there,
Where many days have seen the explosion of flowerbanks,
And, above them, the breathing of bee-wings,
Kissing here this daisy, and then here, this solitary violet.
O! Of these grounds let us stoop and pause,
Forgetting for one moment our purpose and destination,
Following the afternoon's sleepy pull until we are
Sleeping,
sleeping,
Under blue skies.
In all these sounds are crickets, the whistle of an owl, and toads.
It is night and by the moon's light I shall go,
Leaving my stick,
And carrying a solitary violet."

I folded my little composition in half, re-gathered my wits and started back for my chair. The sweat dripped down my shirt sleeves and gave me a chill. I looked up just briefly and caught The Professor's eyes from the back of the room. He had a broad smile and he called out at me.

"Bravo!" he said, and Shelly Fogle echoed him: "Bravo."

I nodded in thanks and sat down, looking at nothing but the desk top in front of me, and then out the window, away from the class. What had he said? Bravo! My heart fell back into my gullet, a deep élan of satisfaction slowly washing over me. Wiping the sweat from my earlobe, I noticed a squirrel shifting anxiously in the bare tree limbs outside. The squirrel looked at me slyly.

"Bravo," the little creature seemed to say. I took a second look, bit my lip, then came back down to earth.

What is it in those words that can pick out the cavern's dog of your mind? I lay in bed and rolled over on my side in the same mattress where Michelle had once rolled over and felt shelter and evil; they were two sides of the same twin. Poe is a madman and a genius. This is every artist's gift, every artist's bane. Like Fred he was a mathematician, a scientist. Like Willie, he guarded his stories with the traps of magic. Like me, he had a love for language.

> *'True -- nervous -- very, very dreadfully nervous I had been and am; but why will you say that I am mad? The disease had sharpened my senses---not destroyed--not dulled them.'*

So he sang, putting up a perfectly formed structure into which I could lose my imagination and my naturally sullen emotions. The icy season in Connecticut had just turned full blown. Just as our season of play closed out on its final act. Not with a bang. Not with a whimper even. Yale, I say, on Saturday, in New Haven: the rich boys, the smart boys, clean and slick and too clever to let any grease stick to 'em. No self-respecting college student in Connecticut liked anyone from Yale. Some of us might aspire to be like them, push for some of that New England old-world wit, but we would never really be them. Any club that wouldn't have us for a member, shouldn't have us for a member. Most of all, as an athlete, we knew they were all wimps. Even the name of the school had a wimpish ring to it. Yeah, they might take over our father's company in two years, figure out a quick and easy cure for the common cold, but they lacked style. Here in the Lassiter football program we'd forsaken any sense of wit for victory. My mind wandered back to the page. Poe rambled on, his dreadful heartbeat booming louder, louder! What was it she'd said, "Don't ever leave me." I heard a noise, it was like a girl's fingernails scraping on my window, or an old lady's. The shadows stopped on the wall, then moved again in their familiar dance, conjuring up a dream; any dream; then a voice: "Leitrea." I shuddered and looked out the slotted blinds. The bare fingers of the tree outside waved slowly in the courtyard lights. I remembered suddenly about a big live oak that sat near a creek in an old girlfriend's backyard, and though it was covered up in moss it had the same long, slender limbs always reaching out for you in the gentlest of winds.They had a tire swing which would sway out over the creek from another of the big tree's limbs (a wide, powerful arm, twisted with strength and age) and she and her sister never tired of riding the pendulum over the clear runnel in the late afternoons. Another screech drew me back to my room, and the 60 watt bulb, and my creepy story. We'd have to win this next one. My boys would have to come through.

We boarded the bus at 10 o'clock on Saturday, the 29th of November. Willie came up the steps right behind me and so we sat next to each other on the ride. Interstate 91 was a direct route to New Haven. We passed through the corner of Middletown and some sharp hills and arrived on the Yale campus in less than an hour and a half. New Haven was alright - every college kidin Connecticut had enjoyed a party or two down there— but we all despised the ancient grounds of the University that sat smack in the town's epicenter like an old and proud homesteader. We looked out the window at Harkness Tower, with its placid belfry looking over us, and Phelps Gate, opening up on New Haven Green, and we were envious and downtrodden. Lassiter gave off its own feeling of American academia, but this place rubbed your face in it. There's such a thing as being too smart, they say. I know Sarge would buy into the theory. We stepped down from the bus and took another look around at the beautiful excerpts of American architecture and history, then dipped into the visitors' locker room, rancid with the odors and echoes so familiar to our kin.

It was important that The Boys have a good game; and they didn't disappoint me.

Fred controlled the entire right side of the defensive line; Jimmy - on the few occasions he'd been called on to punt - struck the ball with clean, high spirals that put the poor receiver into retreat and alarm. Our defensive squad disliked these little snot-nosed lads worse than anybody and gave them a crisp greeting from the central regions. What

I could do but pull down a touchdown pass in the middle of a crow's nest of defenders and walk quietly into the end zone while they stumbled in confusion. We busted them up good and The Coach seemed prouder than ever at the flock he'd herded into the valley.

I sat on my hands on the ride back and looked out the window at the dim lights in the hills. The Coach thought the whole thing was about him; he believed it was his season. I saw Coach Chapman looking at me from a seat up front, his face full of shadows and solicitude. We'd won another one, alright. Put those little bastards in their places, if only for a few hours. But the bus was quiet, too filled up with weariness and broken ideals. The small bulb over Coach Chapman's head suddenly went out, spent of its vigor, and he looked up and turned away. At a stoplight I saw a policeman leaning against his patrol car. He looked back slowly at our bus as we pulled up beside him and I could see him reading the words Lassiter Football on the side of the bus. Suddenly he looked up, straight at me, then he turned and spit onto the street. I had the feeling he wanted to make another gesture in my direction, but he kept his restraint. My head fell against the window as we pulled off and made our way down the ramp towards the interstate. Night had fallen and my eyelids were heavy, on the verge of closing. I remembered an image of Michelle at today's ballgame, jumping enthusiastically on the sideline. She had left a message for me at the dorm over the weekend, but when I'd tried to call her there was no answer. It was near midnight, yet no one was home. She had come by the dorm on Tuesday night, but this time I was out, studying at the library. I remembered an image of her rushing to the stadium concourse with the rest of the squad, screaming hurrahs as we jogged into the locker room at the game's end. She turned and smiled at me, then went into the cheerleaders' dressing room. They all were laughing, throwing their pour-pours at each other. Michelle stood up on a bench and smiled at all the cheerleaders.

"I'm pregnant," she said, throwing her hair back and letting loose another full laugh. She pulled her sweater up and thrust out her chest and before another moment they all began to join her. I heard a voice, my own voice, then a hand, pulling at me . . . not . . . no!

"Colton," Willie said. "What the hell you dreaming?" The image turned to dark.I saw my own dim reflection in the window.

"Jesus!" I said, then turned my head towards Willie. "You won't believe this one."

"What the hell?"

"It's a weird world out there, Willie."

"So I've heard."

I rubbed the sleep from my eyes and took a deep breath, trying to bring back the dream-visions.

"It's a weird world."

Willie smiled and slapped at the back of my head. "So I've heard," he said.

Chapter 18
The year of Elvis

The sports page of the Lassiter Beacon was too well written. They'd learned to be journalists, but not sportswriters. By now, our exploits were turning up in the Hartford Times. I picked up a copy from the Minute Mart and read it on the walk back to the dorm.

COUGARS CRUSH YALE!
FACE BOSTON COLLEGE IN FINAL HOMESTAND

In what could be termed a total domination of both sides of the line of scrimmage, the Lassiter Cougars put down the Yale Bulldogs 44 to 17 Saturday, putting the crowning touch on their league title in front of 12,000 fans at Yale Stadium. More than half of the stands were filled with the faithful from Lassiter.

The Cougars scored on their opening drive when Bucky Shoals took it in from the five on a quarterback keeper, and they never looked back. The Lassiter defense, which has led the league in fewest points scored against it, held Yale to only two first downs in the first half. A fumble on Yale's second possession set up another score, this time by fullback Jerry Lupestein, who took the ball in from the 12.

After an exchange of punts, Shoals found wide receiver John Colton in the middle of a group of defenders for a touchdown strike of 33 yards. Lassiter added a late field goal in the second quarter, making the halftime score 24 - 0. The Yale offense had an equally tough time in the second half, tossing two interceptions and converting only three first downs. Lupestein scored again on a burst up the middle from the 20, place-kicker Reggie Pace drilled two field goals and Bucky Shoals scrambled for a touchdown in the third quarter before most of the first team was pulled out.

Next Saturday the Cougars face perhaps their toughest test of the year against Boston College. BC is 6 and 6 coming into the contest, but has played a much tougher schedule than Lassiter. If Lassiter were to win it would be the first time they had gone undefeated since 1957.

1957. The year of Sputnik; the year of Elvis.

Which event had a greater impact on us Americans? It's hard to say. We had made it through the two most horrible wars in history, had truly arisen as the Last, Best Hope, yet we were still full of innocence, unable to really see the two great societies, the two American Dreams. We are a country of cultures and machines. I don't believe history moves in a circle; I cannot see the curve that moves through today. 1957. It had been a while, yet once again we stood poised, on the verge of another perfect season.

There were many discussions and conversations which would take place during the week before our final game, including several troubling debates within my own mind. I would talk to Professor Strache, and Lisa Rae, and my mother; and I, Jimmy and Fred would spend a late Wednesday night over several pitchers of beer discussing our chances on Saturday and the true nature of the universe. And on Sunday one of my calls to Michelle would finally reach her.

It was just after noon and her voice sounded sleepy. "How are you, girl?"

"Oh . . . I'm fine. What are you doing?"

"Well, I'm trying to catch up with you. "

"You are? I thought you were trying to avoid me."

"Well, you're never in."

"Not true. Sally told me you called. Listen…" There was a pause on the line, as if she were moving the phone to her other ear. "What are you doing? Can I come over?"

"I suppose. I've got no plans. Matter of fact, I wouldn't mind seeing you. Talk about old times."

"Yeah, right. Give me a while. And don't go anywhere." When she arrived at my room and I opened the door we stood and looked at each other for a moment awkwardly. She wore a small, white rabbit-fur jacket and a light blue sweater which carefully matched the color of her eyes. Her golden-streaked hair was down, cascading off her shoulders and mixing with the soft pelt around her. Her face had a natural blush to it; it looked like she'd hardly put on any make-up at all. She put her face on my chest and pushed me inside and I held her closely.

"I'm so glad to see you," she said. Her voice sounded troubled.

"You look great, Michelle."

"I wish." She looked up at me shyly, her big blue eyes as wide as a baby's.

"Do you like me, John?"

"Of course, Michelle." I pulled off her coat and led her to my bed where I sat down beside her. I gave her a quick, soft kiss. But the question bothered me. Did I like her? She was beautiful, and she was in need of a strong hand, but she was nevertheless full of puzzles. I thought I knew her kind. I'd fallen for these Belladonnas before. I'd been snared in their web of love and felt my heart wrapped up in their sweet, milky silk, and then, when the warm fires of comfort had rocked me to dormancy, I'd been quickly stung and poisoned and left hanging as testament above the forest floor: "Beware young traveler who goes there, man of dreams, man of beauty, see her prize and despair." Michelle had all the makings of her kind, namely: physical magnificence, sensuality, delicacy and mystery. She knew she was too sweet for possessing. Some women are raised to be heartbreakers; others are born.

"I missed you. Even while I was home." She paused and wiped away a tear. "How is your father? I heard he was sick."

"Yes, he's okay. He should be home in a little bit."

"Jimmy told me you went home to Lumberton."

"Well, actually I went to Jackson. It was a little nerve-racking, but we all survived it. You know, it was the first time I'd been on a jet."

"You're kidding me, right?"

"No. I wish I was. It was a little strange."

"Shit, honey, I've flown more times that I can count. We're always flying somewhere. So how did you like it?"

"Oh, it was great. Once you learn to relax and enjoy the view."

"Yeah, I suppose. I don't know. Last week was so weird." She looked down and shook her head. "My family Shwew!"

I pulled up her chin so I could see her face. "And what about your fiancé?" I asked her.

She tried to laugh, silently. "That was weird too." She looked me in the eye, thinking for a moment about how to describe the thoughts in her mind. "He's in love with me, John."

I had to laugh."Well, Michelle, he's your fiancé, after all."

"I know, but it's crazy. It's like everything I do. And you know I can't tell him about all this. It would kill him. That's why it's so important that I can still see you. I feel so safe with you. So open. So alive."

"I don't think you know what you feel."

"You know what? You're probably right about that."

I brushed her hair back and admired the sweep of her cheeks. She had a wisp of blonde hair which rode up the sides of her face like a spring breeze. I saw her eyes look past me, towards the window. Her face suddenly grew alight and slowly she stood up and pulled me with her to see the view.

"Look! It's snowing."

In the long yard and the street you could see wisps of snow beginning to fall. The air was calm and the ground cool so it floated quietly and laid still on the grass until its sister flake could float down beside it and begin the arduous process of covering the green and brown and black with a pure and cleansing white.

"It's so lovely," she said, holding my hand, then she pleaded, "Let's go to the park."

"The park?"

"Yes, let's do. Just down the street. Pope Park. You know, behind Delta Chi."

I looked at her and smiled, seeing the child in both of us on this wintry New England day.

We were the only ones in the park -- well, except for an older couple who wandered through for a moment, looking over at us from across a frozen pond, remembering perhaps how it once was when they were young and the snow would start up -- and we held hands under the trees and tasted the snowfall and kissed with the ice on our lips; and Michelle grabbed up a handful of the fresh drift and tried her best to nail me with a reckless toss, but the snow was too unwieldy and her target too warmed up. We finally found a bench to sit and ruminate on, while the sky filled up with the frozen feathers and the night began to fall around us. I'll remember that afternoon in Pope Park for a long time. We were worn of the struggle, afraid of the fight before us and overflowing with a simple love for a simpler life. We sat and kissed, and talked about old times and childhoods, and how much a little thing like a snowfall can connect us to each other, and to this little world around us. Did I like her? Well, I loved her like I loved the seasons, with the same emersion of being that you could feel sometimes when the sun just barely breaks through a wandering cloud with a warm, golden greeting, or when a sudden gust of wind fills up a tree, making it whisper and sing, and sway with premonitions. Michelle was part of this earth, and part of this earth's beauty; and like all parts of this earth she would one day grow older, and disappear.

In his office every bit of his imbroglio leapt out at you as if it were a warning; worse even, worse certainly, than his own library.Papers stuck out from between texts everywhere, both on the shelves and in piles on his desk, and in chairs, and on the floor. A small window and a small desk lamp provided what little light there was, and mostly it lit up the smoke which floated in swirls as The Professor puffed thoughtfully on his pipe.

"I've been thinking about your poem," he said to me, flipping through a stack of papers as if he'd lost a whole stack of assignments somewhere. "It's really not bad. I hope you didn't take me too seriously when I joked about Romanticism and Modern Poetry."

"No. Of course not. I would've had to have understood it, to take it seriously."

I moved some texts from a chair at the corner of the room and sat down. The Professor leaned back and looked at me slyly, one eye almost closed. His chair creaked eerily. "Well, one must take the good with the bad, you know. This is the price of progress. You cannot live in the past, no matter how badly one wants to. And how is your dad?"

"He's fine, Professor. I think he'll be all right. You know, he's a Marine."

"Of course, of course." He paused, leaning forward. "I suppose he's had a big influence on you."

I looked at The Professor's desk, thinking suddenly of the desk Sarge had in his hardware store, every item perfectly arranged, lined up at perfect right angles, two pencils -- one sharpened and one not -- sitting in the top drawer beside a single, dried-out, felt-tip pen.

"Well I guess so. You know how it is with your old man. It's not enough that you have to look like 'em. Half your waking moments you act like 'em." The Professor leaned back once more, distancing himself from my remarks. He threw a hand haphazardly into the mix of smoke and dust as if to mix up all my conjectures.

"You imagine my own father. You think of him as a dairy farmer, or a writer. You look at me, you see him; in him, me. Nothing could be farther from the truth. Yet he is why I am myself; and a teacher." He took a big puff and the smoke billowed out from his pipe and drifted off his shoulder, towards the dark books on the shelves above us.

"I have a problem," I confessed to him. "I don't know where I sit in this whole mess; where I should stand or just watch the whole thing pass by. It's not a family thing -- though God knows my family's got plenty of problems -- it's almost . . . Surreal. I was reading some Poe the other night. This weird tale about the Literary Life of Thingum Bob, Esquire."

"Yes," The Professor replied, "A weird tale, indeed."

"Well, I tried to push through it -- even though it didn't flow evenly (at least to me) -- when suddenly I had another weird notion: that all of us are pushing our ideas out there to a bunch of crazy editors and judges; and coaches and professors and parents. Who's right, finally?"

"Only the guy with the pen."

The Professor studied my face and knocked a thumbtack off the edge of his desk.He rubbed his hand on his chin and closed him eyes for a moment.He spoke, quietly, "Have you decided what you'll be taking next semester?"

"Yeah. I'm thinking about taking Greek Literature."

"Greek? Well, that's a 300 course. Certainly, you can find a more challenging course than that."

"It's an elective," I told him, leaning back, my chair suddenly creaking and moaning. "And I know this, Professor." His eyes opened up, then folded, then he looked at me amiably, his light gray irises reflecting the buttery sun from the window. We sat in his smoky office quietly for a moment, smiling at each other across his littered desk, and for a moment this school was not about graduation and G.P.A.'s and career goals; it was not about assignments and essays and multiple choice exams, or grading on the curve, or figuring out the easiest schedule, or which bar to meet up with your running buddies after your last class, or where you could hang out and see the most legs. It was just a teacher, who was so absorbed by his calling that his mind could drift past a mountain of unfinished housekeeping just to chat with a protégé, and a student who's every interest and curiosity had been seized by the legerdemain of a master.

"You had a problem," The Professor said.

"Yes. It's about The Coach."

"Hmmm. Well, he's a volatile character. Some might even call him overbearing, or self-possessed, or even small-minded I've heard it said."

"Well, he's all those things, and a lot more; and a lot less. He's done some things, stretched some rules, overlooked the truth. I've been very disheartened, but the situation seems too large for me. I don't know how to get into his mind. He's too wrapped up."

"What, if I may ask - before you confuse me even more - what did he do?"

I looked at Professor Strache and tried to put the whole story in order, but it was discombobulated, too volatile to explain. I got the sense that the Professor could turn over rocks with the power of his intellect; it might be too much force to apply with so many fragile egos.

"I can't say, Professor. I just wish I could figure him out."

The Professor turned and looked across his bookshelves, as if hunting for a lost title. He ran his hand across a few bindings, squinting to make the focus, then frowned when he failed to locate whatever he was searching for. "Well, John, you should know this man. Everyone has their whale. Everyone has that one thing. That one thing that wraps them up."

I looked at him, falling forward into even more confusion, swallowed up in this vapory, Cimmerian darkness. I stood and shook his hand, a ritual -- it suddenly struck me - that we had seldom performed (that is, between me and The Professor). His hand was small and warm and his grip firm. I nodded and excused myself, walking into the afternoon brightness of the campus with my mind still wandering though a dozen tales. Everyone has their whale.

But what of this tale? I could imagine a dozen endings. If I'd learned nothing else this season it was the knowledge that this life is full of shifting sands and sudden storms. All I could do was just pray that The Boys, in the end, would come through.

On a chilly Wednesday night a few days before our final game together Jimmy and Fred picked me up for a ride into Hartford for a cold beer at Mrs. Johnson's Bar and Grill. Willie was hanging around the lobby with nothing to do that night, so we took him with us. Only Jimmy could afford to drink much during the season (because he didn't do too much running and therefore didn't have to be in shape) so Fred and myself would usually just have a couple. The rules forbade us to drink at all during the season, but, like the rest of the team, we didn't always follow the rules.

We found us a booth in the back corner of the bar, a vantage point from which we could view most of the action, and we promptly ordered a pitcher of beer. Jimmy knew two or three other students who were enjoying warm conversations and cold beverages and they raised their mugs at us as we settled in and pulled off our thick coats.

The bar filled slowly, providing few distractions for our conversation. I looked from face to face at my collection of friends, wondering what the boys back home would think if they could see me now, exchanging political theories with a black dude and two upper-crust New England whippersnappers with connections all along the northern seaboard. It was indeed an odd mix of confidants, but we blended well and I'd never felt as comfortable or secure with a group of friends anywhere. Perhaps we had all matured. The prospects of pending graduation connected us with expressions of anxiety and brotherhood. Only Willie could keep his eyes wide open, prepared to look on every crazy notion and possible future that presented itself. He had time to change his mind, make mistakes. For us, the time to be foolish was passing quickly.

The last ballgame meant different things to all of us. We could not grasp the prospects of defeat. Fred held the table as he poured everyone a beer from the plastic red-letter inscribed pitcher of Foster's Lager.

"I understand their defensive line averages 250."

I feigned a spit-take and swallowed a gulp loudly. "What do we average?" I asked them. "Are we over 200?" They shook their heads and looked down dejectedly. No one knew how large we were, only that we were certainly smaller at every position. Perhaps only Fred could match up mano-a-mano to his opposing player. Boston College had played Syracuse to one touchdown this season and had beaten Illinois and West Virginia. They had been on a skid over the last four games, but the nucleus remained. They were undoubtedly primed to erupt on a fresh, unsalted victim whose eyes were full of stars. Both teams had something to prove. One of Jimmy's buddies walked over to our table and shook Jimmy's hand.

"What's happening, buddy?" he said, then looking us over he asked us:"You guys with the team?"

"Yeah," Jimmy told him, then proceeded to introduce us. The student looked at us pleasantly and perked up when he heard my name.

"John Colton. Yeah, I've heard of you," he said, pointing at me. My teammates broke into laughter and tried to push me out of the booth.

"We call him Tightrope," Jimmy announced.

"Why's that?"

Fred broke in, "He likes to tie up women." The student looked at us for a moment, baffled.

I asked him:"You in school?"

"Oh yeah. I'm a senior at U Conn. Jimmy and me used to be in a band together. You guys play BC this week, huh?"

Jimmy answered him. "Unless you got some idea on how we can get out of it."

"Not me," he said. "Well, kick their ass, alright? See ya, Jimmy. Good luck, you guys."

"A band?" Willie threw out at Jimmy. Jimmy looked away, as if he didn't hear him.

"What'd' you play?"

Jimmy took a full drink from his mug. "We had a little high school band when I was a senior. It was stupid. I played the trumpet. We thought we were the next Chicago."

"I didn't know you played the trumpet," Fred stated.

I echoed him: "Yeah, I thought it was the sax."

Jimmy laughed, embarrassed for some reason. "Well, that's because I play them both. Also trombone. I could've gone here on a music scholarship, you know that?"

"You're kidding?" Willie said.

"Nope. I'm more talented and less intelligent than any of you ever suspected."

"Well, more talented perhaps," Fred tried to assure him. Willie noticed a group of young coeds working their way up the aisle and he elbowed me to direct my gaze. They looked like freshmen. You could tell by the way their eyes moved cautiously over the crowd and by the way they whispered their comments to each other. Soon our entire booth was looking over awkwardly and it struck me why Willie was so interested in these new arrivals.There was a gorgeous little girl in the group who happened to be black. I watched her offer the group suggestions on where to sit, and I watched Willie roguishly catch her eye, then I saw her look back at him and give a demure smile before they slipped into a booth right beside us and she found a seat facing Willie. Jimmy looked at me with that devilish expression that he could put on at times that said a mouthful without uttering a word. Fred and me looked at him and held our tongues as if exchanging thoughts through telepathy. Fred was the master of the blank expression. To look at him you'd think his mind was in another county; but he understood every iota of what was going on.

How stupid I had been my freshmen year. Feeling sorry for myself as a clumsy foreigner in a bright new land. I looked around Mrs. Johnson's; I believe Willie and this girl were the only two black people in the bar. Lassiter brought people of special talents together from everywhere, but the number of African-Americans who I'd met in my four years there I could count on two hands. Most of them were wide receivers or running backs on the football team, or played basketball. I remembered the night Willie introduced me to some of his old buddies in the stadium parking lot. I might someday stop sounding like a redneck hillbilly, if I worked at it long enough, but Willie would never stop being black.

I guess he'd gotten used to blending in, adapting to the prevalent culture of the moment. He spoke in much better English than me, or most of my teammates for that matter, and he carried himself with a conservative, brisk posture. Who knew if he'd make it through all this mess? How well could anyone adapt to a culture full of such polarity, a world where it seemed you were always alone? I admired Willie's discipline and courage and intelligence. He fit the profile of a survivor.

We finished our spare portions of ale and expressed more of our concerns about the upcoming contest. We tried to prod Willie into making an advance on the girl across from him, but he suddenly turned shy. As we paid the tab and started out Jimmy held us up at the booth with the four freshmen.

"Excuse me," he said, "You're not college students are you?"

They looked at him annoyingly. A couple of them offered an insincere laugh. Jimmy was undeterred. "My name is Jimmy Piehler. We're, uh, on the Lassiter football team. You know, the one that's undefeated and fixing to go into battle against Boston College Saturday?" He hadn't exactly won them over with his charm, but he did get their attention. "Well, there's a good chance we may not return from this battle. The casualty rate has been high. This may be our last chance to know what it's like to be married and have a bride. Would you consider it?"

They laughed and shook their heads. One of them piped up. "We're from Lassiter too." Then she looked at me and pointed.

"Are you John Colton?"I smiled and looked at the ceiling. It's a shame that they were so young and I was so damn old.

"Yes," I said, throwing my arm around Willie and pulling him forward. "And this is Willie Patterson, the fastest wide receiver in the Ivy League." I looked down at Willie's new friend. She had beautifully rounded eyes. "You're name's not Cheryl, is it?" She looked at her friends and smiled. "No. I'm Rebecca."

"You sure you're not Cheryl?"

"Yeah, I'm sure."

"Well, Rebecca -- if that's your real name -- this is Willie Patterson, the fastest wide receiver in the entire Ivy League." Willie reached down and shook her hand politely as I continued. "And this fellow here, well, his name escapes me, but it's not important. We're all doomed men. We must go. But come see us on Saturday. We'll be looking for you in the stands. Especially you, Cheryl. If we survive, perhaps we'll see you at Delta Chi after the game. If not, then please do pray for our souls, especially mine. Adieu."

Fred pushed me up the aisle and out the door. Willie looked back and smiled at Rebecca warmly as we exited.

"What are you, nuts?" Willie asked me.

"My sanity is not the issue. It's your loins you should be concentrating on. I must say, she was quite attractive."

"Nice knobblers," Jimmy added.

Just then a car door slammed shut loudly off to our right. I looked over and spotted an old friend standing with some tall fellow next to a black BMW. Karen's face seemed pale in the blue neon.

"Excuse me, guys," I said and walked in her direction. She turned and looked away as her date led her across the lot.

"Karen," I said as I approached them. "Hold on. I need to tell you something." She stopped suddenly and her date looked at me sullenly. I recognized him from somewhere. I had had him in one of my classes or something.

"What do you want?" the fellow said to me, irritated, refusing to let go of Karen's hand.

"Look, fucker," I told him. "I just came out of there after polishing off two pitchers of Foster's Lager and ogling three dozen virgin coeds. I'm so full of pent up sexual energy and machismo that I don't even care that you're twice as big as me. Think about it. The least thing that's gonna happen to you, is you're gonna ruin your fifty dollar shirt. And if you happen to hurt me in any way, shape or form, then I've got three of the baddest and craziest motherfuckers you'll ever want to see just waiting for an excuse to pummel your face." He looked over just as Fred was yawning and stretching out his enormous biceps. "Believe me boy,

I'm no threat. I'm ancient history to this girl, and I just want two minutes of her time."

Karen pulled away from him and I followed her across the lot. "What are you doing?" she asked petulantly.

"Who's this guy? He looks like Jack Pennyloafers."

"That's Carey Lunz."

"Oh yeah, Lunz. He was the student council president last year. Amazing."

"Don't start on me."

"I'm not. I'm sorry. I'm a little drunk."

"That's your excuse for everything, isn't it?"

"I wish it were that easy, Karen." We stopped beside a pick-up truck and leaned against it.

"I want to tell you something.I just have to let you know some things. What ever has happened between me and Michelle it was about her, not us. She got herself into some serious trouble, Karen. It had nothing to do with me. I know you think I'm crazy, that you'd believe such a story, but perhaps someday you'll see. It was about her, that's all, not us."

"Is that it?" she asked, impatient, turning away.

"And one more thing.Your mother told me some things about you and your family, about how you needed to marry someone with sophistication and money. I'll never have enough of either of those two things for a girl like you, but you know there are times when I really miss you Karen, and I wish things had been different. I don't believe everything your mother told me. Just don't believe everything she tells you. And tell Carey I apologize. Your beauty swept away my emotions. Oh yeah, you can tell him I voted for him, too."

Chapter 19
My own peculiar briar patch

We were down to one. That was the end of it. No more then. This would be my last game as a player; my last chance to step up to the scrimmage line and dig in my cleats; the last time I'd have to endure the rankle of slipping on filthy, sweat-crusted shoulder pads; the last time I'd worry about how snugly my helmet hugged my cranium; the last time I'd go to one knee and straight-flush excitement when The Coach shared his words of inspiration; the very last time I'd huddle up and run the pattern, look for the pigskin and my chance to wade into glory. I was glad in a way that it would soon be over, whatever the final outcome.It no longer seemed like a simple game to me. It had become a job, a burden. If I'd had to play another game just for my own sake, then I would have called it quits; but this game was no longer about me.

It was dark and cold when the buzzer on my alarm clock shook me into consciousness. I bundled a blanket around me and took a peek through the blinds. The snowfall from Sunday had mostly melted, leaving only a few crusted patches on the courtyard. The sky was cottony. The breeze shook the bare tree limbs only slightly. Only moments after I pulled on some clothes Willie came knocking at the door. We trudged side by side down the block towards the Administration Building, clearing the sleep from our eyes.

"Interesting sky today, Willie."

Willie looked up and checked the western horizon. A thick layer of milky clouds blanketed the sky at the farthest reaches of the stratosphere. I looked to the southeast where the rising sun had begun to cast a pink and orange glow across the diffusion. I spotted two lone geese soaring in the direction of the sun. Willie took in a deep, full breath through his nose.

There were no cars out this Saturday morning on our short walk. The air was clear and fresh. "Good day for hunting," Willie heralded. I laughed and pushed him off his metered stride.

"Don't laugh," he warned me, "a morning like this: Grandpa would lead us out along the tree lines separating the fields - some corn stubble on one side perhaps and, who knows, maybe pumpkins on the other - right where we could sneak up on as many as a dozen mallards, or it might be a pheasant covey, and Grandpa would ease out quiet as a old cat, then flush 'em out. The cocks would always rise up late, for some reason - maybe they had it planned out - but they'd gawk and take off like a dart, or swoop right over your head. It took me a while to keep my cool and hold my aim, but Grandpa Zack would fix on a bird, lead it across the field and - BAM! - knock it out of the sky. It was something to see."

"Yeah, it sounds really beautiful."

"Hey, it was. What's wrong, you never done any hunting down there in the swamps?"

"Well, not really. My dad had a problem with firearms. Other than hunting gators with a pocket knife, we kept pretty much to the more docile pursuits: lazing around a creek bed and fishing for bream, or maybe floating across Cowley Lake pulling up a boatful of catfish.

"You talk about patience! My dad would paddle us out in the lake and we'd sit there for two hours without saying two words. He'd shush you if you cleared your throat. I guess I'm too much of a talker to be a good fisherman. I guess I enjoy the stories more than the fish."

We jogged into the cafeteria and blew warm breath on our hands. I noticed an air of apprehension circulating around the entire team as we put down breakfast and once again went over our game plan. Everyone feigned full confidence in our fate, but behind everyone's eyes, including the coaches, you could see a glint of reality, a glint of fear. Boston College had an excellent defensive line. They were large and intimidating. Only Syracuse and Indiana had been able to run on them all year. But there was much more to worry about than just that. They were a 1A school, who played the big boys all year long, every year. We were small fry. So what if we could beat up on a bunch of Ivy League starch-shirts? College football may have been invented in this league, but it had long since graduated to bigger and tougher and richer schools. Most of our players weren't even on scholarship. Hell, most of us would probably graduate on time.

Only Coach Rivers seemed unable to let any of his doubts bubble up from his oily subconscious. He peered down at us as he drew out our blocking schemes and alignments with a face like a bird of prey. He could have been Poe's Raven, croaking relentlessly: 'Nevermore! Nevermore!' He spoke about giving Bucky time to throw, drew out our roll-out 22 hitch, a play we could run in our sleep at this point in the season. Fred would be up against some guy named Maslanka, whose specialty was flattening quarterbacks. He loved the outside rush. Fred sat quietly, doodling with a sawed-off pencil as The Coach forewarned him. Fred was looking forward to this encounter. I could tell. He was a big-league player on a small-time team. He hadn't been challenged all year.

He seemed ready. As for me, there were so many rushes of reflections going on in my mind the words and faces had begun to blur in front of me. This game, and my performance in it, were tertiary considerations. There was an old man back in the swamps fighting a Real battle for his life, and a young, foolish girl with a heart too delicate for brandishing, and there was my own thirst for justice, and the foamy tide of my conscience sweeping in slowly over the dark sands of this long, fateful season.

We rode in the bus over to the stadium and I sat beside Bucky and looked out the window. Bucky tried to appear calm, but I could hear his shoes tapping incessantly on the hard floor. He was a nervous soul and I could find no words of consolation. We filed out and pushed our way slowly inside; no joking and no boyish playfulness in our march. My heart had begun to swell up in my chest and pound rhythmically in my throat. I waited for The Coach and took a moment of his time outside the lockers. Were we all stuffed men? Some folks you just can't read.

You never really know what's gonna happen with your life. The older you get, I suppose, the more uncertain life seems, the more everything appears to be mere chance, the dust-trails of time's wagon. I had begun to wrap my hamstring when Coach Chapman called for Thompson and McClary to step in to the coach's office. I kept watch from the corner of my eye and could see through the glass the pleading of the two infidels. I hurried my dressing and looked through the crowd toward the silent debate. I could tell that everyone was uneasy. It was as if some nasty rumor had reached every ear, as if we were all in on a deep and deadly secret.

I had just turned to pull out my game pads when I heard the commotion behind me. Kyle McClary came busting up the aisle like a bull loose from the gate. He was knocking faces out of his path as he raged towards me. I had a good idea what was on his mind. He was a tough son of a bitch and I knew he wouldn't go down easy. But I guess he'd forgotten: I was raised in the dragon's den. I stepped out and stood before him, watching him charge. ("Use the momentum," Sarge told me.) I feigned a punch, leaned aside and threw him by me headlong into a bank of lockers. He caught the corner of a door square in the face and fell back, dazed. It was a good day for hunting. I took a defensive stance and kept an eye out for Thompson. When McClary tried to rise up I spun and caught him with a side-kick flat on his already damaged nose. His hands flew out and he reeled backwards in pain. I turned around just in time to see Fred clothesline Thompson with a single outstretched arm. Thompson went down to the concrete with a wail. Then suddenly the room was full of coaches, everyone was grabbing everyone and McClary and Thompson were led to the coaches' office, where they were attended to and escorted out to the local clinic. Everyone was intoxicated by the violence, and bewildered. My heart beat settled slightly, but quickly another invitation took up my focus.

The Coach told another lie. The boys had been caught drinking. Were suspected of using drugs. He had to kick them off the team to make a point. Lassiter will not tolerate the uncommitted, even if it costs us the season. We would take on Boston College without our best defensive player and we would play like men, and play to win. The team didn't know what to make of The Coach at that moment. Some thought of him as a hero, others as a fool. Only he and I knew the truth. The door flew open, the crowd roared and we dashed wildly onto the field, full of spirit and danger.

My boys cornered me as we hit the sideline before warming up.

"What happen?" Jimmy asked. "Did the coach finally believe you?"

"Neaw, he's too stubborn to admit he's wrong."

"Well what then? Why did he change his mind?"

"I don't know. I guess I found that one thing. That one thing that wraps him up."

"Wraps him up?" Fred repeated.

"Oh yeah, I just told him that if he didn't let them go, we would throw the game."

"What? Who would throw the game?"

"Us. The Boys, of course."

"You son of a bitch!" Fred accused me.

"It was the one thing he had to have. It was his whale. Victory! And I threatened to take it all away."

Jimmy looked at me and smiled. "You sneaky little bastard."

"Hey, I thought I told you," I said, walking backwards from our huddle, holding up my palms redemptively, "I'm part Indian."

My boys would have to come through. This was not Yale, and the already thin odds had been shortened. We were a team embroiled in confusion and disillusionment, and fear, but now, at least, I could feel something coming together, something I could be proud to be a part of, win or lose. I stood on the sideline stomping my feet to keep them warm as I watched us win the toss and take the opening kick-off. A slender kid from North Hartford High had taken over the role of kick returner, but before Willie could make it to the 18 he found himself tangled up in a conundrum of flying bodies and nearly got his block knocked off. The Coach grabbed me as the offensive squad started on to the field. His grip was like a wounded eagle.

"Alright Colton. No more tricks. You gotta do it this time." At last I'd seen that soft speck of light in his eyes, that glint of reality, that glint of life.

"We're gonna do it alright, coach. But this one's for another old man. You just get me the ball." I wish it were that easy.

Bucky was more nervous than I'd ever seen him. All this talk about the BC defensive line had put him into a tizzy. They were all over Lupestein before he could get out of the backfield. They were blitzing up the middle and closing down every running alley. On third and eleven, The Coach called a slant pattern. Bucky's throw was wild and though I managed to pull it in, I dropped right into the lap of their middle linebacker. He racked me hard and buried me for a gain of only four yards. It was not my day for middle linebackers.

All I can say is thank God there was another slender kid from Hartford who'd given up jazz for football. It might have been the most foolish thing he'd ever done, but then again, when Jimmy Piehler really got a hold of one, it was a thing of beauty to watch, and I'll bet it felt every bit as delightful as hitting every note just right on a long solo. He hit 'em all on this overcast southern New England afternoon, spiraled the ball high and deep, dropped it in on the sidelines, ran the receiver back in circles. He never could stand McClary either and today, when the offense could muster only a single scoring drive in the entire first half, he saved our ass.

The Coach was right about one thing. Bucky was having a hell of a time getting loose to throw. They played a zone defense in the secondary, which was well structured and disciplined, but seemed to be anxious to close in on the running play. They were big at the corners and fast enough, but it didn't take me long to find the lanes. I had checked it out. There was no number 17 in their defensive backfield. I'd get open. I just needed the ball. The longest pass play of the first half, oddly enough, went to Fred Cole, our blocking tight end. He broke free in the right flat, hauled in a wobbly toss and plowed over two cornerbacks and a safety before a linebacker dragged him down. He jostled me as he huffed his way back to the huddle.

"That's how you do it," he said. Our defensive unit had been inspired by the challenge. A sophomore named Coartney had been thrown into the middle of the gauntlet and he rose to the occasion, dashing towards the ball wildly to deflect passes and trip up running plays. We came up with three interceptions in the first half, effectively shutting down the BC passing attack. Our opponents pushed in a score on their first drive, and added two well struck two field goals to lead us at halftime by a score of 13 to 7. But we had settled down. Their enthusiasm had waned. It was slowly dawning on them: we were a real team, and it would be a real ballgame.

Coach Rivers spoke to us quietly at half time. He, too, didn't know what to make of this odd turn of events. His mind seemed in a daze, his words disconnected to his thoughts. Perhaps he understood finally that we were in this thing together. It wasn't about him. It was about us. We would win or lose this one as a Team. At this point he was just another passenger on the boat, riding the currents with the rest of us. Boston College's advantage in size, on both sides of the ball, began to wear us down as the game drew on. They began to move the ball on the ground. They picked up another field goal early, then scored when their quarterback scrambled from the 24, saw daylight and sped free to the end zone. Jimmy tried to keep them back, but he couldn't keep them down. Bucky had been sacked five times and by the start of the fourth quarter his frustration was noticeable. Fred and I tried to keep him focused. He finally got in rhythm and threw me a long pass which I hauled in at their 40 and carried down to the 27, setting up a field goal by the unflappable Reggie Pace. We regained some of our sense of purpose, some small unction of hope. But we were down 23 to 10 with 8:12 in the game. They had the ball on their own 25. I looked across the field. 8:12 on the game clock. After that, then no more.

Eight minutes and twelve seconds could be a season if you knew how to work the clock, and you had the players. But you needed a plan. From the stands we heard the chant of: DEFENSE! DEFENSE! This team we played for our final game had the players. We were outmanned, but we were playing with purpose. Our defense forced them to punt and we stood on the sideline and watched Willie pull the ball in softly back at our own 33 yard line. He started to his right, stopped, then went on, then stopped again. I guess he had a plan. He spun and went across the field towards our sideline, looking for an alley, a whisper of ashen daylight.

He side-stepped a lumbering tackle then took off with long measured strides. Willie was deceptively fast. Players who thought they had the angle on him suddenly found themselves trying to catch him from behind and that was no place to be. No one would catch him this day. He had the moves, and he was playing to win. Coach Chapman was so excited he nearly planted Willie a kiss. It had been his idea to let Willie return kicks and his plan had provided a vital spark to re-light our murky aspirations.

Twenty-three to seventeen now, with six minutes and twenty seconds left, and we'd proven we belonged on the same field; we'd proven we had a trick or two, a player here and there who had the knack. But the season would not be complete until we could get another score, and to score we needed the ball. Our dilemma was no secret to anyone on either side of the field, or in the stands, or perhaps listening in on the radio all over Connecticut and Massachusetts. Six minutes could be a season, or it could tick off with the patience and persistence of the clock in a doctor's waiting room, when you're due next for a flu shot. Nothing could slow down the hands of the game clock except good defense, good tackling. Boston College was wary of the pass at this stage of the game. They'd made too many miscues. This allowed us to hunker down and dig in for the run. Their big lineman and fullbacks pushed us back brutally and squeaked out a first down at their own 32.I looked up at the clock (4:22) and took a gaze up at the stands, taking in for a moment the whole of my last few minutes on the field. I knew the odds very well. We'd given it our best shot, proven our merit. We'd still be champions, win or lose. I watched them break off a sweep for six yards on first down, then stumble for a small gain on their next play.On third and three I looked on impassively, void of emotion, holding down my dreams, when suddenly, out of nowhere, here comes Coartney on a blitz and he's chasing the damn running back towards the sidelines. He catches him deep in the backfield and executes a marvelous tackle, wrapping us his knees like a mummy. Coartney sprung up, raised his fists triumphantly in the air and sprinted off the field. (3:01) I opened up a small tap to my small dream. Their punt was short but angled away from Willie. It was a well-calculated move. They couldn't afford another spark. Our offensive team huddled briefly at the sideline around Coach Chapman. He looked up at us, his face flushed with passion.

"Okay," he said, holding his hands outspread before him, as if calming everyone's nerves, "There's 2:48 left up there. Now we got to think. Bucky, if you're in trouble, throw it out of bounds. We can't afford the sack. If you're near the sidelines, go out of bounds. We've got one time out; I'll tell you when I want it. Now let's start off with a 17 Fly. Alright! Let's do it!" We broke and headed for our huddle on the field.

"17 Fly," Bucky called out hoarsely. That was me. There was no doubting the storm our little craft had drifted into, nor who would have to pilot us through the rocks if we were to make it to safety. I was the money man. I had the moves. We lined up over the ball; Bucky took the snap then dropped straight back for the pass. After a short hitch, I took off down the right sideline, gaining a step on the defender and looking over my shoulder for the ball. But it never rose up from the backfield.

Instead I heard a groan from the stands as Bucky was brought down quickly by a blitzing linebacker six yards deep.

Bucky got up slowly, rubbing his side and grimacing. He cursed and spat in the huddle as the next play came in. Coach C called a quick out, a faster pattern with less opportunity for a sack, short enough for me to slip in under the coverage and close to the sideline where we could stop the clock. It was a good call and we worked it well. I grabbed the ball seven yards downfield and gained another two before slipping out of bounds.

It was third and six, but the whole field was fourth down territory. I was more worried about the clock (2:33). The play came in: Split right, motion right, 60 stop. Another good play call but this time it didn't work as planned. Lupestein and I would cross the middle, attracting the secondary's attention and then Fred would slide out to the right flat. It was the same play we'd run successfully in the second quarter. Unfortunately, BC also remembered the play. Their outside linebacker shadowed Fred every step of the pattern and Bucky wisely threw the ball over their heads out of bounds.

Fourth down and 2:20 left. That was all there was. If it wasn't over yet, it was damn close. The call came in. "80, roll-hitch," our right guard recited to Bucky, breathing heavily.

Bucky repeated the call: "88 roll-hitch. Ready, break!" But it was the wrong call. It hit me suddenly and I stopped in my tracks as the huddle broke.

"Wait!" I shouted at everyone. "It was 80 roll-hitch, 80!"

Bucky looked at me, totally bewildered. Everyone stopped, halfway to the line. "It was 80," I told him. Someone yelled, "Let's go! The clock!" I threw up my hands and jogged to my split right position and the Lassiter Cougars lined up at the scrimmage line, ready for the snap of the ball on what might be our last play, in our last game, in my last season. It was a fitting end to a season so tangled up with controversy and confusion. Football is a game of chance, a game of players bouncing off each other chaotically, like molecules in a beaker. Both the 88 roll-hitch and the 80 were rollout passes, only each rolled to a different side. It was a recipe for disaster. I looked up into the stands one last time and took my standing position toeing the scrimmage line, halfway from

Fred to the sideline. On the snap I sprinted up field, working my arms as if to break into a fly pattern. Then, about 12 yards up the field, I stopped on a dime and came back to the ball. In the backfield I saw Bucky smash into Lupestein and then stumble. Everyone on the field was going in different directions. Bucky put a hand to the turf and righted himself, then he spotted me coming to him. I suppose it was too late to be nervous. He set and fired a crisp spiral, perfectly placed at the numbers. Then I spun and surveyed the field, the green and luscious Open Field, my second home, my own peculiar briar patch, and my heart pounded and my eyes lit up when I saw all the room to move. I cut for the middle, then stopped, then cut back in the same direction, then stopped again and made for the sideline (but I was not through, only getting things set up) then I broke through a linebacker's meaty but laggard grasp and started the dance. I moved every way they weren't, then back where they should've been, till I saw the last man sizing up the obliquity (it was all trigonometry I wanted to tell him -- perhaps draw out a graph to make it all come clear -- but there was no time for that) so I cut back behind him and left him to his own analysis. After that; then no one. Just me and the yard markers and the goal line, a sight I knew I'd never see before me again in this life.

I can remember when I was a kid the many times my friends and I would run up and down the dirt roads which sprawled all around Lumberton. There was this one old path that wound through the forest not too far from our house that I always loved the best. It had grayish sandy soil, mixed with chalky red clay and under the overhanging oak trees and magnolias the earth would be cool to our bare feet. The sound of jays and cicadas would fill up the canopy, serenading every creature that crept through the dusty woods. There was a creek just off the end of the road and often we'd find ourselves racing towards the cooling gurgle, jumping up and grabbing handfuls of the Spanish moss as we scurried toward relief. I'd carry that long beard of moss with me like a prize, digging my feet into the soil and pushing out ahead of the pack so I could be the first to break free of the shade, rip off my shirt and plunge wildly into the stream with a howl. Well, now I found myself racing towards the goal line, carrying the football like another prize, as if I held all the broken dreams and unfulfilled promises of this season cradled under one arm, as if I took with me toward the end zone a healing salve for every wound. I was still fast. And I still had the moves. The crowd erupted as I broke free and sprinted alone toward the goal line, rising as one and cheering me on to triumph. Our team raced onto the field and nearly carried me back to the sidelines. Everywhere was pandemonium. Tightrope had come through. As I pushed through my teammates, slapping at their hands and taking in their congratulations, I caught sight of a familiar face standing at the edge of the stands. He was grinning at me broadly behind his thick glasses and giving me two thumbs up. I hopped the fence and made my way closer, then I tossed him the ball. Bobby Dregorian caught the ball awkwardly with both hands and pulled it to him admiringly. He smiled at me warmly, a tear in his eye. I turned back to the field just in time to see Reggie Pace casually add on the margin of victory. The Boys had come through.

Chapter 20
But who would believe such a crazy tale?

So ended my football career.Not with a whimper, but with a bang. I hung up my cleats for the last time and walked out of that filthy, malodorous, echo chamber we called a locker room with no regrets. I could go back to being a regular human, no monkey on my back. I wasn't the best guy ever to catch passes at Lassiter College, nor even the most talented player on this year's team. There were several players who outshone my flickering light game after game. But I had come here to learn other games, master new moves. I could walk away from the game with satisfaction. It had not been all good times and laughs, triumph and glory, but at least I gave 'em a few things to talk about and -- for the most part - played the game by the rules.

I called everyone after our last win and then sent everyone a copy of the same letter with clippings from all the local newspapers. I felt like they would want all the angles on the game, (plus my name was in half the headlines). I tried to be philosophical about the victory and the perfect season.

Hello to all:

Well, this will be the last time you see my name in the newspaper I suppose for a long while. (Unless, of course, I get thrown in jail some night for hanging out with the wrong crowd; but then I'll save those clippings for my own scrapbook.) You might get the impression from these accounts that it was a game filled with drama and heroics, and you'd be right. BC was tough and big; but we had luck on our side. On the last play there was a mix-up in the huddle on which play we were running. Half the team was going one way, and half the team another. I guess it was fairly typical of my football career. Well anyway, I hope everyone down there is doing well. I will be down for Christmas so save me some turkey and cranberry. I look so forward to seeing everyone. It has been a long and laborious season and I look forward to a rest with some old friends.

Love to all, John

On the long bus ride back home for Christmas, I divided my time between sleeping, reading the cheap paperback Willie had loaned me (I was in no mood for serious literature) and gazing out the window contemplating the three and half years I'd invested at Lassiter and what would become of me when my short time left there had ticked off the clock. Most of what I studied at Lassiter was knowledge that I'd quickly forgotten, or put way back on the back shelves of my memory banks. It was always hard for me to really remember all the specifics of what I studied: dates, names, places, theories. But it all sticks with you somehow. Somehow I felt a general sense of things from everything I'd learned and forgotten, a sense of how the world works and doesn't work. Perhaps we learn most and deepest about those things which we hold dearest and are of the most interest. Perhaps it takes a teacher like Professor Strache to animate a subject in such a way that even the uninspired catch on to the music and walk away humming the tune. The old man had taught me how to read, and a little bit about how to write, and a lot about how to teach. I was proud to be his student and honored to be considered a friend. He was the best of our little school.

I thought about Michelle and Karen, and how much my heart throbbed when an image of either face crossed my mind, and how much I wished the paths of all our lives had crossed under different circumstances. What would become of us? I thought to myself on that long ride home. I did not know.

We were all troubled souls. How does a man ever find a bride? Where is my gentle light in the wood?

I looked out the window and saw a country bar lit up by neon signs outside of Knoxville. Two cowboys were holding a discussion in the gravel lot, each with a boot up on the side-rail of a full-decked pick-up truck. I thought suddenly about the time me and Jimmy had stumbled upon Coach Chapman in that country bar north of Lassiter. Me and Jimmy had had some times. I'd miss that ole' boy. He was one of a kind. What a triumvirate we had: Jimmy, Fred and Me. Here's to n'er do-wells and troublemakers. I rubbed the fog from my breath off the window and looked over at the old, gray-haired lady beside me. She was looking at me from the corner of her eye. Her lips were moving, but I heard no sound, only the grinding of the diesel engine as the vessel lumbered down the mountain toward Chattanooga.

We were a lucky family that Christmas. We all sat around the table Christmas Eve, our heads bowed and eyes closed as Momma gave thanks, and truly this was one Christmas to be thankful. Lisa and Roger and Jamie joined us for Momma's Christmas turkey for the first time at the big, old table that my parents had picked up some thirty years ago for less than eighty dollars. Invariably my father would tell us the story and remind us that it would sell for more than a thousand in today's furniture market. On that Christmas Eve Lisa Rae and I looked at each other as he told the story once again and we almost broke into laughter. Sarge was holding up well.Roger listened to my father's story patiently and nodded as though impressed. Roger would know about such things. He was a banker and could tell you about things of value. My Momma always lit four red candles on the table and they gave off a fluttering, yellow light. Little Jaimie's face was so soft and warm he looked almost waxy. He was a well-behaved little kid and he seemed taken in by the simple, country elegance of my parent's Christmas dinner. I filled up my plate and tasted Momma's sweet potato pie. I looked at her with a smile on my lips and then looked around the table at our simple family enjoying a simple meal, and I held back a tear and prayed a silent prayer.

Well, the rest of that school year flew by with a blurring rapidity; the clock didn't stop for any time-outs. More snow snared me in the dormitory, where I could spread out and read more of Edgar Allan Poe's mysteries and fables, and marvel at the chilling details and the smooth-sweep of the words.I tried my hand at a few stories, but it was not as easy as it looked. Soon, before I was ready, spring came on the campus, and across the town, and all of Connecticut. It bloomed with a potency and complexion far beyond the mild transpositions we witnessed in Mississippi. The flowers of Hartford came to life and the barren trees in the rolling countryside threw out their buds and their flapping, emerald leaves like flags in the March wind and the sky passed a tale of renewal and warmth and possibilities.

All things change with the seasons. Karen McIntyre had accepted Carey Zimmerman's invitation to be engaged to be married. Michelle Puckett, as I had guessed, was still full of surprises. She dumped me for Jimmy Piehler, my best friend. But it was not a lamenting loss; we'd had some times and I had protected my spirit. I knew her kind, and I knew a thing or two about my own heart. We were all better off.

The year ended not with a bang, but with a whimper. They always held a sport's banquet at the end of the Lassiter school year, to honor all the Lassiter athletes and give the coaches and the alumni a chance to get flushed and make an ass of themselves before the school year closed. I attended reluctantly and our table snuck in a flask of tequila which we passed liberally and often. They put us up front because they thought we were leaders, but our table was packed with short-timers who held few allegiances. Jimmy and Michelle were there, and Fred and Cathy; Reggie Pace sat beside me, with his latest conquest, Gabriella, while I sat modestly between them, dateless and biding my time.

They always invited some prospective athletes to this wrap-up banquet, small-time jocks from the area that they hoped to cajole into accepting a glassy scholarship and a four-year degree. No one at our table could give them much respect; we were too jaded, and, most of us, too drunk. Our vaunted Dean spoke, then Coach Rivers, and then they picked out a couple of the most prodigious and dependable jocks to say a word or two from the basketball and football teams. Lupestein had been chosen to speak on our behalf and I looked behind me to catch some smiles when suddenly I heard a chant coming up in the old, dust-soaked student union.

"Tightrope! Tightrope!" they began to yell. I put my hands on my face and my head on the table. They, too, had had too much to drink. "Tightrope! Tightrope!" Fred stood up beside me and dragged me to my feet, picking up the roar from the guests. "Tightrope! Tightrope!" they cheered. My mind was foggy. I didn't know what to make of it. I held out my hands and looked at Lupestein as he motioned for me to come on up. This was not my forum, and I was not a speechmaker. Perhaps if I just gave my thanks.

I walked awkwardly up the aisle and maneuvered the steps to the podium, looking dimly over the audience. I spotted, up front, Karen and her fiancé, and I saw Coach Rivers, sitting beside Coach Chapman and some well-angled blonde. Standing in the back I noticed, for the first time, The Professor, standing with his arm draped over his demure and delicate wife Carolyn. These faces were all emotions and alarms and dreams. Us Colton's were not speakers. I grabbed both hands on the podium and tried to gain my bearings.

"I don't know what to tell you," I began, throwing up my hands, as if apologizing for my lack of grandiloquence. My voice echoed in deep, somber waves off the oft-repainted walls. "I'm just a stupid country boy from the sticks. They used to play football in Mississippi just like they do up here. Imagine that! Shocks the sensibilities. We didn't have any real game play in mind; just a bunch of crazy jocks jostling for position. I'm not a speaker…" I looked at Lupestein, who had found a seat down the aisle. "But, I don't know, I guess I learned a thing or two up here. You can't ever know someone till you know what wraps them up. If you're thinking about coming up here and getting an education, it's probably not a bad thing." I stopped for a moment and looked out once again over this mute and docile assembly. "But I wouldn't recommend coming here to play football. I wouldn't recommend that to even my worse friend. You can learn a thing or two about English. It's a good school for that, alright."

And with that I let it be, and gave the congregation a broad smile, thinking about all I'd endured and all the tequila I'd drunk, then I stepped down graciously and made my way out of the hall.

It was a crazy season and a weird and wild year. Everyone seemed mixed up. I heard Sarge went deep sea fishing with Roger and Lisa Rae. They even got Bill Holland to join them and he caught a mackerel, while Jaimie stood on the back-deck full of wonder. They let me out of Lassiter, and awarded me a starched-white diploma, but I was just about as lost as when I'd taken on the charter. Perhaps I'd take on the challenge. Perhaps I'd try my hand at teaching a bunch of upstarts how to spell and, if they'd let me, how to write. Perhaps one day I'd try to get down all the facts of this strange story for someone else to read. Hah! But who would believe such a crazy tale? Whatever I finally decided to do, and wherever I finally settled down, I felt good about the weird and wild future ahead of me. I was beginning to learn how to really look at the sky. And besides, I had the moves.

CPSIA information can be obtained
at www.ICGtesting.com
Printed in the USA
BVHW04s1348230918
528267BV00018B/119/P